FRACTURED SOULS

HELLBENT HALO

BOOK 1

E.A. Copen

This is a work of fiction. Names, persons, places, and incidents are all used fictitiously and are the imagination of the author. Any resemblance to persons living or dead, events or locales, is coincidental and non-intentional, unless otherwise specifically noted.

FRACTURED SOULS

For information or to report typos, write to the publisher:
eacopen@grimcatpress.com

ISBN: 978-1-7353290-2-4

This one is for me. Sorry, everybody.

JOSIAH

Most professionals wouldn't stop to light a cigarette while being stalked by a demon. I'd never been known for my professionalism, though.

Flame sparked from my fingers, sizzling when the snow flurries struck it. I pressed the end of my cigarette to the fire and inhaled sweet relief while the demon followed me twenty paces behind. He'd been following me since the Saratoga Avenue stop, cap pulled low, hands shoved in his pockets, collar turned up, working too hard at avoiding detection. Conspicuous as a fart in an elevator, really. But that's demons for you. Not very bright.

If the magic alarmed him, he didn't show it, nor did he slow his advance when I stopped. I let him close the distance just a little before moving on.

If I'd been in any other city, I'd have turned down an alley and ducked behind a dumpster to wait for him. I'd found Brooklyn surprisingly lacking in accessible alleyways. The buildings were too close together for one thing. You could hardly tell where one left off and the other began. Crammed together like everything else in the damn city, like the need for living space and fresh air was an afterthought. In the rare gaps that did exist, someone went and put up an iron gate, which wouldn't do. Iron was bad for magic; I'd be asking for it if I climbed over one. Besides, I was more worried about running into an American with a gun than the idiot tailing me. If iron was bad for magic, guns were worse. Guns made me dead. Couldn't get paid if I was dead.

Graffiti was scrawled over a corrugated metal door under a pink awning to my right, the mark of a budding urban artist. I reached out to brush my fingers over the cool metal as I passed and decided to fill the silence with a whistle. It was late, and the weatherman was calling for a blizzard. For the time being, snow drifted calmly from the sky, blanketing the streets in silence. The shopkeeps had all shut down early to go buy bread and milk for the Snowpocalypse. Iron bars slid by on my right as I passed another darkened window. I wished I had a stick to draw over them. A little music would liven up the chase at least.

At the corner stood an old grocery and another corrugated metal door with more graffiti. I touched the door and moved on, slowing my pace. Had to give the poor bastard a fighting chance, didn't I?

He closed as I neared the middle of the block. Ahead, a blue sign announcing a transit stop kept a silent and lonely vigil in front of a building with a faded sign advertising a bail bondsman. Yet another business hiding behind a corrugated shell all decked out in urban spray paint scrawl. I walked up to it and stopped short, waiting for the demon to close.

Footsteps stopped at the sidewalk.

"Evenin', mate," I said without turning around. "How you goin'?"

The demon stopped and raised his face. It was long and drawn, skin the color of ash. He'd been in that meat suit a while. Maybe too long to have a proper handle on speech.

"If you were tryin' to tail me, you failed. No worries, mate. Happens to the best of us. Well, not to me. But I don't follow fuckwit demons about." I tapped a long column of ash from the cigarette. "What is it then?"

"Huh?" It took me a moment to realize he'd spoken, and the sound wasn't a simple grunt. So, the bastard was capable of speech after all.

"What'd you want?" I put the cigarette back between my lips and puffed, wishing I'd had the sense to go somewhere warm instead of Brooklyn.

He stared at me without blinking. "I'm to take you to the boss."

"And if I don't want to go?"

The demon drew his hands out of his pockets and cracked meaty knuckles. "I make you."

"Oh, yeah? You and what army?"

"Hell's army."

I sighed and flicked the cigarette off into the bushes before turning back to face him. "Look, it's been a long day. I got bumped to Economy on my flight up from Atlanta and shoved into an exit row.

D'ya know how exhausting it is sitting in an exit row? And then the traffic. Christ, don't get me started. Bloody Americans don't know how to drive. Don't suppose you have to worry about that, do ya? Just jump bodies as you please."

"Are you coming or what, asshole?" the demon demanded.

"How about a counter-proposal?" I lifted my hand and let it hover over the metal door. "You go back to your boss and tell him to fuck off, and I don't blow the whole block to kingdom come, yeah?"

The demon raised his head, eyes widening. Fear crossed the meat suit's face. "You're bluffing. There are still people here. Human souls."

He was right about that. Fifty-eight thousand people were crammed into just over a square mile that made up the Brownsville neighborhood, some of them sleeping quietly in their beds above the very shops I'd just spent the last hour arming on my stroll around the block. Women, children, young and old. The demolition spell wouldn't discriminate if I activated it. All I had to do was touch the last charge to begin the countdown.

I raised an eyebrow. "You must be new, so let me give you a quick biography. Name's Josiah Quinn. I'm Australian, not English. I know, the accent is a bit confusing to most people at first. I like long strolls through empty neighborhoods, general mayhem, loose women, and loud music. Humanity can get fucked for all I care. Your boss wants to torture me? You can pry my lifeless body from the wreckage. Now, what's it to be?" I pushed my hand closer.

"Don't!" The demon raised his hands.

That's what I thought, fuckwit. Like most demons, he wasn't very bright, but even he was smart enough to know dead souls were worthless. A poor suburb in a high crime area like Brownsville was easy currency for any demon looking to make a quick score. Promise the poor bastards a quick ticket to a better life or even just an afternoon's distraction, and they'd sell their souls for the idea alone. Never mind how pissed his superiors would be when the God Squad showed up to investigate. Pricks, the lot of them.

He waved his arms animatedly. "He just wants to talk!"

I hesitated. "Who's he?"

Sweat beaded on the demon's forehead. I inched my hand closer to the metal door.

"Daniel Monahan!" He squeezed his eyes shut.

The name shocked my heart into double time. Memories of a skinny teenage redhead two years my senior marched through my mind. How long had it been since I heard his name on anyone's lips? I hadn't had the heart to utter it myself since that night on the rooftop eighteen years ago. The night everything changed.

No, I could deal with that later. Right now, I had more pressing problems. I shook the memory from my head and focused on the demon in front of me.

He lowered his hands but didn't take his eyes off the door. "What is it you want me to do? I can't go back empty-handed."

"You can go back with a message. You tell Danny this stops. No more tails. Once it does, I'll find him. We'll talk. And in the meantime, there's something else I want."

Relief touched the corners of his eyes. "What?"

"August Jessup."

He made a face as if he'd just swallowed a live jellyfish. "What the fuck is an August Jessup?"

"He's a mate. Specializes in the forgery of official American documents. Identification documents. Word on the street is he cut a deal with one of you idiots. I need to find him."

It was just like old Augie to sign his life away when the feds came sniffing around. He was the best forger in the city, but a coward and an addict. I always did say he'd sell his soul for a fix. As it turned out, I was right.

"I don't know anyone by that name, but give me twenty-four hours, and I can find him. But you have to meet with Danny before that as a sign of good faith."

I pretended to consider it a moment before I withdrew my hand. "Twelve."

He shook his head. "There're eight and a half million people in this city, man! I can't find one guy with the snap of my fingers!"

"Twelve hours or no deal." When it came to demons, it was best to be firm. They usually caved rather than negotiate. Most didn't have a sense of what anything was worth. Mindless soldiers, most demons.

The demon sighed and lowered his hands. His shoulders slumped. "Fine, you win. Do you know the Casablanca? It opens at five. I can have him there at opening. Best I can do."

I offered my hand to the demon instead. "It's a date."

He looked uneasy but shook on it anyway. The bastard's hand was cool and clammy. Nothing worse than shaking a sweaty hand. He tried to pull away.

I held tight. "Suggest you get on it, mate. I don't like to ask twice."

A sheen passed over the meat suit's eyes. His hand went limp in mine, and I released it. He blinked once and looked around with the same shocked expression they all had when the demons cleared out. "What the hell?" His eyes fell on me. "Who the fuck are you?"

I offered my most charming smile and lit another cigarette. "I'm the guy you're going to pay to go away unless you want to have a very bad day."

His eyes widened, and he bristled before digging out his wallet.

Easiest fifty bucks I'd ever made.

After the fella stumbled off in a chilled panic to get away from me, I pressed my palm to the corrugated iron door and gave it a pulse of magic, watching the spell fizzle and die in a show of sparks. Good thing the bastard didn't call my bluff.

The metro back was unusually empty and quiet. I shared the car with a couple of teenagers looking to score for a party before the snow hit, and a man wearing three coats in desperate need of a bath. Stepping out of the subway car and onto the platform left me choking on stifled air. I tapped out another cigarette to light up but paused. Half a pack left. I'd need more just in case we got snowed in and the shops stayed closed.

Snowed in with a succubus, I mused, putting the pack back undisturbed. There were worse ways to spend a long holiday weekend. Then again, she'd been in a foul mood when I left, even though I'd brought her dinner. You'd think she'd be more grateful to the man who rescued her from Hell.

On the way out, I stopped by the line of beggars and listened to a young man play the guitar. He was good, but not great. I'd been in his shoes once, desperate for a dollar and a dream. The twitch in his bloodshot eyes and his rotten teeth might've marked him as a tweaker but I dropped him a tenner anyway. If he could find relief from the human condition for that price, more power to him.

I stopped at a twenty-four-hour pharmacy to pick up another pack of smokes and tossed a chocolate bar up on the register. If I was feeding my addiction, might as well get one for her too.

The streets in the heart of Brooklyn were a little busier. People were still rushing about, preparing for the worst with their heads tucked, fear and worry etched on their features. They moved driven by a singular purpose: stock up for the winter. Ensure survival for the pack. Don't look anyone in the eye; he might take the last six-pack on the shelf before you. Gotta hurry or I'll miss the footie. Football, I guess it was there. Christ, that wasn't even the right word, was it? I'd never get the lingo right.

Loaded down with my bag of sins, I rang
myself into the flat we'd borrowed from an old
mate of mine. He was out of the country at the
moment, Honduras or El Salvador or wherever it
was he was from. Couldn't recall. Narrow stairs
creaked underfoot as I ascended. Dogs barked
behind closed doors while old men shouted at them
in quick Spanish. Televisions recited the same
weather report that'd been playing all day in
muffled tones on the other side of thin walls.

On the landing, I passed the man who had
introduced himself as Marv when we first arrived.
He was snoring with his hand resting limply on an
empty bottle. Poor man lived in the flat above us,
but his wife ran the roost. You could set your clock
by their evening argument. She'd kick him out, he'd
drink himself to sleep on the landing, and she'd take
him back tomorrow, sure as the sunrise.

A door slammed open on the next floor and a
half-dressed man stumbled out in a hurry. He was
too nicely dressed to be slumming it in low-rent
apartments like these, but I'd figured my succubus
roommate wouldn't go for any of the locals. Dark
hair, expensive suit, in good shape, and no ring. A
few drinks, a photo, two hundred dollars, the
promise of a good time and he was down for
whatever. I'd practically gift-wrapped him for her,
so why was the idiot running scared?

He tripped down the first two stars only to keep
himself upright by grabbing my shoulders.
Recognition sparked as he looked at me. He
retracted his hands, dug into his pockets and pulled
out three crumpled Benjamins. "Here! Just keep that

bitch away from me!"

"I only paid you two, mate."

"Keep it!" The man ran down the stairs fast enough he knocked over Marv's bottle.

I watched him go and sighed.

The flat was a mess. On his hurry out, the businessman had knocked over a shelf and all the pictures on it. Glass shards crunched underfoot as I came through the door. "Honey, I'm home."

A glass smashed into the wall next to me. Maybe all the broken glass wasn't from the pictures then.

At the end of the hallway stood a woman in a fuzzy white bathrobe. Dark hair sat in a messy bun while darker eyes fumed. Her full lips twisted into an enraged sneer. "You son of a bitch!"

"Am I to take it he wasn't up to snuff, then?" I nudged aside more glass and closed the door behind me. "You prefer blonds, Khaleda? Is that it?"

"I should rip out your guts and strangle you with them! You selfish prick!"

"Women then? Let's make a party of it. I don't mind."

The succubus screamed and charged to throw a punch. I dropped my bag, grabbed her pathetic attempt at a right hook, and twisted her arm, pressing her against the wall. Had she been at full strength, she could've overpowered me easily. Lucky for me, she hadn't fed in over a week now.

She tried to throw her weight back, but I had too good a hold, and the space was too narrow. "I hate you!"

"No, you don't. You hate that I'm not letting

you sit in here and wallow in your own self-pity until you die." Her struggling pushed me back a step, and I felt glass crunch. "Stop it or you'll cut your feet, and I'm not picking glass out of them!"

She rested her forehead against the wall, muscles growing slack. Poor girl, she'd barely even put up a fight. She must've been bad off.

"Khaleda?"

"Let me go, Josiah."

I did as she asked but kept my hands up in case she decided to renew the fight. She didn't, choosing instead to turn around and press her back to the wall. Her robe had slid open during our scuffle, leaving it clear she wasn't wearing anything underneath. Maybe they'd gotten further than I thought. Lucky bastard. She was a beautiful devil.

"Dammit," Khaleda muttered when she saw me looking and covered up before crossing her arms. "Can't you even pretend to be a decent person?"

"No." I picked up the bag and pulled out the chocolate bar, offering it to her. "Truce?"

She squinted, shook her head, and marched off with a disgusted sigh.

"Come on! It's imported," I shouted, dragging myself after her.

When I stepped into the living area, I had to pause. Freshly snuffed candles sat in a brass candelabra on the coffee table. On either side of the candelabra stood an empty wine glass. The rest of the bottle was in Khaleda's hand, draining fast into her mouth while she reclined on a sofa. She'd gone all out trying to seduce the poor bastard too. Must've used everything but her magic. If she'd spelled him, he'd never have been able to run. But why didn't she use her magic?

I sighed and sank into the love seat across from her. "All right, where'd it all go wrong?"

Khaleda pulled the wine bottle from her lips and waved it around. "With me. It's always me."

The bottom dropped out from under my heart, letting the icy chunks of whatever was left sink into my stomach. Even I couldn't help but feel bad for her with what she was going through. I still didn't know the full extent of what had happened to her while she was in Hell, just that she was tortured by demons at her father's behest. When your father was Lucifer Morningstar, even stupid demons could be motivated to come up with inventive punishments. Still, it was sometimes the simplest tortures that hurt worst.

For all my experience with the supernatural, I had no idea how to help her cope. Hell, I didn't know how to get her to talk. She didn't eat, she didn't sleep, and without using her succubus powers to feed her magic, she grew weaker every day.

It wasn't my job to fix her. I'd only been paid to rescue her, but in my mind, a rescue meant ensuring her safe return to a general state of acceptable normality. Nothing about her was back to normal.

"Khaleda, please." I kept my tone gentle. "I know you don't want to talk to me, but let me bring someone else for you to talk to. Someone who will understand."

She offered a bitter laugh. "And who's going to understand? You know another succubus perhaps?

Someone else who's been to Hell?"

"I meant a woman. A trauma counselor, maybe."

She sat up to offer me a sneer. "I'm not a fucking headcase, Josiah. It's not just in my head."

"I didn't say you were." I leaned back in my chair, tapped out a cigarette, and lit it while she curled up with her bottle. "You've got to replenish your reserves, Khaleda. If you don't, you will eventually die."

"Yeah, well, you don't have to pay men to sleep with me, Josiah. Especially assholes like that."

I cringed. That idiot had told her? No wonder she was pissed at me. She wasn't supposed to find out about that. "Well, at least things are good to go for your identity documents. I'm supposed to meet Augie tomorrow. By the way, you know if you're just waiting for a decent partner, say the word, and I'm there."

She jumped to her feet. "Fuck you."

"That's the idea."

She flipped me off with both hands before storming back to the bedroom and slamming the door hard enough that it probably woke Marv on the landing.

I sighed and leaned back in the recliner. She'd come around eventually.

When I was sure she was gone for good, I moved to the sofa and got out my laptop. Danny Monahan. Christ, eighteen years and I'd barely thought of him. Once, we'd been inseparable, bound by a shared love of pushing the boundaries of our magic. How many lazy teenage afternoons had we spent inscribing circles and practicing our chanting on rooftops in L.A.? That sun-bleached summer had been one of the best of my life.

And Danny was good. Most of what I had learned at the beginning, I'd learned from him. Though we were close in age, he'd been miles ahead of me when it came to the craft. It wasn't just the spells either. Danny understood magic theory on a level no one else in our doomed little group did. He could craft new spells no one had thought of before and bridge gaps of knowledge that had persisted since the Victorian era. God, he was smart. I'd have never gotten into it as deep as I had without Danny. We were best mates. More, even.

Until the day everything changed.

Danny and I had shared more than a love of magic. We had the same teacher, Christian Lenore, and Christian was a jealous man. Once Danny and I were equal in power and knowledge, Christian took me under his wing directly, and I surpassed Danny. It drove a wedge between us, one from which we'd never recover.

I still remembered the night it all went wrong. Standing up on the rooftop of Christian's flat inside our respective circles. The air was heavy with the promise of a thunderstorm, but there was already plenty of thunder and lightning between us. I didn't want to fight him, but Christian made us, forced us to pit our skills against each other with everyone else watching. I had no choice.

I opened my eyes and pulled the burned-out cigarette from between my lips. Danny's face stared back at me from the laptop screen. He'd aged more gracefully than me. Filled out more in the chest with his teenage years behind him, grew his face a little longer, jawline more defined. He wore his thirties like a mantle of power. Or maybe that was just the six thousand-dollar suit he wore for the interview with Forbes. He looked different, but I recognized those smart blue eyes and the knowing smirk.

Danny was the CEO of a Fortune 500 company now. He had come up in the world. Out of nowhere, it seemed. Five years ago, no one knew who the hell he was. Now, he was a celebrity with a financial empire to rival men twice his age. The article called him New York's most eligible bachelor. How does a person build an empire that quickly in a shithole town like New York? I'd have dismissed it as luck, but I knew Danny. Danny wouldn't have, couldn't have, given up magic. He was involved with the demons of New York, and he knew I was in town since he'd sent them to find me. In my world, there was no such thing as a coincidence.

The bedroom door suddenly burst open, and Khaleda ran out, headed for the bathroom with her hand over her mouth. Telltale retching sounds followed as she emptied her stomach. Aces, now she was a sick *and* moody succubus. Just my luck.

I stood with another sigh and went to lean on the bathroom door, waiting for her to be done. "Told you to ease up on the wine."

She coughed and leaned back from the toilet so that I could see her face. Red streaked from the corners of her eyes and along the side of her neck from her ears. More dribbled down her chin. I thought it might be the wine at first until I realized it was far too dark.

That was blood, not wine.

"I think I need help," she managed before doubling over again.

2

JOSIAH

The witch rang a bell and tapped on a skin drum with feathers hanging from it. It was a sham mostly—I'd never placed must stock in traditional healers—but Harmony was legit. Her magic was more based on the ability to read auras than any actual healing, and the musical accompaniment was a show to make me feel like I was getting my money's worth.

Harmony closed her eyes and waved her hands over Khaleda's prone body on the sofa. She tossed her head back, sending golden hair cascading down her back and revealing the delicate lines of her neck. If I didn't know for a fact she was a lesbian, I'd have been interested. Of course, I hadn't touched a woman in more than four months now. The hooker three doors down was almost tempting at that point.

I crossed my arms. "What is it?"

"Don't know yet." Harmony winced and moved her fingers as if she were weaving a basket and not feeling out an aura.

"It's because she's not feeding, right?"

Khaleda shifted her head to look at me. "Shut up and let the woman work, Josiah."

"That's odd," Harmony said, twisting two fingers in the air.

"What is it?" Khaleda shifted her attention back to the other woman, her body growing rigid. She was trying to hide how worried she was, but it was clearly written on every inch of her face to anyone who'd known her more than five minutes.

Harmony lowered her hands and opened her eyes. "I don't know how to explain it, but your aura is incomplete. There are pieces missing. Holes torn in you so wide, the psychic pain you're in must be terrible." Her eyes slid to me and narrowed. "What did you do to her?"

"Me?" I growled. "What makes you think I've had anything to do with it? All I've done is try to help the woman!"

She helped Khaleda sit up and walked around the sofa to squat in front of her. The posture made her jeans slip down enough to reveal a tramp stamp I'd have liked to get a closer look at. She had nice legs, especially in those heels. What was it with jeans and heels anyway? "Khaleda, you don't have to stay with this dickhead. You need to heal."

"Fuckin' hell," I muttered and took myself to the kitchen to pour myself a drink.

In any other case, I probably deserved to have

suspicion thrown at me, but I barely knew Khaleda. Every moment I'd spent with her had been me trying to get her set up to get out of my hair. She'd already made it clear she wasn't going to sleep with me, and that she didn't like me. It was a wonder I'd helped her as much as I had. I could've dumped her in Tulsa and let her buy her own damn airfare to wherever she wanted to go.

There it is, Josiah. There's the reason you don't have any friends. Christ, I am a dickhead. I popped the top on the last bottle of wine. Better in me than her. "She was in Hell before I found her, by the way. If her aura's incomplete, then the damage stems from damage to the soul."

"It's not just damage. It's *missing*." Harmony stood and leaned over the small space between the sofa and the kitchen counter to snag the bottle from me.

"I was drinking that!"

She wiggled the bottle between her fingers. "Were you planning on paying me for my time?"

I sighed. "Fine. Take the damn bottle. I don't like red anyway. Just don't give her any more. The last thing she needs is to get pissed again."

Khaleda shot me a look that told me that was exactly what she wanted to do.

There was nothing else to drink, so I settled for a smoke while Harmony planted herself on the sofa next to Khaleda, legs crossed. The two women conversed in hushed tones about girl things while I considered the news.

When I'd found her, she was pinned to a rock. Khaleda had yet to detail all the abuse she'd

suffered at the hands of her tormenters, and I didn't
ask. I wasn't much good at carrying my own
emotional baggage, so I'd figured adding hers
wasn't wise. It didn't take a genius to figure most of
it out though. I'd met enough demons to know the
first few things that would cross their minds when
they were handed the Devil's daughter to play with.

In theory, a demon's job was to break down
living souls for processing in the underworld.
Different underworlds completed the task in
different ways, but pain and suffering were always
the fastest, most preferred methods. Pieces didn't
just break off though. Someone would've had to
take it by force. We needed to know who if she
wanted it back.

It's not my problem. I took a long drag on the
cigarette wishing I'd thought to make coffee to go
with it. She hasn't asked for my help, and I don't
owe her. Maybe it would be better if I just got her
documents tomorrow and left as we agreed.

Yet I didn't want to leave her alone and hurting
without any direction. She still hadn't found the will
to feed. She'd barely made an effort to bathe. Most
of her calories still came from the wine she'd
convinced me to buy. If I left, she'd be dead inside
a week.

What's it to me if she dies? I never promised to
keep her alive. It's her choice to behave like a child.

Except I knew that wasn't right either.
Someone had broken something inside this woman.
They'd broken more than just her body and soul.
Bastards had broken her will and ripped away her
self-respect. That was too low, even for me.

I leaned my elbows on the counter and tapped some ash from the cigarette. "So, there are pieces of your soul missing, Khaleda. What do you plan to do about that?"

She shrugged and hugged herself, rubbing her shoulders as if she were cold. "It's probably gone. I suppose this is just me now."

Harmony frowned and rubbed Khaleda's back.

I crushed the cigarette on the countertop. "Bugger that. We're getting it back."

Khaleda tossed her head back and laughed.

Not the reaction I was hoping for. "Hear me out. If it's not there, that means it's somewhere else."

"Brilliant deduction." Harmony rolled her eyes.

"I'm not finished. Now, it's either been processed in Hell, or someone is holding onto it. My bet is that someone has it. She's the Devil's daughter, a potential Queen of Hell if her old man was killed."

Khaleda's face sobered. "But he *is* dead. And I don't want to rule Hell."

I'd been there when it happened. Watched the bastard go down with a whimper when a mate of mine challenged him to a duel he couldn't win. Lazarus was a better man than me, walking through Hell to save his woman. I didn't think I'd walk to the corner store for anyone I'd ever slept with, let alone through Hell.

I nodded. "And any forward-thinking demon would've seen that coming and prepared himself a little get-out-of-trouble-free insurance. As for the second half of that statement, most demons won't care what you want. They'll either seek to support your claim or try to kill you to make sure you're not a threat."

Shit, there was that too, wasn't there? She was in no shape to fight off a legion of demons if they came calling. Sooner or later, they would.

Khaleda found her feet. "Let them come. I stood by my father for twenty years as his personal assassin. They know my face, they know what I can do, how many of them I've killed. I'll kill them all until they learn to leave me the fuck alone!" She swiped her hand through the air, but the movement threw her off balance, and Harmony had to help her back to the sofa.

I crossed my arms. "Not like that you're not. How drunk are you right now?"

She hung her head. "Less since I vomited."

"Khaleda," said Harmony, taking her hand, "I think he's right. You need to be whole. You can't fight them until you are. And even if you don't want the missing pieces of your soul back, don't you at least want to live? You've got to stop this. You have to take care of yourself. If you don't, you'll fade away until one day you just die."

Khaleda flexed her jaw. Her fingers closed firmly around Harmony's squeezing until Harmony sucked in a shocked breath. Harmony's eyes widened and her body stiffened, head tilting back. I didn't realize what was happening until Khaleda lifted her head and the two of them locked lips.

No matter what any fella says in public, in private, we're all animals, and every animal's got his fantasy of choice. Two attractive women making out on a friend's sofa while said friend is out of town wasn't my top choice, but it was definitely in my top five. Though I wasn't involved in the scene unfolding in front of me, some primal part of my brain was convinced otherwise.

I leaned forward putting my chin in my hands. "Well, then. Looks like I had your type all wrong, didn't I?"

Harmony's eyes snapped open and she tried to pull away, but Khaleda grabbed her by the hair and deepened the kiss. It was the first sign that not all was as kosher as it seemed. When Harmony tried to push Khaleda away, she found herself pinned to the back of the sofa by the wrists, easily overpowered. She let out a muffled, panicked sound and tried desperately to get free.

Suddenly, I understood why the man I'd left here with her paid me to keep her away from him. This was no longer just a sexy makeout session.

I pushed away from the counter and walked over to grab Khaleda's shoulder firmly. "That's enough."

Khaleda shrugged my hand away.

Harmony squeezed her eyes shut, letting tears fall.

"I said she's had enough!" I grabbed Khaleda by both shoulders and yanked her off the sofa.

She crashed into the coffee table head-first. Cheap chipboard snapped and twisted under her weight, and she lay there dazed.

Before I could see if both of them were all right, Harmony shoved me away, scooped up her purse and ran for the door. I called after her, but all

I got was a slammed door in response.

"Well, bugger." Harmony was no pushover, and Khaleda had snared her with little more than a brush of skin, turning her into a near helpless victim. If I hadn't intervened, Khaleda might've drained the life out of the poor girl.

I stepped over to the sofa where I stretched out, putting my shoes on one arm and head on the other. "Well, at least Harmony's vegan. You won't ruin your figure."

"Ungh." She put a hand on her head. "What happened? Why am I on the floor?"

"You and Harmony," I said, tapping out another cigarette to light. "She was into it at first, but seems you don't know when to stop, Khaleda."

She sat up, drawing her knees to her chest and putting her head in her hands. "God, I can't live like this. I need control. I need to be strong again."

"You need your soul back."

She said nothing.

I smoked in silence for a moment, giving her the time to ask. When she didn't, I sat up. "If you want my help, it doesn't come free."

She lowered her head, focusing on the spilled bottle of wine emptying its contents on the floor. "You know I haven't got any money."

"I'm willing to extend you a line of credit. You can work it off."

Khaleda raised her eyes and stared at me.

Maybe it was me, but the sad look on her face made my heart change tempo. Some primitive part of me wanted to rush to her side and assure her that everything would be just fine. We would fix this, her and me.

Instead, I picked up the overturned bottle of wine and took a swig of what was left. "What's it to be?"

"You're a fucking asshole, Josiah."

"I'm the only asshole you've got, sweetheart. For the right price."

"Fine." She stood on unsteady legs. "Prick."

"Bitch."

Khaleda gave a frustrated growl and stormed off to the bathroom, slamming the door behind her. If she didn't stop slamming doors, I was going to have to replace one of them before we left.

A minute later, I closed my eyes against the muffled sound of her sobbing. She was right about me. I was a real bastard.

3

KHALEDA

Steam rose from the water around me. No matter how many baths or showers I took, no matter how many bottles of wine I emptied, I still felt unclean. Ever since Josiah had brought me back from Hell, all I ever felt was numb.

Rescued. I scooped the water in my hand and watched it slip through my fingers. That was the word everyone used for what he'd done. But I didn't feel like I'd been saved either.

I picked up the plastic bristled scrub brush and rubbed it against my arms until the skin was red. I was Lucifer Morningstar's daughter. His death didn't change that. Didn't change what he'd let them do to me, that he'd sent me away, that I had betrayed him. He'd made me into the monster I was, and I hated him. So why did I still cry every time I realized he was dead?

I scrubbed harder.

Josiah's constant badgering didn't help. He'd thrust that man into the apartment and run off to buy more cigarettes, retreating as if he'd just tossed a leg of lamb into a feral lion's cage. Feed on him, he'd demanded. Drain away his life, his free will, everything that makes him human. Rape the poor bastard's mind and never mind that his body wants you, that he doesn't know what you are and won't until it's too late.

The plastic handle of the scrub brush snapped in my hand. I threw it against the wall with a growl and decided to wash my hair instead. When was the last time I'd done that? Had I done it at all since coming back? Maybe. Mostly, I'd been trying to stay drunk so I had an excuse not to talk to Josiah. The man was infuriating. Why the fuck was he still around anyway? Acting like he had some right to protect me. I didn't need his protection, not with the number of bodies I'd left in my wake. My father—

I choked off the thought before it completed. Fuck my father, and fuck Josiah if he thought he could tell me what to do. I was going to get better, and I was going to make it just so I could prove I didn't need them.

Stewing in the bathtub wasn't going to get me there. I stood and reached for the towel hanging on the hook only to cringe and pull my hand back once I touched it. Gross. When was the last time that thing was washed? I glanced down into the milky water swirling down the drain. When was the last time *I* was washed?

Without drying off, I stepped out of the tub and

wiped the mirror clean to look at myself. Once, I'd
been beautiful, able to bed anyone I wanted with a
casual glance and a crooked finger. Now, with my
butchered hair, gaunt face, and dead, sunken eyes, it
was a wonder even the tiny spark of magic that
remained in me could get me a glance. The face in
the mirror wasn't Khaleda Morningstar. She was
dead. Died the day Lucifer turned her out and
decided she should learn a lesson. That woman,
whoever she'd been, was weak and spoiled,
dependent entirely on the idiot men around her for
everything she had. She lived and died for her failed
chance at revenge.

One of my obsidian knives peeked out from
behind the toothbrush holder where I'd left it just in
case. I grabbed it and yanked a strand of my hair
straight away from my head before sawing through
it. That belonged to her, too. All that beautiful hair
that she'd been so proud of. All the bruises, the
heartache, the dead brother, the dead mother.

I cut them away with the knife and let them fall
with the hair into the sink.

Something crashed through the apartment
outside, and I spun toward the door, knife raised.
Whatever it was hadn't come from the door. Maybe
Josiah had just fallen over something. Glass
shattered followed by more splintering wood and
the bark of gunfire. Muffled, one-two precision
shots. Small caliber with a silencer. A handgun in
the hands of a pro killer with a single purpose in
mind: eliminate the target.

The sounds of a struggle were coming from the
living room. If I could get through the bathroom

door without making any noise, they'd never see me coming.

I gripped the doorknob and turned it, quickly, quietly. Pulling up on the door as I swung it open lessened the weight on the hinges and let it open silently. Broken glass and splinters from the broken door littered the hallway to my left from where I'd thrown the glass at Josiah, but the path to the right was clear. I swung into the hallway, the familiar weight of the blade in front of me at a relaxed distance.

Adrenaline surged, and everything came into focus as soon as I saw the scene. There were two of them. The closest had his back to me. He was on the floor, his hands around Josiah's skinny neck. The other stood in the doorway to the bedroom, armed with a Sig Sauer with a silencer and telescopic sight attached. Both wore black tactical armor, complete with helmets. Weak points would be joints, neck, face, groin. Modern plate armor: good for stopping bullets but not so good for enchanted obsidian blades.

The information flashed through my brain in the time it took me to cross the room and bury the blade in the first man's thick neck, right where it met his shoulder. His hands went slack around Josiah's neck as dark, arterial blood spurted. Not dead, but he'd be unconscious inside fifteen seconds and dead inside two minutes. First threat neutralized.

I grabbed him by the back of his Kevlar vest and jerked him up, pulling his body tight against mine to catch the first three shots from the second intruder. Tap, tap, tap. Two to the chest and one to the head like a good soldier. My human shield's face exploded as the third shot hit, sending chunks of brain and shattered teeth to the floor. With a growl, I shoved the dead weight forward and let the body crash into the gunman. In the narrow doorway, he had nowhere to go but back a step, and to move effectively, he had to lower his weapon.

I got my opening and ran for it, leaping over the still bleeding body of the first man to drive my knife at the face of the second. He tried to get the gun up in time, but I was faster than he'd ever be. His plastic face mask took the brunt of the impact of the blade, but I'd never meant to cut him. All I needed was an inch of skin. The idiot tried to position his gun again, but it was no use. I had him.

I wrapped my fingers around his exposed throat, met his eyes, and let the magic do the rest.

His muscles tensed, body growing rigid, pupils dilating. Pulse fluttered under my fingers, racing to catch some fleeting feeling his mind had convinced him was real. A breath and I was inside his mind, slithering around in his memory, tongue lashing out to taste a life that wasn't mine. Emotion beaded on the surface of his being, an unshakable, unwavering faith laced with the sweet realization that I was there, inside of him, penetrating to where I wasn't supposed to be.

He struggled, but not for long. They never did.

Beneath me, his body shuddered, surrendering, becoming food to feed the Hunger. Images flashed through my brain at breakneck speed, too fast to absorb at the moment even if I had wanted to. I didn't. The only thing that mattered was finishing, sating the Hunger for another few seconds so it would die inside. It whipped out of me, a living thing, ripping, tearing, chewing on the poor unsuspecting human.

No. Need him alive. Need answers.

The gun fell from his fingers as I exhaled and pulled back. The Hunger rebelled, demanding more. We were incomplete. We needed more of him, more power, more satisfaction. It was strong, stronger than it had ever been. Everything I had went to taming the beast in my body, pushing it back into its cage until, with another shuddering breath through pursed lips, it quieted.

"Fuck me," Josiah ground out in a deeper than normal voice behind me. "What a way to go."

I looked down at the quivering mound of flesh that had once been a man under me. Deep brown eyes stared into nothing, unfocused. His mouth moved, forming incomprehensible words with no sound. Perspiration coated his face, soaked his body as he gasped in breaths like a man drowning. Everything that he had been was gone, inside me now. I'd killed everything that mattered. Guilt stabbed at my heart.

Not that Josiah understood or cared. I could feel desire pulsing from him like a living thing. Watching me destroy this man, this living creature, it had turned him on.

Heat flooded my face along with inexplicable anger as I stood. "He's not dead."

"Too bad. That's one you want to kill."

"Who are they?" I grabbed an oversized shirt

from the floor and pulled it on without turning to
face him. Blood dripped onto the collar from my
nose. I wiped it away and tried to swallow the angry
nausea and dizziness. Feeding wasn't supposed to
make me feel feverish and sick. "The armor is
meant to look like law enforcement. SWAT
probably, except SWAT doesn't use silencers and
move in teams of two."

Josiah's answer was a grunt.

I tugged the shirt down, wishing he'd stop
looking at me like that. With hunger in his eyes. Go
smoke, you idiot. You don't want me to fuck you,
not unless you want to wind up like the drooling
meatball on the floor.

He rubbed a hand over his face. "*Manus Dei.*
God's Hand."

"Is that supposed to mean something to me?"

"Means that trick was probably the closest he's
gotten to getting lucky in a long time. Most are ex-
Special Forces. Navy SEALS. Former KGB. British
SAS. Handpicked for special duty directly under the
command of an arm of the Vatican that doesn't
officially exist, supplied by shadow governments.
About half of them are willing hosts to angels. The
other half are murderous zealots." He stepped over
the dead one to squat beside the murmuring man.

I crossed my arms. "Holy warriors? What do
they want with me?"

"Is he coherent?"

I pressed my lips together and turned away,
closing my eyes. A memory played in my brain,
projected by the piece of him I'd taken. In it, he
knelt before a man clothed in white, hands folded as

if in prayer. Raw power radiated from the man in front of him, creating a sense of…reverence. Loyalty. Dedication. This soldier would die to protect the faith if God demanded it.

I swallowed. "He'll come down from it in a minute, but he'll never be himself again. If you want to interrogate him, we can."

Josiah sighed and stood. "I'll get some rope, then."

"You won't need it. He belongs to me now."

There it was, the appraising look laced with fear. *I told you I was dangerous.*

I avoided looking straight at him because I was still remembering this other man's life, feeling his faith, his fears, his hope for a better world. Unclean. That word was attached in his memory to me. He was right. "Just take him out to the living room. Let me get dressed."

Josiah dragged the man out of the bedroom and came back to close the door. Pointless gesture. He'd already seen me naked more than once now. That wasn't what bothered me. It was those stupid, small, almost gentlemanly gestures like closing the door or bringing me a chocolate bar. He would do something so selfless and then turn around and try to pay a stranger to sleep with me. It was as if he was saying, "Go get laid and you'll feel better." Typical male pig attitude, as if sex were the cure for all the bullshit in the world.

The thought made me so furious, I ripped the first pair of underwear I tried to put on. With a sigh, I tossed them aside and put on another pair. Dressed in a loose-fitting white t-shirt and gray sweats—the least sexy thing I could think of—I ventured out of the bedroom to face the two men.

Josiah hid behind the counter in the kitchen, leaning over it with his cigarettes and a glass of water. He'd supplied the other man with water too, but he left it untouched. He wouldn't drink unless I told him to now. At the sight of me, the soldier leaned forward, anticipation plastered on his face.

"What's your name?" I asked him. I didn't need to know. Father had never liked it when I asked for names. He wanted me to call them something demeaning. Slave, dog, bitch, anything that would further strip them of what little humanity remained. But Father was dead. I was in charge now, and I could do things my way.

"Private Victis Deramo," he answered in Latin. "I apologize. I don't use English much anymore. I can do German or Italian if it is easier."

I glanced over my shoulder at Josiah. "How's your Latin?"

He shrugged. "Better than my German."

"Latin is fine," I said to Victis. "Are there any more of your people in the building?"

"No, mistress."

I hesitated. No, 'mistress' wasn't the right translation for that form. Teacher. What the hell did he mean by that?

"Are any more coming?" Josiah asked in perfect Latin.

Victis didn't answer.

Josiah swore, and I smirked. Serves him right for trying to take over my interrogation. I repeated the question for Victis.

"If I don't report in before dawn, yes," he said. "There are two cohorts in the city with orders to hunt the Nephilim."

Nephilim? I thought all of them were dead. Legend had it that a group of angels had once descended to Earth and stupidly fell in love with human women. They taught humans forbidden knowledge and went on to have bastard children with them. When God found out, he sent a whole legion of loyal angels to murder their offending brethren along with their women and children only to wash away the slaughter with the Great Flood. Nephilim were supposed to be giants, the half-human, half-angel offspring of those unions thousands of years ago.

"They won't hurt you, Teacher," Victis offered. "I'll protect you."

"That won't be necessary, Victis." I turned my back on him and faced Josiah. The red ring around his neck was darkening into a bruise. "Nephilim? Do they mean you?"

He cleared his throat. "It's not like I put it on my business cards. Josiah Quinn: Nephilim and master of the dark arts. What kind of idiot would I be?"

I crossed my arms. "You could've told me, especially that there might be people after you."

"I could've. But you didn't ask. You were too busy drinking yourself silly and telling me to fuck off."

I rolled my eyes and turned back to Victis. "Victis, you're a member of this God's Hand group?"

He straightened. "I am a legionnaire of the fifth degree."

"God's Hand is a bunch of militant loonies," Josiah clarified in English. "Zealot dogs without a proper leash. You should kill him, and we should go."

I ignored him. "How did you find us?"

Victis nodded to Josiah. "Mr. Monahan is a known associate of his. Monahan's employees have been under surveillance since we received an anonymous tip that Mr. Quinn was in the U.S. We assumed the two of them would meet while he was Stateside."

"Are you shittin' me? I haven't talked to Danny in twenty fuckin' years! Known associate!"

I bit my lip to keep from smiling at his irritation. The more g's he dropped and the deeper he delved into his slang, the more upset Josiah was. He was probably telling the truth, but there was no reason to let Victis on to that. "So you tracked him here. How?"

"He met with one of Mr. Monahan's freelancers this afternoon in Brownsville. The sniper team deployed, but couldn't get a clear shot. Lucius and I were to eradicate him here and make it look like a robbery gone wrong."

"Why?" Josiah's tone was icy. "I've not done anything to you lot. If anything, I've scored more points for your side by helping kick the Devil's arse."

My breath caught, but I let it go. I couldn't let him see that it upset me. Josiah would use it against me. "Answer him."

Victis shook his head. "I don't question why. The Hand points. I shoot."

Josiah swore under his breath.

"Thank you, Victis." There were no more questions that he could answer.

I felt it, the wall in his mind. He didn't question his superiors because a good soldier didn't need to know why. He only needed to know how. My father had tried to turn me into that kind of soldier. Go seduce this man. Kill this woman. Seduce then kill. Get close to this one and learn his weaknesses. Report them back to me. Like a dog, I'd obeyed, though I hated it. I'd said I'd never let anyone use me like that again, yet here I was, using Victis. Killing him would be kind.

His eyes lit up when I reached to touch him, the same excitement of a puppy on seeing his master.

Josiah grabbed my arm before I could brush a hand against Victis' cheek and end it. He must've moved so quietly I didn't hear him. "What're you doing?"

Victis jumped to his feet, a fire burning in his eyes. His coiled muscle and fierce expression screamed there would be violence if I didn't tell him to back down.

"Victis?" I kept my voice even, calm, even though my heart was pounding in my ears. Too much contact too soon after feeding the Hunger. It had woken at Josiah's touch and threatened to surface again. The Hunger knew he was different, a power we had never tasted. It whispered to me, promising this one would sustain us for more than a day. *Reach out. Take him. Make him ours.*

"Yes, Teacher?"

I squashed the Hunger. "Go into the bedroom and cover your ears. I don't want you to hear us."

He hesitated, but he couldn't disobey. Victis left the living room, stepped over his dead co-worker, and went into the bedroom, shutting the door behind him.

As soon as he'd had enough time to do as he was told, I pulled my arm away from Josiah. "You said it yourself. He needs to die."

"But what if he doesn't?" Josiah gestured to the closed bedroom door with his chin. "You heard him. If he doesn't report back, they'll send others. God's Hand isn't going to leave us alone just because they failed. They have endless resources. They will hunt us down no matter where we go."

"There is no *us*. God's Hand is your problem."

"And a fucked-up soul is yours." He jabbed a finger into my chest. "If you want my help putting yourself back together, then you're as much in the shit as I am."

"What do you want me to do, Josiah? Send him back? He's helpless. He can't function without me, and I've got no use for a slave whose only interest is in pleasing me!"

"But you do need a shield and someone who can fight. I'm no good for it. Magic, I can do. I can put up a good front, but in a gunfight, I'm worthless."

"I can defend myself." I gestured to the dead man whose blood was soaking into the carpet.

He crossed his arms. "When you're asleep? And what about if you decide on a little snack? My guess is, you're vulnerable when you feed. When you were feeding on both Harmony and Victis, I could've slit your throat. You need someone to watch your back, and I can't do it all the time. Not to mention this Victis fella knows the ins and outs of God's Hand and has access to surveillance teams and equipment that will prove useful."

I threw my hands up. "How does any of this help me get the lost pieces of my soul back?"

"I don't know yet," Josiah said, shaking his head. "But if you kill him, you're killing something that could potentially help us down the road."

He was right. It made me feel like a monster, but I knew he was right. Hell would be coming for me. My father's warlords would want to eliminate me to strengthen their claims. This God's Hand group was also going to be a thorn in our sides going forward. Hunted by Hell, in hiding from Heaven, we were going to need all the allies we could get.

I sighed and lowered my chin to my chest. "Okay, but we can't stay here. They know about this place, and now the front door is busted, and there's a body here. Eventually, someone's going to find it."

Josiah gave me one of his troublesome grins. "I know just the place."

4

JOSIAH

We should've skipped town. If it'd been anyone other than Danny, I would have in a heartbeat. I'd tangled with God's Hand before, and the only way to give them the slip was to spend eight weeks in Siberia. Not something I would choose to do again.

So, instead, Khaleda packed up what little she'd acquired since coming to Earth—mostly oversized and unflattering clothing—and her pet and we left. With the news that we were likely being watched, I didn't trust public transit, but none of us had cars of our own. Victis had come in a company vehicle that was being tracked, so we left it.

I wove a cloaking spell over us. They weren't my specialty, and it wouldn't hold if Khaleda was more than a foot from me, but it would discourage anyone from looking too closely. Couldn't do anything about the cameras. That was Victis' department.

Cleaned up and out of the body armor, he still wasn't a looker. More the grizzled soldier type, all scars, body hair, and hard muscle. But he had sharp eyes, and a direct manner of speaking, which I appreciated. He directed us away from the cameras, taking us out the back of the building where an awning covered us as long as we slinked along the fence. With a little luck, a lot of planning, and switching cars three times, we made it to Chinatown and the Old Gong Hotel.

The Old Gong occupied the top three stories of a five-story building, with a Chinese grocery taking up the bottom floor. The floor between the hotel and grocery might've been apartments or storage. It was hard to tell which since my Mandarin was shaky at best. Khaleda spoke it well enough to get us checked in with the agitated man at the desk, who we'd clearly woken. It was closing in on dawn, and he kept trying to insist he didn't run "that kind of place." He didn't want to take cash. In the end, he took the three Benjamins I had left and called it a deposit. Expensive for a crummy, one-star room in Chinatown, but at least we were paid up for two nights.

We reached the room and Khaleda flipped on the lights with a frown, eyeing the single bed. "It's even smaller than the last place."

"It's New York," I said, shouldering past her. "You want more than fifty square feet, you pay through the nose. Be thankful we got a room with a private bath."

She was right, though. Linoleum flooring made the place look more like a hospital room than a hotel. The singular window was maybe a foot wide but made up for it by stretching floor to ceiling. If I slid by the foot of the bed carefully, I could avoid brushing against the television, but three people couldn't stand in the open space without being in each other's way.

I tossed my bag on the bed and gestured for them to come in. "You stand out in the hall, the other guests won't be able to get by you."

Khaleda glared at me. "It's four in the morning. Normal people aren't moving through the halls." She griped, but she came in.

Victis followed her, looking grim, and closed the door behind him, keeping his back to it and staring longingly at the bed.

Khaleda sank to the bed, spreading her fingers over the thin comforter and crossing her legs. "I want you to go back to your command center, Victis. Tell them where to find your friend's body so they can give him a proper burial."

"Yes, Teacher." He hesitated, glancing at me. "What should I tell them about the Nephilim?"

"You can tell them this." I offered him a middle finger without looking away from my bag. "What's the Latin for that?"

Khaleda shoved my hand away from her. "Tell them he overpowered you with a knockout spell and escaped. If they want to know why he left you alive, tell them he was too busy running away to check and you played dead. You saw him get into a cab, but you didn't catch the number. You changed your clothes so you could leave without seeming suspicious. Did you get all that?"

He nodded. "Yes, Teacher."

"Good."

Smart girl, hiding the lie inside the truth.

The man beamed like a dog who'd caught a fox.

"When your shift is over, you're not to come back here," Khaleda said.

Victis' smile faded, his face shifting to panic. "But... Where should I go?" Before she could speak, he dove to his knees in front of her, folding his hands as if in prayer. "Don't send me away from you, please. I love you."

"Victis..."

"Please, Teacher. I'll do whatever you ask. If I've offended you, tell me what I can do to fix it. I'll do it, whatever it is."

Khaleda closed her eyes as if she were in pain. Poor girl. Maybe I should've let her kill him. She reached to brush her fingers against his cheek, and he leaned into her hand as if it were the only thing keeping him from falling. "I want you to go back to your old life until I call you, Victis. Pretend to be your old self and do whatever you have to. I promise I'll call you soon."

He gripped her fingers and turned his head to kiss her knuckles, shaking. "Yes, Teacher. Don't forget me."

"I won't."

He stood and crept with careful backpedaling to the door, exiting through it without ever giving

Khaleda his back.

She stared at the closed door. "He'll be dead by tomorrow."

"Bastard might surprise you. He looks tough." I opened my bag and dug through the contents to find some chalk. "Anyone ever break free of that bewitching thing you do?"

"No," she said, shaking her head.

I considered it. "You slept with Lazarus, and he wasn't a mindless idiot. Well, let me revise that statement. He wasn't brainless mush like Victis."

In fact, Lazarus Kerrigan was a scary man. He was a Horseman, one of the foursome said to be the heralds of the end times. Having met the man, I believed it. He wasn't someone I wanted to cross. Lucky for humanity, he had no idea how much power he truly had and chose to waste it on senseless things like truth, justice, and video games. He was all right.

Khaleda's eyes followed me as I walked around the bed and knelt on the floor to begin drawing my circle. "Lazarus is the Pale Horseman, and we were using sex to quick charge an item for a spell, so the item in question took most of the energy."

"Sounds like fun."

"Only if you're a masochist."

"Is he?" I reached where she sat on the bed and looked up at her.

She'd either have to move so I could finish the circle or I'd have to stop drawing. If she stayed, I'd just sit there with her legs in front of me and work hard at remembering the way she stood over the first soldier with her knife in his neck. Naked, covered in blood, the raging storm of a hundred battles in her eyes, those lovely muscles flexing beneath tight, wet skin…

Khaleda raised an eyebrow and stayed right where she was. "Is he what?"

"A bloody masochist, woman. Try to keep up."

She wrinkled her nose, looking like she'd just eaten a whole spoonful of vegemite in one go. "I'm not going to discuss anybody's kinks with you, pervert."

"I figure he must be. He did willingly climb into bed with an ice queen. Wonder it didn't freeze off. Did it?"

Her disgusted expression deepened, and she stood with a huff to storm to the tiny window.

Victory for me.

As I finished the circle, drawing the chalk over the wall to complete the other side, I stole a glance at her backside. While it was a nice view, it wasn't near as nice in the sweats as it might be in a dress. A nice short one and a pair of heels. She could put her hair up and—

A wave of cold hit me, rushing down my spine. "You cut your hair."

Khaleda instinctually reached up to run her fingers through the shorter do as if I'd just paid her a compliment. "So?"

"Where is it?"

"What do you—" She paused halfway through turning around, eyes growing wide. "Shit, it's in the fucking sink!"

Stupid girl. She should've been more careful! Not only would the fresh trim give away that

someone else had been in the apartment with me
when the Hand went to search the place, but it'd be
an easy way for them to track her down.

There was nothing to be done about it now
except try to block the spell. That meant either
shaving her bald or drastically altering the
composition of her hair.

"I need peroxide and foil." She stormed over to
where I was working, standing on the bed and held
out her hand expectantly.

With a sigh, I handed over my last thirty dollars
in cash. It was worth it to have the place to myself
for a few minutes. She left in a determined flurry,
not even realizing the significance of the moment. It
was the first time she'd gone out to do anything on
her own since coming back from Hell. Maybe there
was hope for her yet.

After she left, I finished my circle and lay on
the bed, staring at the ceiling with my hands on my
chest. Sleep seemed impossible. If I'd had the room
to myself, I might've indulged in a quick wank just
to relieve some of the pressure that was building
from dealing with that woman.

At first, I'd chalked it all up to her trip to Hell.
Maybe it was the missing bits of soul too. But I had
the distinct feeling that even once she was whole,
she'd still be an entitled bitch. I wasn't even under
her spell and I'd just forked over the last of my
money. What for? For her vanity. We should've just
cut it all off. It'd grow back.

It wasn't going to get me anything. She hated
my guts. Even when she was desperate, even when
she needed to feed, she'd never given me more than

an insult. Not that I cared. I wasn't in it for that. I could get what I needed on any street corner for less than what I'd handed her and still have cash left to smoke. The sex—or lack of—wasn't the problem.

What was it then that was making my skin crawl with an unscratchable itch? Why was it I'd flown all the way here with her, set her up with whatever she wanted? Why did I give a shit when she cried behind closed doors?

The only reason I wanted to fuck her was because that's what I'd do with any other woman. But Khaleda wasn't any other woman. She was the one I couldn't have. I couldn't decide if that was why I wanted her so badly or not. I wasn't a kid who should've been drawn to something just because it was forbidden and dangerous.

And she was no Danny Monahan.

I sat up with a sigh. "Fuck me, I'd better get this done before she comes back."

The leather bag I carried around with me was no ordinary bag. It contained near limitless space thanks to a spell that had been woven into the leather by the manufacturer. The cow the leather had come from had been raised on a steady diet of grass from consecrated ground in Nepal and chanted over daily. When it was slaughtered and skinned, it was done in a special ritual. Another ritual for tanning the hide in the urine of a holy man, another for the thread... Everything about the bag was drenched in magic, which had made it take strong spells with ease.

It was Danny who made the bag into a bottomless object with extra-dimensional space. He

gave it to me for my sixteenth birthday. The
memory of that always brought a smile, no matter
how many years passed. It'd been the one happy
moment before life went to shit. Oh, to go back and
be young again…

But even with all my power, I couldn't change
the past. Not for me, not for Khaleda, and not for
Danny.

I opened the bag again and drew out the small
plastic container I'd been hiding from Khaleda ever
since we'd met. "Hello, lovely. If you promise not
to get into trouble, I'll let you out for a walkabout."

With care, I popped the lid on the container and
extended my senses into it, flooding the rectangular
plastic space with familiar magic before reaching in.
Milly might've been a lovely girl, docile as they
come, but two weeks in that cramped space with
only limited outings would be enough to test
anyone's patience. Luckily, she had the run of the
place as long as she stayed in the bag, making her
tiny plastic container four, maybe five times as
large on the inside. More than enough for a
tarantula her size.

Delicate little legs tapped at my fingers. Tiny
hairs tickled my palm as she crawled up and met my
magic with her own. Being reunited with Milly was
a welcome relief, as she was the only creature I
could stand to touch when things got overwhelming.
She was gentle but strong, less aggressive than a
cat, and surprisingly more tolerable than a dog.

I let her perch on my shoulder while I moved
my arms about over the circle, flexing both
magically and physically. Extend, retract. Touch

and go. Feel the energy of the room, release. Take, return. It was a basic centering exercise, much like breathing in yoga, or a morning jog for a marathon runner. No effort at all for me, but a prerequisite to keep sharp. In magic, basics were everything. If you didn't have a good handle on that, might as well not try. Some idiots were born with natural talent or stumbled into it by accident. Me? Left to my own devices, I'd never have done anything other than parlor tricks to get laid.

Another push of magic directed at the circle and I held it there, feeling the power spread over the faint lines I had drawn and spread into a full dome. Encased in the familiar warm glow of my own power, I relaxed. This was what I knew.

I closed my eyes and threw out a hand, letting the power kiss my fingers like a lover a moment before I bent it to my will with a verbal command, just the way Danny had taught me. The spell drove into the space I'd created, probing, searching for an escape. I held the circle and gave it none, forcing it back to the center. Even there, it tried to wriggle out of my grasp and disobey. I lashed it back into submission, my voice raw from the effort.

Sweat formed on my chest and on the back of my neck. Familiar euphoria hovered on the edge of my consciousness. I could complete the summoning now. There was plenty of power there, and I'd done all the work, but I wasn't ready to let it go. I had more to burn off, and this spell was too small, too tight for what I needed. What I needed was big magic, raw, violent and angry, the kind that would shred my skin and make me bleed if I made a mistake.

Milly shifted on my shoulder, subtly reminding me that such a spell wasn't required. Her way of saying, *Save it for the real fight, fuckwit.*

I held the magic in a ball just a moment longer, until the strain of it made my skin burn and muscles quake. When I let it go, the summoning exploded in three short bursts of power, each one stronger than the last, a hammer on Hell's door.

Flame sparked in the center of the circle, hovering just above the bed and coalescing into a form vaguely like that of a German Shepherd. The demon dog's eyes flashed red, and he tilted his head to the side quizzically. "Having a bit of fun, Josiah?"

"Just blowing off some steam." That's right. Ignore the shaky hands and heavy breathing. A ciggy and I'd be back to normal like nothing'd happened at all. I lit one before continuing. "How's it been, Valefor? How're the kids?"

The demon showed me his fangs. "Dead. You and the Pale Horseman made short work of them on your last trip through."

Shit. Better apologize. "Sorry about that, mate. Just business. Hard to tell one hellhound from another when they're all trying to eat you."

"I'll make more. Now, what do you want?"

How to approach this? Valefor wasn't loyal by any means. No demon could be. As soon as we were done speaking, he'd run to whatever master he was serving in Hell and report that we'd spoken. That much was a given every time we talked. Still, I knew Valefor well enough to trust him not to shack up with anyone too awful. While the bastard didn't have any morals, he did have agendas, being King of the Hellhounds and the faithful companion of the next King or Queen of Hell among them.

And since I'd woven a binding spell into the summoning, he couldn't run off until I released him to do so, which meant I had him for as long as I wanted.

I plucked the cigarette from my lips and offered it to him. "You'll never guess who I ran into while I was in Hell last."

Human-like fingers reached out to grab the smoke and huff on it. "Don't fuck with me, Josiah. I know you and the Pale Horseman walked out with Khaleda Morningstar. Everybody knows. Half of Hell is still mourning Lucifer's passing. The other half has already sworn allegiances to people who want to kill you. Or kill her. Some want both."

"No kidding? Well, that's a problem, see, as I'd like to go on living."

Valefor puffed on the cigarette and blew out perfect rings of smoke. "Then you shouldn't have helped kill Lucifer Morningstar."

That was Valefor for you. Honest to a fault. I knew I'd signed my death warrant with that job, but maybe I could get out of it if I played my cards right.

Milly's legs tapped on the pulse in my neck. *Quit stalling and ask.*

I cleared my throat. "Thing is, Khaleda seems to be missing part of her soul. You know anything about that?"

Valefor's ears perked. I'd surprised him.

"Morningstar didn't authorize that."

"Figured as much. The two demons I found with her are dead. If they'd had a piece, the Horseman I was with would've noticed. I thought someone else might have it. You know who oversaw her punishment?"

The demon grunted and made a bird out of smoke in the air. "Well, whoever it was, they're idiots. Something like that would be too hot to move down here. Khaleda's in the running to take over. Anyone caught holding onto something that belonged to her can count the days left in his lifespan on one hand."

Guess that made sense. Most of Hell probably didn't know she had no interest in wearing her father's crown. They'd fear her. She'd have an established reputation as a killer, despite Lucifer's damage to it.

I held out my hand, gesturing for him to hand the ciggy back. "So where would they take it? Here?"

Valefor took one last puff before handing it back. The damn thing was little more than a stub already. Greedy bastard. "Souls are good currency. Hers would be worth a lot, especially to a mortal looking to expand his power base in the supernatural world, or some minor god. Not to mention, it could be used as blackmail. Anybody would want it, but it'd be a dangerous thing to hold onto. You'd have to have balls the size of coconuts and a private army to back it up. Khaleda's not known for being kind to people who betray her."

Oh, she's a handful all right. "Thanks for the

info. I'll look into it. Say, who're you working for these days with old Lucy gone?"

He shrugged. I'd never seen a dog shrug before. "Lying low for now. Let the bastards kill each other, and when the dust settles, the Hellhounds will support whoever's got the best odds. I don't like to hedge my bets. You know that."

"I do." Same old Valefor. I dropped the ciggy to the linoleum floor and ground it out. "Give the wife my love, would you?"

He grinned, showing pointed teeth. "Try not to die, Josiah. I enjoy our little chats. Now release me before I burn this whole block down."

Hellhounds. Fuckin' drama queens.

I spread my arms, murmured the chant in reverse, and called the power back to me. The circle broke, shattered with the withdrawal of power. New calm settled in the air as if the world itself had exhaled. Milly crawled down to hang on my chest over my still-pounding heart, and I collapsed on the bed, exhausted.

An hour of sleep, maybe two, and I'd be ready to go again. Hopefully, Khaleda could bleach her hair by herself, because I wasn't getting up to play salon.

My body humming with the satisfaction of spent magic, I drifted off into a well-deserved sleep.

5

KHALEDA

I came through the door of the hotel room and found Josiah passed out on the bed. He didn't even wake up when I slammed the door. How could he be so tired after doing nothing? I was the only one who'd actually done any fighting. All he did was get himself choked, smoke, and draw trouble. Why did I need him again?

I shifted the towel on my shoulders and wrapped a strip of foil on a strand of hair. *Because he knows people. I don't.* He'd promised to get me a passport, ID, and social security number that would hold up under even the highest scrutiny. That was the only reason I'd put up with him as long as I had.

Then there was this business with God's Hand. He'd called them a Special Forces arm of the Vatican. Since when did the Vatican have an army? I'd been around the world, murdered countless diplomats, commanders, and dictators and never run into them.

Maybe it's because of what he is. I leaned through the bathroom door to glance at him, sprawled out on the bed, face-down and snoring. He wasn't much to look at, was he? A haggard face with permanent worry lines carved into his forehead, pronounced aquiline nose, always enough facial hair to look more scruffy than rugged... Josiah leaned more toward waifish than powerful in build. He was about as threatening as a coat rack to look at.

Yet he'd been instrumental in helping kill Father. I'd felt his magic wrap around me when he carried me out of Hell, cradling me like a second pair of strong, protecting arms. It felt like a thick, impenetrable shield. He'd held it steady enough it barely seemed like any effort at all. The things I'd seen him do when he set his mind to it made it seem like he rivaled the Horsemen in power.

Maybe he wasn't much to look at, but he was the best mage I'd ever met. If he was worried about God's Hand tracking us down, I should be more concerned.

With my hair set, I shut the bathroom door and slid off the sweats. While I was at the drugstore, I picked up a few razors and decided it was high time to start taking care of myself, especially if I was going to be around Josiah. He'd find any reason to pick at me, critical bastard. I wasn't going to give him the satisfaction, not anymore. He'd be pissed I spent his money on expensive pink razors. Good. I'd make sure to leave the razors out where he'd see them just so he'd know.

I should've gotten more wine too, I thought and put my leg up on the side of the bathtub to shave it.

Something moved on the shower curtain just above eye level. I raised my gaze and locked eyes with a big, hairy spider the size of my hand. The razor clattered into the tub, and I let out an involuntary scream before jumping back.

The bathroom door crashed open, and a wide-eyed Josiah teetered in the doorway, brown hair sticking straight up. He looked at me.

I pointed at the spider. Inside, I was already cussing myself out. I should've had better control. Shrieking over a spider? Oh, he was going to have a field day with that.

"Milly!" Josiah exclaimed and shouldered past me to scoop the spider off the shower curtain. "Fuck me, I must've fallen asleep without putting the old girl up."

I closed my eyes, sucked in a breath through my nose and counted to three. "Josiah, why the fuck is there a tarantula in our hotel room?"

"She wouldn't've hurt you, Khaleda. Poor girl, you've scared her!"

"*I* scared *her*?" I glared at him, jaw unhinged.

He urged the spider onto his shoulder and she scampered behind his collar. "She weighs less than half a pound, and she's no bigger than a teacup! Of course, she's scared of you! Look at 'er!"

I started to scream for him to take his damn spider and get out, but hesitated, watching as he fiddled with the tarantula, trying to get her to come out. Instead, the little eight-legged monster cowered behind him like a frightened child while he cooed at it. It was the first time I'd seen him care about another living creature's well-being. Well, maybe there was more to this asshole than first seemed. I filed that information away for later use.

Instead of yelling, which would get me nowhere, I crossed my arms. "Sorry I scared your spider. Now, would you please go?"

His face twitched as if he'd been slapped before a smug smile crept onto his lips. "Someone mark the calendar. I believe that was a genuine apology followed by a 'please.' You've expanded your vocabulary!"

"Fuck you. Get out." I pointed to the door.

"There's my girl."

"I'm not your girl! I'm not your anything!" I shoved him toward the door only to step back when the spider reared up as if to attack.

"Easy, girl," Josiah said to the spider. "She's on our side." He turned around on the other side of the door and gave me a wink.

I slammed the door in his face. A spider for a pet. Could he be any weirder? Something was broken in that man's brain.

Because I could, I took extra long in the bathroom, going over various revenge scenarios in my mind. There was no way he'd just fallen asleep and forgotten about the giant spider he'd left to roam the room. It was a play, a dig at me, maybe even an excuse for him to get a chance to see me naked again. He'd been trying to get in my pants since we'd landed in New York, despite shoving everyone else at me too. Yet every scenario I could come up with left him impervious. He was virtually unshakable. No matter what I did to him, he'd just light up a cigarette, make a quip and pretend it didn't bother him. I'd never seen him shaken, but he'd leave an opening sometime. No man was perfect. I'd find the chink in his armor, just as I'd done to a thousand other men. And when I did, he'd regret crossing me.

I smiled to myself as I finished up my hair. *Be careful what you wish for, Josiah.*

***

When I came out of the bathroom, the spider was gone. Josiah stood beside the bed, staring at an image on the laptop screen, hands on his skinny hips.

I stopped dead in my tracks to take him in. He'd changed his clothes. I'd never seen him in anything other than a dirty t-shirt, plain black pants, and work boots. Today, he'd put on a sharp navy blue button-down and dress pants. *Ironed* dress pants. Did our room even have an iron?

"Who died?" I asked, coming to stand beside him.

He dropped his hands from his hips. "What? No one."

"You look like you're dressed for a funeral. Or maybe chaperone a high school dance. I can't decide."

He smoothed his hands over the shirt. I'd touched a nerve. Interesting.

"I think I look good in blue. Better than you look as a blonde," he said.

Nice try. I'm not so shallow I need you to

approve of my hair color, asshole. I gestured to the screen. "Who's he?"

"Daniel Monahan, CEO of Monahan Investments."

I waited for him to offer more, but he was unusually tight-lipped. He hadn't closed the screen yet, so I took another look. Monahan had the look of your typical thirty-something rich asshole. Thick, dramatic hair, charcoal suit, broad shoulders, confident smirk, and an aura that radiated money. The kind of asshole who'd try to fuck every woman he met with his eyes first and then flash around his checkbook to get them to crawl into bed with him. I'd dealt with enough assholes like him to know how to play the empty-headed and lonely woman on his arm. Just the kind of man Father would've thrown me at to break.

"And why do we care about some CEO?" I asked.

Josiah finally realized I was staring and closed the screen. "You don't. He's not your problem, but he is someone I need to settle with. He might be able to help get God's Hand off our backs so we can go our separate ways once I get your papers in a few hours."

So, he was trying to get rid of me. Good, the sooner we were apart, the better off we'd both be. "I take it you're going to see him? You made an appointment?"

He chuckled. "An appointment? Oh, I wouldn't worry. He'll see me."

"He'll see *us*." I concentrated and touched the hem of my shirt. Magic flowed out of me, shifting

the threads, thinning the material, and drawing it
tighter across my chest. The neckline plunged just
far enough to show a little cleavage. With another
touch and more magic, I changed the boring sweats
into a light gray pencil skirt and black stockings.
Once I molded my flip flops into a pair of stiletto
heels, I was every male office worker's fantasy. I
just needed a pair of dark glasses and it'd be
perfect.

Josiah stared. "Well, I was going to say no, but
it's hard to argue with *that*."

That's right, Josiah. I'm not letting you slip
away to waste an afternoon on nothing again. This
time, I'm going to keep an eye on you. I smirked
and went back to the bathroom to fix my hair.

6

JOSIAH

Monahan Investments was a Wall Street firm situated on the fiftieth floor of the Monahan Building, which sat directly across from the Trump Building, not to be confused with the Trump Tower over on Fifth Avenue. The Trump Building was an impressive seventy-five stories of brick and mortar. Monahan's was seventy-six stories tall. It boasted bigger windows, a grander entrance, and more flags all without the ostentatious gold leaf present in the building across the street.

Danny-boy was doing all right for himself, it seemed. I stood on the cobbled pedestrian street, looking up at the imposing structure, letting myself get dizzy. My stomach sank into my toes and my breath caught. Standing in the shadow of that monstrous thing brought back ancient memories of another high-rise on the other side of the country.

What was it about those bloody tall buildings that made my chest hurt?

Khaleda stopped next to me but didn't look up. A look crossed her face, somewhere between irritation and outright revulsion as she looked at the building. "What is it about men and oversized phallic-looking buildings?"

Guess size didn't impress her. She didn't understand how it was. It wasn't about whose was bigger. It was just about being *bigger*. There was always somebody to beat comparatively speaking, and no one would've understood that better than a man's man like Danny. His motto always had been bigger is better.

God, I wished I'd thought to smoke one before coming here.

"'Spose they look like dicks because that's what's inside," I said with a shrug.

Khaleda did that thing, the laugh without a laugh all women did when they weren't impressed. "In my experience, the more a man finds the need to project the size of his cock, the smaller it is."

"It's not all about size, though, is it?"

"Feeling a bit self-conscious, are we?" She flipped some of her new platinum locks behind her shoulder and smirked at me.

I returned her grin with one of my own. "Meet me in the janitor's closet, and you can see for yourself."

"I'll be sure to bring a magnifying glass."

We strolled into the lobby, which was about what you'd expect. Marble floors, lots of spotless reflective services, red carpet leading to an information desk only to turn and guide unsuspecting people to the open mouths of elevators waiting to gobble them up. We'd arrived in the early afternoon, just after when most bigwigs would've returned from their lunch appointments and prior to when they'd begin winding down their day.

The pretty brunette behind the information desk flashed us a welcome smile. "Can I help you?"

Time to turn on the Aussie charm. Americans loved it. "G'day, love. 'ow're you this arvo? That's a lovely jumper there."

Khaleda shot me the glimmer of an irritated glance as I leaned into the podium with a big, stupid grin.

The girl's retail-friendly smile shifted to one of surprise and delight. She touched the gray sweater she wore. "Oh, this? We call it a sweater here."

"Really? I s'pose you need one here, what with the snow 'n' cold comin' in. Must be awful on days like today, yeah? And workin' on a holiday weekend, too. They pay you extra for that, yeah?"

She started to say something, then stopped to think a moment. "Between you and me, I'm an intern. They don't pay me at all."

"A shame, that is." I leaned in. "'Scuse my French, but why is it these arseholes at the top can sit around and play golf in their dunders, making more per second than most of us sorry souls will in a year? It's not fair, really."

Her cheeks flushed. "Oh, I don't know. I just answer the phones and give directions."

"And you should be paid fer it." I pointed at

her. "Don't let 'em push you around. You're worth more than this. A pretty girl like you could go anywhere in this town."

Her smile returned, and she touched her hair. "You think so?"

"I know so. What's your name, lovely?"

"Gina." Her eyes flicked to Khaleda, her expression suddenly unsure. Was I flirting with her or just being nice?

"Well, Gina, I'm off to meet with Mr. Monahan upstairs. I'll be sure to give him a piece of my mind about not paying the interns in this building when I see him. Promise." I drew an X over my chest.

She glanced at the computer screen in front of her, considering asking me whether I had an appointment. If I'd buttered her up correctly, she'd forget about it. Gina looked back at me, and I gave her my best lopsided trust-me-unconditionally grin. "He's on the fiftieth floor. Take the elevators on the right."

"Thanks, Gina." I winked at her and turned away.

I followed the red carpet to a narrow hallway with spotless stainless-steel elevators on either side. After thumbing the up button, I stepped back to wait with Khaleda.

"That was sneaky of you," she said, glancing at me. "You know she's just going to phone upstairs ahead of us, right?"

Security was likely to meet us as soon as we stepped off the elevators. I'd hoped to meet some of Danny's staff, so I could evaluate the security of the building, just in case, but getting thrown out wasn't going to work for me.

The elevator doors opened, and we stepped into the yawning mouth. I pressed the button for the fiftieth floor. "That's where you'll come in, Khaleda. We can't leave without seeing him."

"How much of a scene do you want me to make?"

I cringed. A scene? Depending on what she meant... "Don't get the coppers called on us."

"I think I can manage that." She tugged her shirt down and tucked it into the skirt which she hiked up just enough to be suggestive without being indecent.

For a flash of a second, the skirt snagged on the lacy tops of her stockings which only came to mid-thigh before they met a garter where she'd tucked one of her obsidian daggers. How fast could she get to that? She'd moved fast against the God's Hand freaks; fast enough they hadn't even had time to react. Faster than I could've. Bastards had surprised me while I was asleep.

She caught me staring at the tiny snag in the fabric and narrowed her eyes at me. "Don't even think it."

"Unless you've got some power I don't know about, I'm still free to think and imagine. And I've got a very active imagination."

"It's never going to happen, Josiah." She tugged the skirt down and crossed her arms. "You're not my type."

I sighed and leaned against the elevator railing as we sailed upward in a metal box suspended by a metal string. "As far as I can tell, you don't have a type. Men, women, pious and hippies alike. Clear it up for me, Khaleda. What is it you're looking for in a partner?"

Her face lightened, and her lips turned up in the type of smile most people only show when no one is looking. "Someone boring. Somewhere quiet. Away from magic."

"Bull. You'd kill yourself with some average Joe. He'd be too easy for you."

She bristled. "It doesn't matter. What I want is irrelevant. What I am is what matters."

"And what's that?"

"A monster."

I was about to correct her when the elevator slid to a stop. She spent a quick moment composing herself before the doors slid open. As predicted, two buff fellas in uniform were waiting for us.

The one on the right gestured us forward. "Step out of the elevator."

As we did, Khaleda slid her hand onto his beefy forearm and smiled. Velvety soft magic slapped me in the face. I gritted my teeth against the urge to drop to the floor and sit at her feet like the dog I was.

The guard, however, just stared at her hand on him. "I need to see some identification."

Khaleda's face jerked. She was as surprised as I was that the magic hadn't instantly made him hers.

I put a hand on Khaleda's shoulder and pulled her back a step, placing myself between her and the guards. "Look, fellas, there's no need. I'm an old friend of Danny's. He's not expectin' me, I know that, but I'm only in town for a short minute. Just let him know I'm here. Josiah Quinn."

The guard on the left showed me his teeth. "IDs. Now."

"Come on, mate. Just three minutes. It's all I need."

More security closed in from the opposite direction, pushing us back into the elevator. The petite blonde woman at the receptionist desk picked up the phone and punched a single number, muttering into the phone. Christ, what a day for Khaleda's magic to fail.

One of the security guards grabbed my arm. "Joey?"

I cringed at the nickname. The big goons let me go though, so I adjusted my shirt and turned around to find Danny had come out of his office personally wearing a million-dollar smile. My heart turned into an excited mass of butterflies at the sight of him. "Hello, Danny-boy."

7

JOSIAH

Danny's office wasn't as big as I expected. You watch those shows on the telly, and all the executive types have these huge, modern offices done up in white with big windows and modern chairs. Not Danny. His was small enough to feel intimate while still being large enough to communicate his position effectively. The wall to my right was a giant plate glass window, but the view wasn't breathtaking. It was just a city view.

Snow swirled by. Heavy gray clouds pressed down on the city, promising more before the day was out, but the weather held back for now. Maybe it'd hold until after my meeting at Casablanca's.

"Sorry about the security," Danny said as we sat. "Can't be too careful in New York these days. The post-Nine-Eleven world is a dangerous place. Can I get you anything to drink?"

Khaleda offered a shy smile and declined. She'd already slipped into whatever character she was going to play. She thought she could seduce Danny with the right personality or turn of phrase, and I didn't have the heart to tell her otherwise.

"Bourbon if you've got it." I sat in one of the armchairs across from Danny's desk. Not bad.

He went to the bookcase that took up the wall directly behind his desk "Still no ice?"

"Not unless you want a black eye," I replied with a smile. I couldn't help it. The old banter was easy to fall into.

Danny poured two glasses, one with ice and one without and offered me the straight tumbler. "I see you're still carrying that old bag around."

I glanced down at the spelled bag sitting by my foot. "Haven't found one better, I guess."

He nodded before sitting in his chair, focused on Khaleda. When Danny focused on someone, it wasn't just a look. It was a predatory gesture, like placing a target on the other person's forehead. He flashed his shark teeth and pretended it was a smile. "Well, aren't you going to introduce me to your friend?"

"This is Annie Bennet," I lied.

Khaleda took Danny's hand when he offered it. "So pleased to meet you, Mr. Monahan. Joey's told me good things."

I clenched the tumbler in my hand tighter. I was going to make her pay for every time she called me Joey.

"Oh, he has? That's surprising, given how we left things." Danny leaned back in his chair. "We didn't part on good terms."

I shrugged. "Well, it's been twenty years."

"Eighteen," he corrected. "Eighteen years, six months, and eleven days since the last time I saw you. I do believe the last thing you ever said to me was that I should slink off and die."

Damn him and his near-perfect memory. I sipped from the glass and hoped it would lessen the tension in the air. I'd have sold my soul for a cigarette at that moment. "We were kids, Danny."

"It's Daniel now." He adjusted his tie. "But you're right. Who can expect teenagers to know what they want, right?"

The phrase was an ice-cold slap in the face. It triggered a memory I'd pushed into the deepest, darkest recesses of recollection.

Tiny bedroom. Heavy air. It smells like smoke and sex. There are four of us crammed into the room: me, Evette, Hannah, and Danny. It's so hot that everything feels covered in sweat, even the wall, though it feels cool against my back. The girls urge us on. How do you know if you've never tried it?

Danny knows. He's always known. It's as much a part of him as the air we're both breathing.

But I don't. I don't know anything. I'm fifteen. I know I like magic and Metallica, but that's about it. How are teenagers supposed to know anything about anything?

"Come on," Evette urges. "Hannah and me kissed. It's only a kiss."

But it's not. My heart is jackhammering in my chest so loud, I swear they can all hear it. It's not just a kiss, some small thing that means nothing. This is *Danny,* and I can't breathe because he's too close.

The memory fell back into darkness, and I shrugged. "It was a long time ago, wasn't it? You seem to have done okay for yourself in the meantime. CEO. Good for you."

He put his glass on the desk. "Let's cut the shit. You didn't come here to congratulate me. You came because my freelancer caught up with you yesterday. What are you doing in my city?"

"Your city?" He was bloody rich and amazing with magic, but last I heard no one person owned New York.

All expression left Danny's face, transforming him into a blank slate, a businessman on the verge of negotiating a deal. "Why are you here, Josiah? Business or pleasure?"

When I didn't respond, his attention went to Khaleda for a moment, considering something before he turned back to me. "You feel like a cigarette with that bourbon?"

I stood a little too fast and felt dizzy but smiled anyway. "Fuck yes."

***

We went to the roof for a smoke. Seventy-six stories up in the cold for a bloody dose of nicotine. Maybe I should quit.

Danny went to the edge of the roof and put one foot up on the narrow lip, leaning over it. The red cherry glow of his cigarette against the gray

afternoon sky seemed like the only color. He'd
shrugged on a long gray coat. Black pants, black
shoes… He always did like the darker colors. "It's
not personal, Joey. I promise."

"Just business. Is that it?" I struck a flame on
my lighter and held it to the end of my own
cigarette, watching the paper curl and burn away.

"Everything is just business anymore. Know
who comes and goes and everything he's capable
of. It's how I learned to survive. Christian taught
me that. Never let it get personal."

I frowned and walked to the edge with him.
Christian was the one nightmare we'd both
survived. A common enemy, something that
should've united us when all it did was push us
apart. "Christian's dead."

"I know. I heard. Heard you killed him. That
true?" Dark eyes scrutinized me. Was I a threat?
Had I killed Christian to take his place?

*Is that what this is, Danny-Boy? You think I'm
him?* "He went too far. He murdered Evette to fuel
his magic. Poor bastard thought if he had enough
power he could become a god."

"He was a cult leader. What'd you expect?"

I shrugged. "I don't know. I wasn't in it for the
religion."

He smiled, a warm, genuine smile, not the
shark grin from earlier. "No, not you. You were
there for the magic. And Christian had that. He was
good."

"You were better." I regretted saying it as soon
as it fell out of my mouth. It felt like too heavy a
compliment, even if it were true.

"I *am* better. Here, watch." He took a step back and kicked some snow aside to reveal a perfect circle had been laid on the roof. Was it steel? No, too much iron in steel. It'd have to be silver. Shit, he'd gone all out.

Danny drew in the magic and expelled it with all the ease of a breath, a big grin on his face. "Go on! Hit me with something!"

I sighed. "Danny, are ya sure, mate?"

"Don't call me mate unless you mean it, Joey. Now hit me!"

Fine, ya dipstick. You want me to hit you? I'll hit you. I flicked the half-smoked cigarette off to a snowy corner of the roof and shrugged off my coat, so I'd have freedom of movement.

"Don't hold back," he taunted. "I can take it."

I closed my eyes and extended a hand toward the snow swirling its way downward. Cold licked at my exposed skin. Snowflakes touched my hand and melted, trickling under my cuffs as icy water. The magic formed around my hand, a velvet glove with plenty of power. I formed it into a single stroke of energy and sent it careening toward Danny with a command word.

The beam of frozen magic struck the edge of Danny's circle and sailed straight through. Panic gripped me for a fraction of a moment. I'd sent something too strong. The poor bastard had overestimated his reach.

But Danny batted it aside with a laugh and shouted, "Again! Something harder this time!"

I obliged, this time with a shot of black fire.

"Please!" He moved his arms, spreading his

fingers wide to suspend the fire in place. With a few quick movements, he took control over my spell and made the fire march in a circle. Another twitch of his fingers and the fire changed into a dozen black butterflies that exploded into fireworks.

Another spell and we were back in L.A., boys of fifteen and seventeen on a rooftop in unbearable heat, battering each other with fire, ice, and electric current. We batted raw magic back and forth, speeding up the exchange until eventually the spell would career out of control and we'd have to race to shut it down before it killed someone. It was easy magic, but no less deadly for its ease. One wrong move and I could kill him. One miscalculation on his part and it could be me careening off that rooftop. And still, we traded spells laughing like grade school boys.

I didn't know how long we stayed up on that rooftop, slinging spells at each other, but we didn't stop until we were both senselessly drained and slick with sweat. We lay in a snow drift, staring up at the way our cigarette smoke seemed to cut the flurries in two.

"I haven't done that in forever," he said with a big, dumb grin.

I hadn't either, but I didn't say as much. Now that we weren't knee deep in the magic, all I could think about were the eighteen years that had passed and how much he'd changed since the last time I saw him. "What're you doing employing demons, mate?"

He raised a hand to the sky and made a fist. "I wanted this building, so I worked until I could buy it. Then I decided I wanted to organize all the shithead demons in this city, so I did. They all work for me now. Christian never would've thought I could. I know he's dead, but I needed to know that I could. That I could have whatever I wanted, no holds barred. I get what I want now, Josiah. Everything I want."

"That's fire you're playing with, Danny-Boy. You're going to get burned."

"I can handle it." He lowered his fist, and we lay there in silence for a long moment before he continued, "You wouldn't have come to me if I hadn't sent him, would you?"

"And why would you want to talk to me after all this time?" It didn't make sense. I was the reason he'd had to leave our little group. After I defeated him in a duel and took his spot as Christian's second, he chose banishment rather than to accept the defeat. I'd robbed him of more than just his dignity when I beat him in that duel. I'd taken away his teacher, his future in magic. Or so I thought.

"Because you're the only person who's ever understood magic the way I do." He shook his head. "Everyone else wants to use it as a means to an end, or else just wants to keep their magic under wraps. Like it's some fucking secret. It doesn't have to be. Give me twenty minutes and a big enough battery, and I can rule more than just the demons in Manhattan. I could have New York City. I could have the whole damn country. I could run Hell itself."

I sat up, suddenly cold. "If this is a run away with me and take over the world speech—"

"Why not? The idiots running things right now are making a mess of things. We always talked about how we could use magic to fix things. Why not do it? Now that there's a position opened up, we can. The two of us together, we'd be unstoppable. It'd just like old times."

I stood and shook melting snow from my clothes before kicking aside a snow drift to retrieve my coat. "No offense, Danny, but I'm not that pig-headed adolescent boy with delusions of grandeur that I was eighteen years ago. I can barely run my own life. I've got no interest in running anyone else's."

Danny sat up, but he didn't move from where he was.

I made for the door down from the roof and pulled it open. "Thanks for the spar, Danny-Boy. Good luck with taking over the world."

"Josiah!" He fought to his feet, a strange gleam in his eyes. "I meant what I said. I want you back. The way we were before Christian fucked us up. And I always get what I want."

Something stabbed at my heart, an old, scabbed-over wound that went so deep, it almost killed me once. "Not today, mate."

I pulled open the door and left him alone on the roof all over again.

8

KHALEDA

Josiah and Daniel didn't leave me alone in the office but made me go sit in the lobby and watch Josiah's bag. I spent the entire time angrily flipping through magazines under the watchful eye of the Monahan security team. He'd dragged me all the way downtown in the cold and ditched me again. Even forcing myself to go along with him hadn't stopped him from running off to waste our time.

This side trip didn't help me get my soul back any faster, and it had nothing to do with me other than the trouble Josiah had gotten me into. If he'd just left me alone, God's Hand never would've noticed me to begin with.

If he'd left you alone, you'd be dead, I reminded myself. Those first few days after he carried me out of Hell were a blur, but I clearly remembered him sitting with me, forcing hot soup down my throat. When I first refused to bathe, he shoved me into the shower, leaned against the glass shower door, and smoked a cigarette to keep me from getting out. He'd insisted he wasn't taking me to the airport covered in four days of sweat and vomit. I hadn't even wanted to go to the damn airport. At the time, I hadn't wanted to do anything.

I turned the page. He liked to pretend he was a selfish bastard, but somewhere, deep down, he had to care about something.

Footsteps came down the narrow row of cubicles, and Josiah appeared walking heavier than normal. He'd drawn his hands into fists. Underneath his coat, his nice shirt was patchy and wet. I'd never seen him look so pissed.

I kept my calm and gently put the magazine aside to stand.

"We're going," he announced and paused to collect his bag.

I wanted to ask him what happened, but the guards and secretary were staring. With a smile, I turned and followed Josiah to the elevators, reaching him just as he jammed his whole fist into the down button. "I take it you and Danny aren't getting the band back together?"

"Fuck this cold," he growled. "And fuck this city. The sooner I can get out of this place, the better. Can't fuckin' breathe here."

I'm sure that has nothing to do with the cigarettes you're always sucking down. Normally, I'd have said that out loud, but he didn't seem in the mood for verbal sparring. It was no fun to poke at him if he was already angry. There'd be no challenge.

We got into the elevator. He was too distracted by whatever was pissing him off to hit the button, so I did.

"Did you talk to him about God's Hand?" I asked, stepping away from the array of buttons.

He crossed his arms and stared at the elevator doors as if he could melt them with his gaze.

"Josiah! Did you talk to Danny Monahan about helping us with God's Hand?"

"He's no help."

He didn't ask, the ass. I sighed. "Okay then, do you at least have a plan to track down the missing parts of my soul? Or am I own my own for that too?"

"I've got a plan." His voice was flat, deflated as if the whole world were crushing him into a pancake. What the hell had gone on between the two of them?

I had to do something to bring him back to the present, or I was going to lose the only help I had, but what? The only things Josiah cared about were himself and that stupid spider. Threatening him would just make him dig his heels in harder, and if he even thought I was going to hurt his precious arachnid, he'd flip his lid. Maybe if I could get him to shift his focus to the work, give him something to work toward, he'd stop brooding.

I leaned against the back of the elevator. "What's your plan?"

He shrugged. "Modified tracking spell. Wherever your soul is, it should be easy to form a sympathetic link since we've still got some to work

with. The biggest challenge will be extracting a
sample to work with. I can't just pull out bits of
your soul, but I will need to have unrestricted access
for an unspecified period of time. It's delicate work,
and once I begin, there can't be any interruptions.
It'll also take a significant amount of power. For
anyone looking, we'll be a beacon the entire time
I'm working."

Meaning if God's Hand was actively looking
for us, they'd find us. No wonder he wanted to get
them off our case before looking for the lost pieces
of my soul. He could've told me that. Well, at least
there was a way forward.

The elevator jerked to a stop and the lights
flickered before dying. When they came back up, it
was only the emergency lighting. We'd only made
it as far as the twenty-second floor. I leaned forward
and tapped the lobby button, but the display didn't
respond. Someone had cut power to our elevator. I
looked over at Josiah.

He squinted. "Bugger."

Something heavy impacted the top of the
elevator car. We retreated to the corners. If whoever
it was up there had guns, we were fucked.
Something sharp grated against the metal, making it
scream at a frequency that hurt my teeth. I cringed
and covered my ears.

Above, the ceiling peeled back, opening as if
we stood inside a tin can. A bone-chilling roar
shook the car, and a lion stuck its head into the
opening, flashing huge teeth. Wait…a lion? Why
the hell was there a lion in an elevator shaft?

Huge claws tore at the wall as it tried to pull

itself into the car with us. I drew the dagger from my garter and threw it. The blade spun and struck the lion's paw, pinning it to the elevator wall. It roared. Powerful muscles flexed, shifting under the skin and rolling like waves. Fur disappeared, and the proportions shifted until the paw became a human hand. Another hand reached into the car and pulled the knife out.

A lion shifter. Great.

Josiah finally found the sense to back away from the lion and join me on my side of the elevator car. "You got any silver on you?"

"No. You?"

He pushed his sleeves up. "Keep it busy."

I was about to ask him how I was supposed to keep a four-hundred-pound man-lion busy with the beast dropped into the car with us. He stood on his leonine hind legs like a man, though the only thing human about him were his arms, and even they were slowly shifting back to their animal form. Dagger-like claws sprouted, and sharp teeth snapped before his cat lips stretched into a smile.

He thought I was unarmed. Idiot. Even without my knives, I was my own weapon.

The lion slashed at me, but I ducked low, avoiding his strike with ease and throwing myself inside his range to deliver a precise strike to his stomach. It was a wall of hard muscle, and he knew how to flex to take the punch. With that mane of thick hair, his throat wasn't a viable target, but his balls were. I followed the punch with a kick that left him dropping to all fours. The move would've crushed me if I didn't slip away toward the front of the elevator at the last second.

Claws grazed my back in three lines of heat. I wasn't fast enough. Another swipe took my legs from under me, and I landed face-down in a puddle of my own blood. The lion's muscles coiled, preparing to strike.

Josiah struck first. Bright blue flame sprouted in his hand, and he tossed it at the lion. All that fur went up as if he'd been soaked in gasoline and the lion exploded into a blue fireball, but he didn't burn. He opened his mouth and inhaled sucking all the fire up before spitting it back at Josiah in a stream of sticky magic napalm.

Josiah leaped out of the way, managing only to get his clothing singed. He landed on the floor next to me, patting out the flames.

"Quit dicking around and kill it!" I snarled. Despite trying to stem the flow of blood with a firm grip, I'd already lost enough blood that I was feeling dizzy. My role in the fight was over.

The lion shifter swiped at Josiah who rolled out of the way, leaving streaks of blood over the elevator floor. He kicked at the lion, but it was a pointless gesture. The lion just caught his leg and squeezed, trying to crush the bone.

It was a mistake to leave Josiah's hands free. He slammed his palm into the blood pooling next to him with a shout. Thick, black magic swirled up inside the elevator car, dark and foul enough it made my stomach turn. The power swirled and surged, pulling at my own magic. I fought the urge to answer whatever he'd just called, and my mind reeled with the effort.

The lion shifter's eyes went wide as the magic hit him, and he tried to shake it off as it were water.

"*Kneel!*" Josiah barked, except he didn't say it in English or any other Earth language for that matter. He'd used a language native to Hell and her demons.

The shifter grimaced, mouth fighting to form words. "You think you can command me? With your demonic speech?"

Josiah gritted his teeth and extended a blood-soaked hand toward the lion, continuing in the same language. "Kneel, you son of a bitch!"

The lion sank to his knees, eyes wide with terror his voice didn't betray. "You can't escape. We see all. We know all. Someone will kill you."

Josiah stood on shaky legs and staggered to the other side of the elevator to grab my dagger from where the lion had dropped it. "Yeah, maybe," he said, stepping up behind the lion shifter. "But it isn't going to be you."

He plunged the dagger into the beast's neck, just above its chest and sawed through muscle, tendon, and gristle. The shifter roared and snarled, but whatever magic Josiah had worked kept it from fighting back. Blue light lit the wound as the shifter's body tried to heal the damage, but the dagger cut too deep too fast. In the space of a minute, he'd severed the head to the spine. With a snarl, he snapped bone and tore the head free, tossing it aside.

The body shrank back into the body of a naked man built like a soldier. On his chest was a tattoo, a handprint. Underneath, in a curling script, it read:

Manus Dei. God's Hand.

Josiah went to his knees in front of me. "Let's get you patched up."

Pantyhose make a decent tourniquet in a bind. The claws hadn't nicked any arteries, so I thought I'd be fine with some stitches. For now, the stockings would have to do. I stripped them off and let Josiah do most of the work, mostly because the injury was awkward for me to get at. I thought he'd make some smart remark as he was prone to do. Instead, he worked with the quiet and thoughtful efficiency of someone used to patching up serious wounds in bloody elevators.

While he finished tying the stocking around my thigh, I studied the dead shifter in the elevator and thought of Victis. "Why was a shifter working for God's Hand hiding in your friend's building?"

"He's not my friend," Josiah answered a little too quickly for it to be true. "And I don't know. Danny's organizing the demons in Manhattan. Seems to be at odds with him working with an organization like God's Hand."

He had a point. If Monahan was working with demons, zealots wouldn't want anything to do with him. Still, it couldn't be chance. Angels and demons didn't work together, but they didn't just ignore each other either. The two forces were diametrically opposed. They couldn't help but fight each other, so why had this soldier ignored the man gathering demons to him to attack us?

"Why is he organizing demons?"

Josiah shrugged. "Power. Money. Control. Typical bullshit." He was staring at the way my blood-soaked shirt stuck to my chest.

Here I was, covered head to toe in blood and we were sitting less than a foot from a decapitated body, and all he could think about was sex. Most people would be in the corner vomiting from the smell or the panic of having to deal with an assassin, but not him. I couldn't decide if it was pathetic and disgusting or interesting.

"So God's Hand should be trying to stop him," I pointed out. "Instead they're trying to kill us. What've they got against you?"

"Nothing other than my entire existence."

"They seem to be taking it rather personally."

"Zealots aren't known for rational thinking." He stood and offered me a hand. His palm was stained deep red with the dead man's blood.

I slid my palm into his and used the railing in the elevator to pull myself up without putting any weight on my injured leg. He gestured for me to turn around. I hesitated.

"Need to see about the scratches on your back, sweetheart," he explained.

Right. That stupid lion had swiped my upper back too. The injury still burned, but it wasn't bleeding as bad, so I'd almost forgotten about it.

I turned around and gripped the railing in the corner. "What was that spell you used?"

"Difficult. I pulled on the residual power in your blood. You felt it?"

I nodded and then suppressed a shudder as he brushed my hair aside. Breath tickled the back of my neck as he leaned in for a closer look. My monster stretched inside as if waking from a long sleep. "I didn't know you could do that."

"You'd be surprised what I can do." He passed his hands over the three cuts in my back, filling them with a faint buzz of magic.

My heart thumped in my throat. I swallowed it and turned my head to give him a sharp warning look over my shoulder. "How does it look?"

"Oh, everything back here looks amazing as always."

"Creep." I turned around, expecting him to move away, but he didn't back off.

"Icy bitch."

We stared each other down for a moment before he took a deep breath and a step back.

"So," he began, walking through the blood to retrieve his bag. Miraculously, the stupid bag didn't have a spot of blood on it. "We'll have to get out of here one way or another. How's the leg? Strong enough to take a bit of weight?"

Josiah dug through his bag and came out with a crowbar.

"Seriously?" I growled. "You have that in there, but you don't have a tourniquet or a proper bandage?"

He looked at me as if I'd just suggested he chop off his own arm. "If I'm ever so bad off I need a tourniquet, I'd never find it before I passed out. As for bandages, what are you complaining about? It's dealt with."

Of course, it would never occur to him that anyone else would need a tourniquet or bandage. God forbid he should have an ounce of sympathy for any living thing with less than eight legs.

He used the crowbar to pry open the elevator doors. The elevator car had stopped between floors, so he hoisted me up on his shoulders to climb out. As I pulled myself to freedom, I couldn't help but picture the elevator cable suddenly snapping, sending the car careening down the last twenty plus floors. If that happened, it'd snap my spine. Maybe I'd get lucky, and it'd break Josiah's neck when he climbed through.

No such luck, of course, but a girl could hope.

Once we were both on solid ground again, we found ourselves on an empty office floor. Probably closed for the long holiday weekend. Tomorrow was Thanksgiving. Small blessing, I guess. At least we wouldn't have people running to call the cops about the bloodstained people in the lobby.

Rather than take an elevator the last twenty-three stories, Josiah thought it would be better if we took the stairs. He wasn't the one walking around in heels with a bleeding gash on her leg. I could've strangled him, except I had to keep one arm around his neck as we navigated the stairs. It was the only way to keep weight off my injured leg. Every step still hurt.

I gritted my teeth as we moved from the landing of the fourteenth floor to the next set of stairs. "If I never see a set of stairs again, it'll be too soon."

Josiah grunted. "You should let up on the wine, sweetheart. You're getting heavy."

"And you smell like you've forgotten how to shower."

"Says the woman I had to force into the bath a

few days ago."

Point for Josiah, but I didn't acknowledge it aloud. "So, what's the history with you and this guy anyway?"

"We were in a cult together in L.A."

I looked over at him as he struggled with my weight. A cult? He didn't strike me as the cultist type.

"Didn't feel like a cult at the time," he quickly explained. "All either of us cared about was the magic. And the girls. Lots of magic in the nineties was in cult circles. Assholes with a drop of power figured out they could get more of it by luring kids with sex and drugs. Drug them up, take their blood, turn yourself into a god."

"Like the Manson family?"

He shook his head. The move threw me off balance, and I had to brace against the railing for a moment. "We didn't kill anyone. Christian was careful. Never asked for blood directly. He got most of what he wanted willingly. Bastard gathered runaways with magical talent. Promised us the world. Offered us anything we wanted. Money, influence, sex, drugs, music. Whatever. Then, when we were too far in, then came the bloodletting. He made us fight each other."

"For drugs?"

"For his love and approval."

That's the tension between him and Monahan, I realized. They'd shared the same father figure only to have that father reject Monahan in favor of Josiah. After time on the street, at such a tender age, they would've been desperate for acceptance and approval from a father figure, and the bastard who took them in used it against them. It was conjured loyalty, bought and paid for with pain and blood. Just like Father had done with me.

I suddenly understood Josiah on a level that felt too intimate.

I broke away to lean on the wall and turned to him. His hair was plastered to his forehead with sweat. "I can walk myself if you slow down. I just need the railing."

He coughed, rubbed his chest, and made a sweeping gesture forward. "After you, Princess."

Ass. I try to be nice, and he shoves it back in my face like an insult.

We walked the last thirteen stories mostly in silence. On the second floor, I stumbled, and he tried to help me, but I shoved him away. I didn't need him. Not until I ran out of railing anyway. On the bottom floor, I tried my leg and almost fell.

He caught me by the elbow. "Hit me if you're inclined. Either way, you need me. I'll throw you over my shoulder and carry you out if you make too much of a fuss."

I jerked my arm away. "As if you could. You were red in the face just from me leaning on you."

"I carried you out of Hell. I'll carry you out of here."

I didn't have a good retort for that, so I snapped my mouth shut and linked my arm in his. "Fine, but if you grab my ass, I'll break your fingers."

He grinned and winked at me. "How many fingers are we talkin' about?"

"All of them," I said through clenched teeth.

"Might be worth it."

Gina was still at the desk when we walked by, two bloodied and battle-hardened people. Her already pale face turned white, and she jumped to her feet.

"No cause for alarm, Gina," Josiah offered. "But you might want to hold off on asking for a raise for a few."

She immediately picked up the phone to call the police.

9

KHALEDA

I stumbled out to Wall Street with Josiah into a wall of white. On the opposite side of the street, two businessmen hurried by, briefcases in one hand, phones tucked to their ears. Sirens screamed in the distance, drawing closer by the second. Response time in Manhattan was impressive.

Josiah pulled right while I tried to drag him to the left. We turned on each other, trading threatening glares. He was thinking about hitting me. *Go on, make it count. I hope it's worth spending the rest of your life in prison.*

A yellow cab screeched to a stop where Wall Street ran into Williams and laid on the horn. We spun toward it and saw Victis leaning out the window, gesturing to us. That stupid bastard! Where had he gotten a cab? Not that I had time to complain. I was too busy limping toward him.

Josiah jerked open the back door, shoved me inside and threw himself in just as the red and blue came sliding down the street.

"Drive!" I shouted, and Josiah pulled the door closed.

Victis hit the gas, and we spun in place, fishtailing a moment before the vehicle jerked forward. We were cruising down the narrow, snow-covered street in no time. Well, crawling. There was too much snow on the road to go faster than twenty miles an hour.

My leg ached. I shifted so I could stretch it out, careful not to bump into Josiah. "What are you doing, Victis?"

He tried to tuck his head between his shoulders. "I came to warn you, Teacher. They sent someone to kill you."

"We know," Josiah snapped. "Lion shifter, eh? Any more surprises we should know about?"

"Yes, there seems to be a disagreement about how you should be handled. One of the local commanders, Commander Petra, wants to kill you. Commander Decimus wants you brought in alive for questioning. They argued."

"Can I take it this Commander Petra won?"

Victis shook his head. "There still hasn't been a consensus. I believe the divide goes higher. There has been talk of a schism within the order."

I focused on the passing buildings. It had really started to come down, covering the city in a wet white blanket. The cars normally parked on both sides of the street were absent while mounds of snow took their place. Getting around in the weather would be tough. Maybe that'd work in our favor and I'd be able to get a good night's sleep.

We went over a bump that jostled my leg, and I hissed through my teeth in pain. I'd have to heal. Dammit all, the only way to do that was going to be to draw energy from someone else. Considering my options were to either further damage Victis or slink down to Josiah's level, that wasn't going to happen anytime soon.

"Can you magic those wounds closed?" Josiah asked.

I narrowed my eyes at him. "Don't you think I would've done that already if I could've?"

"You aren't at the top of your game though, are you? You still haven't had a proper feeding."

Give it a rest. I folded my arms and turned my attention back to the window.

"Come on, Khaleda. I'm not trying to be an asshole for once. I'm only pointing out the obvious. You're dead weight if you're injured. We still need each other."

"A couple of stitches and I'll be fine," I lied.

Victis slowed to take the next turn and head south.

Josiah tapped on the grate. "We're not going back to Chinatown just yet, mate. I've got someone I've got to meet at Casablanca's in Brooklyn at five."

He had to be kidding. We were covered in blood. Though he was putting on a good front, he had to be hurting after that fight. If we got attacked again, we'd be screwed.

"Dressed like that?" I gestured to his clothes. "I

thought we were avoiding the police."

I took his grunt to be an affirmative acknowledgment until he started unbuttoning his shirt. He shrugged it off, revealing a pale canvas littered with art. Lines and circles intersected over his shoulders, arms, and chest accompanied by writing in Latin. Here and there, an alchemical symbol interrupted the symmetry. The most complex circle lay in the center of his chest and intersected several smaller circles. It was the only circle on his body no line intersected. An anchoring spell, but for what?

I couldn't guess at the meaning for the rest of them. That type of magic wasn't my expertise, but the tattoos were everywhere, stretching from wrist to shoulder and down to his belt. When he bent forward to retrieve his bag, I saw even more on his upper back.

I'd always thought of him as waifish and thin, but he had a surprising amount of muscle definition, especially in the arms. If he'd dress in something other than those sloppy shirts and loose jeans, he'd be something to look at.

"You keep staring, and I might start to blush." Josiah grinned.

I tore my eyes away and glued them to the back of Victis' head. "I was only wondering about all the tattoos. You didn't have them before."

"When I was in Naraka, you mean." He took a package of baby wipes out of his bag and used them to clean some blood off his face.

Naraka. I hadn't even wanted to say the place's name. Of all the kingdoms in Hell, that place was the worst. It's where he'd found me hanging on a rock with six-inch spikes driven into my hands. I stared at the white scars on my palms. That place was awful. It stripped everything from you; your dignity, your hopes, and your clothes. It was so hot they just burned away. I wasn't coherent enough to notice much during the rescue, but it was difficult not to notice being rescued by two naked men.

"My physical body wasn't in Naraka," he continued and cleaned his hands with another wipe. "That was just a projection, one I create with my own will. I can make myself up with all the ink, but there's generally no point in focusing too much on the aesthetics. They're for protecting my body while I'm away."

"Good. Now I can say with certainty I've never seen you naked."

"That can always be arranged." He shifted so he could drop his blood-soaked pants.

I should've turned away. After all, I didn't have any interest in seeing him without his clothes on. But the tattoos left me curious. How far did they go?

"You want me to take anything else off, princess?" He winked at me.

I rolled my eyes. "Please don't. I don't want to throw up in the cab."

He got his pants on by the time we reached the Brooklyn Bridge. It was iced over, and we had to slow down or risk sliding, but we made it across. Coming back might be another story. I hoped this trip to get my papers wouldn't take long. Not only was the weather getting worse, but my leg was starting to ache. I carefully lifted the stocking holding me together to check on it. The bleeding had mostly stopped, but I was worried walking on it would just tear it open again. Thankfully, I'd planned on waiting in the car while he went in.

"So what happens once I have my papers?" I asked.

Josiah pulled on a plain white t-shirt to go with his black jeans. "All depends on you. What d'you want?"

The question struck me like lightning, making my muscles go rigid and my heart pump faster. Panic settled in my chest like a balloon full to bursting. The only thing I'd ever wanted was to kill my father and save my brother, but they were both dead now. I couldn't avenge my brother either because he chose his path. I had nothing, and I knew no one. If I walked away, I'd be completely alone in the world with no purpose.

What did normal women do? Get a job. Get married. Raise a family, none of which I had any interest in. I couldn't see myself showing up to sit behind a desk and answer phones every day. I needed more than that, and yet I didn't know what. Something exciting, something that made my heart beat quicker and let me forget all the terrible shit I'd been through. But what?

"I don't know," was all I could say.

10

JOSIAH

She was lost, drowning in possibilities while the past dragged her to the bottom of the deepest trench. It was written all over her face. I'd smoked and drank and fucked that feeling away enough times to recognize it. The year after I left Christian's cult was a haze of self-destructive days, spent mostly on the verge of suicide. I didn't want to die, but I didn't have a reason to live either. If she was in that same place, I couldn't just let her go off on her own, everything else aside.

I placed my hand on top of hers. It was meant to be a comforting gesture.

Khaleda jerked her hand away and wrinkled her nose at me. Lip curled, body recoiled, she looked at me as if I were covered in oozing boils. "What the fuck?"

She doesn't want to be comforted, ya big dumb

fuckwit. No more than you ever did. Comfort isn't purpose. A life's purpose was something I couldn't offer, but maybe I could get her through the next few days.

I pulled one of the cleaning wipes and offered it to her. "Clean up, will ya? You look like shit."

She jerked the wipe out of my hand. "I hate you, you know that?"

I smiled to myself. Hate was as good a purpose as any, at least for a few days.

The Casablanca wasn't in the worst Brooklyn neighborhood, but it wasn't a great place either. Sitting in the two hundred block of Malcolm X Boulevard, it was within spitting distance of both an elementary school and a church. Plan your outing right, and you could drink yourself silly, hit the confessional, and then pick little Johnny up from school all in the same afternoon.

With it being the day before Thanksgiving and all the snow, the block was deserted but for the hardcore drinking crowd sliding into the Casablanca for a drink. Mostly middle-aged men, old enough to have drunk away their better years, but still young enough to fear growing old. My kind of crowd.

Khaleda had Victis stop in the street to let me out. Plan was, they'd drive around the block a few times and I'd go in, get the papers, and leave. Women. Always trying to hurry everyone else. Still, she needed some stitches and I was knackered from all the magic, so maybe it was for the best.

Cold wind bit at my nose and the tips of my ears as I stepped out of the cab into the street. I turned the collar of my coat up to keep the wind at bay and tucked my head low. It was a short trek up the sidewalk, but I was plenty chilled when I opened the door to bask in the relative warmth.

The bar was more of a long, cramped room with sparse but slightly rustic décor. Wooden chandeliers full of soft electric lights meant to look like flame swung and turned in the wind that followed me in. Mismatched stools and a couple of chairs sat in front of a slab of a bar. Aside from the bartender—a kid in his mid-twenties—there were only three patrons in the bar.

I didn't know what August Jessup looked like, or if he was even there. The demon I'd conned had promised me he'd be there, but he was a demon. Their word wasn't exactly binding.

I stood in the doorway, holding the door open until everyone stopped what they were doing and looked up. "Cold enough for ya gents?"

The bartender scowled. So did the two fellas at the bar. The third man, who'd seated himself at the only table, pulled his cap down further and tried to disappear. *Found you.*

I let the door swing shut and went to join him. Just to make sure, I stopped by the table and put my hands in my pockets to warm them. "August Jessup?"

An older man with sagging skin over sharp features raised dark eyes to me. He looked like he hadn't slept in a week. "Tell me Josiah Quinn's not your real name."

"Unfortunately for both of us, it is." I pulled out the chair across from him and sat down. "I'm told you're the best forger in the city."

"Best on the Eastern Seaboard," he boasted. "And the most expensive. You have money?"

"I wouldn't come to you if I didn't." I brought out the picture I'd grabbed from my bag earlier. It was a candid shot of Khaleda taken just a few days after she'd come back. She was half-drunk in the photo, but it was the best I could do. "This is her."

He frowned down at the picture, grunted and took a swig from his beer. "She your girlfriend? Too pretty to be a sister."

"She's a friend. The documents need to hold up internationally."

He gave me a measured look, sizing me up. Was I good for it? Was I a cop? "I can do that, but seein' as I'm taking such a risk, I'm going to need half the payment upfront."

"I'm not carrying it around with me, mate. That'd be suicide in this economy."

The door to the bar opened, and two big fellas stepped in. They were both wearing jackets too expensive to be slumming it in this part of town, and they walked like they were carrying. Another man followed them into the bar. He was twice as wide and stood tall enough he had to duck to come inside. He folded his hands in front of him and planted himself in front of the door. The two suits scanned the place, settled on me and started forward.

I turned back to August. A blue sheen passed over his eyes, and he sported a big grin full of perfect teeth. He lifted the photo of Khaleda. Bright blue fire sprang up between his fingers, melting the photo.

Fuck me, this was a setup.

11

JOSIAH

I lit a cigarette.

The thugs stopped a few paces behind me, blocking any chance of an exit. To my left, the other two patrons turned on their stools to face me. The bartender put down the glass he was working on polishing and leaned back to cross his arms over an inscribed iron cross hanging around his neck.

"Which one are you then?" I asked the monster across the table from me. Maybe the meat suit's name was August Jessup, but whatever was riding him was something else.

He let the ashes of the photo fall to the table. "My name is Commander Decimus Tullius, primus of the *Ordo Aracani*, legatus of the *Manus Dei*."

"Aces. With all those titles, you've got the credentials to tell the rest of your people to fuck off."

The two big fellas behind me shifted forward.

Commander Decimus waved his hand, calling off his dogs. "We're not here to fight."

"Too bad." I blew out a heavy mouthful of smoke. "Six on one could be interesting. Made short work of your lion friend, by the way. And the two you sent to break into the flat."

He twisted his thin lips into a sly smile. "Now, that's a lie. Victis was just fine when I saw him a few hours ago, although I suspect he's been compromised. Your succubus friend dominated his mind and robbed him of his free will not so long before you relocated to that disgusting motel in Chinatown. The three of you shared a short exchange before you went to see your associate, Mr. Monahan, where he discussed his desire to rule the city. How am I doing?"

A spell. That'd be the only way he could've known all that. Even if he'd had me followed, he wouldn't know about the rooftop. Danny and I had been alone. It'd have to be a damn good spying spell if I didn't know about it.

I leaned one arm over the back of my chair and said nothing. Usually, when you say nothing, the idiot making the offer can't help himself. He just kept talking to fill the space.

"You see, Josiah," the commander continued, "I could've had you killed at any time. While you were in transit to the hotel. While you were asleep on the bed. While you were consorting with demons."

"You've made your point." I finished up the ciggy and crushed it out on the table, wishing I'd

thought to get a drink before all this started.
"You've been watching me, waiting to make a
move. Why not just kill me then?"

He was silent.

I sighed. "You want something from me. The
God Squad doesn't sully itself chatting with half-
breeds like me unless they need something they
can't do. What's the matter? Hands tied? Your little
quid pro quo agreement with the man downstairs
got you in a bind?"

"You know the agreement." He folded his
hands on the table. "Heaven doesn't interfere with
events on Earth directly, and Hell abides by the
same rules. We influence. We whisper and suggest.
No more, no less."

If only everyone abided by that agreement,
maybe humanity wouldn't be such a dumpster fire.
Unfortunately, they only stuck to the letter of the
law and not the spirit. Even with the agreement in
place, everyone walked all over it. Possession was
supposed to be off the table for both sides unless
they had expressed consent. Problem was, angels
would whisper, make deals and promises to get
what they wanted. If that failed, they'd torture their
victims with nightmares until they snapped and
agreed. At least demons laid it all out. Let me in, or
I'll huff, and I'll puff, and I'll empty your bank
account.

"And this sorry bloke you're inhabiting let you
in willingly?" I gestured to his meat suit.

The commander grinned. "August Jessup was
eager to make amends for his wrongdoings. It's
amazing what a quick view of Hell can do to

convince most people. Not you, though. You go to Hell and treat it like it's a vacation. You and that sorry excuse for a Horseman in New Orleans."

"If you've got a problem with the Pale Horseman, I suggest you take it up with him," I said, standing. "I'm not his nanny."

Big hands thumped onto my shoulders and forced me back into my seat. I landed hard enough to hurt my tailbone.

Commander Decimus frowned. "What you two did in Hell caused us a problem. A civil war has erupted down there. There are those in Heaven who want to take advantage of the turmoil and strike now before the demons have a chance to organize. They'd like nothing more than an all-out war."

That couldn't be good. If Heaven and Hell clashed in a full-on war, they'd have nowhere to do it but on Earth. With that much magic being thrown around, they'd wreck the place. As much as I hated humans, I was pretty keen on saving the planet, seeing as how I was one of the sorry bastards living on it. Heaven couldn't be allowed to declare war on Hell. I wasn't ready for an apocalypse. I still had things I wanted to do.

I shifted in my seat. "You don't agree?"

He spread his hands and leaned back. "I'm a traditionalist. I don't like change. I say keep things as they are. Let Hell sort itself out and cut a deal with the new Devil when he or she rises. I'd rather re-negotiate a treaty than bury half my men for Michael's glory hunt."

"And what's any of this got to do with me or Monahan?"

He pressed his lips into a thin line and squinted, considering. "The title of Devil isn't something that needs to be fought for and won, nor can it be earned. There is no prerequisite to hold it, only a need for power. Power enough to command legions of demons. Power Mr. Monahan is rapidly acquiring."

My stomach turned over and knotted itself into a pretzel. So that was Danny-boy's end game. I'd felt how strong he'd become, strong enough to rival me and I wasn't entirely human. I wasn't powerful enough to march into Hell and take over, not even if I'd wanted, but there were ways to gain that power. Both he and I knew that intimately. Our old mentor, Christian Lenore, once sought to become a god, drawing power to him through ritual and sacrifice. For someone like Danny, someone smart with a natural talent and a raw drive for success at any cost, attaining the Devil's mantle wouldn't be so impossible.

What are you doing, Danny? Why become the next Devil? Whatever happened to magic for magic's sake? The Danny Monahan I'd known eighteen years ago would've never wanted to rule anything but himself. But then, Christian broke us all. Christian had a penchant for showing us what we couldn't have, giving us a taste, and then taking it all away until he felt we earned it. Danny couldn't be the same person he was, not after Christian twisted him. Neither of us was.

"You think Monahan wants to be the next Lucifer?"

"We don't think," Decimus said. "We know.

Last week, we captured one of his demons and interrogated it. Daniel Monahan is more powerful than you know. It's not just the demons in Manhattan, Josiah."

Of course not. He'd need a whole legion of them, maybe more if he planned on storming Hell. Question was, why were they following him? He was human. Yeah, he had powers, but demons generally considered humans little more than meat. Following a human into battle was unheard of, not without a significant deal. I'd have guessed Danny was possessed himself, except I'd just come from seeing him. He showed no hints of being possessed, nor did his magic feel like it had been touched by demonic forces. It only felt stronger.

I tapped my fingers on the tabletop. "What's he got on all these demons to make them fall in line? He's good with magic, but not that good."

"Think about it, Josiah." Decimus leaned forward again. "Anyone who wants a shot at Lucifer's crown needs soldiers, yes. He needs to be powerful, true. But he also needs a universal currency, a means by which he increases his power exponentially."

The sour taste of bile touched my tongue. Souls. He was talking about souls. Gods had a tendency to stockpile them, powerful demons and angels too. The more souls someone held, the more raw power they had at their disposal. Find a way to break them down, infuse them into yourself, and there'd be nothing you couldn't do. If the demons were following Danny, he must've had a significant stockpile.

But how? Removing souls was no easy task. As far as I knew, only the Four Horsemen could do it. There were ways to broker deals with underworld deities for more, but they wouldn't move them in the quantity someone like Danny would need to have a go at Hell.

I shook my head. "No. He'd need thousands of souls. If he had that much, d'ya think he'd be here? Where's a human get that many souls? It's fuckin' impossible."

Decimus snapped his fingers and held out his hand, prompting one of the guys at the bar to get up and slip a piece of paper into his waiting palm. "I can tell you exactly how many souls Daniel Monahan has at his disposal." He unfolded the slip of paper and read, "Nine million three-hundred and one thousand and seven."

"Nine *million*?" I almost choked on the word.

He lowered the paper. "Otherwise known as the current population of New York City. The number's likely to get higher as the weekend goes on. The airports have shut down, stranding thousands. Roads will be blocked due to the snowstorm. That doesn't even take into account anyone who's traveled here from out of the city for the holiday. There could be closer to ten million here now."

Christ on Christmas. Ten million souls. How, though? All those people were still alive. Unless... No. He'd need a circle at least five miles wide, bigger than any circle I'd ever seen. The amount of blood it would take to power a circle that size was staggering.

"He's going to kill everyone in the city,

Josiah," said Decimus, curling his long fingers into fists. "And soon. He absolutely must be stopped."

It finally occurred to me what this was all about. I threw back my head and let out a laugh. "Oh, you fuckwit! You can't lay a hand on him, can you? He's a bloody *mortal!* All the power of Heaven and you can't do shit to save one city. So you come to me, eh? The half-breed bastard Nephilim. Back him into a corner. Make him do your dirty work, right?"

Decimus frowned. "Commander Petra didn't want me to come to you at all. She wanted to eliminate you to keep you from working together. Her belief is that Monahan will approach you with an offer, one that you'll have to accept. One that will help him kill everyone in this city. And she thinks you'll do it to save your own skin. I like to think you're not that broken yet."

I scowled at the angel sitting across from me. "You want me to kill a friend after your people chased me all over the city and tried to kill me. Twice!"

He struck the table with a fist. "I told you those weren't my men!"

"But you didn't fuckin' stop them, now did you?"

Decimus sat in silence, rage coming off him in waves. He thought he had me backed into a corner. Work with him, save the city, and he'd call off Petra's killers. All I had to do was take Danny out and the city would be safe. He could go back to his bosses a hero.

Except I didn't have to do shit. I could walk.

More than that, I could help Danny get what he wanted. And why not? Wasn't a soul in New York who gave a damn about me. The world could do with ten million fewer assholes. Might be nice to have someone in charge downstairs that actually liked me, seeing as that's where I was headed when I finally died. Could be Danny might do a lot of good as the King of Hell.

"I want something in return."

"Of course." Decimus folded his hands on the table. "I wouldn't ask you to work for free. Your very soul is on the line here, Josiah. Right now, your sins all but guarantee you a place in Hell. You don't want that. Why would you? You've spent nearly half your life sending demons back there, making many enemies. Your recent trip there also didn't make you any friends. What if I could promise you a place in Heaven instead?"

I crossed my arms. "You'd do that? For a half-breed?"

"I'd do it for the price of your soul."

Of course, he would. The soul of a half-breed angel would be worth a lot, especially to some middle-management jackass like Decimus. It wouldn't just be power for him, but a trophy. He could wave it in Michael's face that he'd succeeded in slaying the last of the Nephilim where Michael had failed.

If I went along with that, however, I'd be signing my own death warrant. There was no good way for this to end. Either I fought and died in that bar, or I'd delay it a few more days. Maybe with a few days to think about it, I'd find a way out, at least.

I stood, pushing my chair back. "Let's get one thing straight. I'm not your pawn, you self-righteous cunt. I don't jump when you snap your fingers. I don't come running when you ring a bell. I don't fuckin' work for you and I never will. You and all the winged pricks upstairs can eat a dick for all I care."

The suits behind me stepped forward, reaching for me. Decimus shook his head, halting their advance.

"So can every asshole in this city," I continued. "It's not my fuckin' city. I'm just here for a stop-off. If I do this—and I'm not saying I will—then I do it my way. And my way isn't pretty. It won't get you any pats on the back from Michael or the Big Guy."

He nodded once. "Understood."

"I'm not finished. I also want thirty grand and all the identity documents Jessup promised me."

"Done." He extended a hand.

"There're two things I won't do, Deci. That's take checks and shake hands."

"Very well." He cleared his throat and stood. "I give you my oath before God and these witnesses. If you agree to stop Daniel Monahan from killing everyone in this city, I will personally see to it that Heaven allows you to leave the city alive."

"And the girl," I insisted. "Khaleda's with me. The agreement covers her or I walk."

"And Khaleda Morningstar. You have free rein to handle the situation as you see fit without consequence from Heaven. Thirty thousand dollars

American will be deposited into your account within twelve hours, and Khaleda's identity documents will be yours upon completion of the task. Are we in agreement?"

I studied his expression. "I don't buy the humble, pious angel act."

Decimus sighed. "Nevertheless, that's the truth. There are some of us who still believe in free will and love humans. Despite what he'd have you believe, Michael and his cohorts don't represent the majority. I don't want war. Most of us don't."

"And me? You content to live and let live when it comes to us half-breeds?"

He looked at me as if I'd just forced him to swallow a dirty gym sock. "You're a mistake, one that needs correcting. Considering your lifestyle, I also believe you'll become a self-correcting mistake soon enough. Feel free to continue smoking, boozing, and fucking your way around the world, Josiah Quinn. Eventually, it will catch up to you. And when it does, your soul belongs to me."

He adjusted his jacket and pushed past me, headed for the door. Decimus' two suits flanked him while the doorman held the door.

The angel paused in front of the open door to turn back to me. "Of course, feel free to prove me wrong too. Heaven could use a man of your talents, you know, and you'll have to choose a side eventually."

I tucked my hands into my pockets. "You know the great thing about free will, mate? It means I'm free not to choose, too."

He tugged his cap down. "And that's a choice

all its own. We'll be in touch."

Decimus the angel walked out of the bar.

12

KHALEDA

Josiah got in the cab, slammed the door and demanded I tell Victis to take us back to the hotel.

"Did you work out my papers?"

The fire in his eyes made my breath catch. He could've matched Father's wrath at that moment. "Later."

I tapped the grate. "Take us back."

We didn't speak. Not as we drove through the heavy snow, not as Victis parked the cab in an overnight lot at the end of the block, not as we got out and walked the icy sidewalk back to the hotel. Victis hung back with me while Josiah walked ahead of us, a silent storm of swirling white rage. He was so upset, he didn't even smoke. Whatever had happened in that bar, it had gotten to him.

I let him take more of a lead the further we

walked and leaned on Victis instead.

"Why are you with him?" Victis asked me.

"He saved me." Was that really it? It didn't feel like enough of a reason to have gone all the way across the country with a man I barely knew. I didn't know anyone else. Well, not anyone else who would've helped me. While I had some contacts I could tap, I had no idea if Father had gotten to them after he decided on my punishment. Once he let those demons carry me away, he could've told them any story he liked and they would've believed it. "He promised to help me get the missing part of my soul back."

"Is he actually doing that?"

I shrugged, or tried to. It was damn near impossible with him half-carrying me. "Honestly, I have no idea what he's up to half the time. I think he was going to, but then God's Hand got involved. We've spent so much time running from them, he hasn't had time."

Was I really defending that asshole to the man I'd brainwashed? I didn't owe Josiah anything, especially since he hadn't delivered on his promise. If I told Victis to take me back to the cab and get me out of the city, it'd be hours before he even noticed I was gone. He was so absorbed in his own problems, he'd forgotten I was limping along on an injured leg. Bastard.

"He said there was a ritual," I continued. "Just a modified tracking spell. But when he starts it, we'll be a beacon. Anyone who's looking for us will find us."

"*Manus Dei* likely already knows where you

are. They have spells that can track Nephilim and demons. There's no hiding from them." He sounded as if he were proud.

If I hadn't been relying on him to help me walk, I'd have hit him. Even with all my influence, he was still one of them. "Josiah killed one of you. A lion shifter."

Victis' expression hardened. His jaw flexed. "Did you know him?"

"Rufus." Victis' voice was rough. "Good soldier. One of Petra's best. How did he die?"

"I helped Josiah decapitate him." It wasn't a lie, not precisely. Josiah had used my power to hold him still while he sawed off his head. The memory of how easily he'd done it made my stomach sour. "Does that change your opinion of me?"

Victis shook his head. "I love you. Him, I hate. If you'd give me your blessing, Teacher, I would kill him. You can be free of him."

We reached the hotel. Victis opened the door for me like a perfect gentleman, despite the death threat he'd just uttered. I pulled myself through the door and he followed me. With him at my back, I should've felt at peace. Even if he'd wanted to, he couldn't hurt me. That was the nature of my power. I'd made him fall so hopelessly in love with me that he'd have brought me the moon if I asked. He would kill my enemies without a second thought, and yet he *was* my enemy. With his dying breath, he would profess his love for me, a false love. One I invented and fried his brain to convince was real. How did that make me any different from Father?

I shook the thought from my mind. I was

nothing like him.

Victis came and took my arm.

I jerked it away and spun around to face him. "I forbid you to hurt Josiah under any circumstances. Do you understand?"

He ground his teeth so hard I could hear them creaking and groaning. "Yes, Teacher."

"You're not to report back to God's Hand either. From now on, you're mine. You no longer belong to them."

His eyes widened. "I…"

Victis' love for me would override his faith. He was mine, and I wouldn't share him with murderous zealots. I was his god now. It was his only chance at surviving. If they found him out, they'd execute him.

For a minute, I thought he'd break into tears, but he swallowed whatever emotion he felt. "Yes, Teacher."

He helped me back to the room and opened the door for me there, too.

I expected to enter and find Josiah passed out on the bed or maybe pacing if he was still too wound up. Instead, the bathroom door was closed and locked. The sound of the shower running and rattling the pipes filled the tiny room.

"I suppose he decided a shower was more prudent than stitching up my leg," I grumbled as Victis helped me onto the bed.

He knelt in front of me. "I heard what he said. If you fed more from me, it would help you. Please, Teacher. Whatever you need, I'll do it."

His offer was an icy knife to the gut. It stabbed

at me and made my stomach turn at the same time. The poor man didn't mean what he was saying. How could he when he didn't understand what he was asking? He couldn't truly consent to anything, not when he was under my influence. It'd never mattered to Father. He'd always said it was better to ask forgiveness than permission. Not that he'd ever apologized for anything. Not the Prince of Darkness and King of Lies.

I took Victis by the chin and tipped his head down to kiss the top of his head. "Thank you, Victis, but I can't. If you were yourself, you'd never let me touch you, let alone feed from you. What I did to you was wrong. I wish I could release you, but there's no spell in Heaven, Hell, or on Earth that can undo what I've done."

"God forgives all, Teacher. No matter how dark a stain the sin leaves, the Heavenly Father can wash it all away with His holy blood." He took my hands and smiled up at me, a big, empty smile.

I wanted to smile back. When he'd been himself, he must've had an infectious laugh. Everyone around him would've loved him. *This man is someone's son too. Someone's brother. I had no right to do this to him.* I turned away. "I don't think God wants anything to do with me."

"God already loves you. All you have to do is accept his love. Don't you want to be loved?"

Yes. That's what I want. The thought surfaced before I could stop it. It was impossible for someone like me. Not just because of what I would do to anyone who loved me, but what it would do to *me*. To love and be loved was more than just a metaphorical weakness when it came to being a succubus. If I so much as brushed hands with someone who truly loved another, and was loved in return, I would sprout blisters. It burned me like fire.

I wanted it more than anything in the world, to know what that felt like, but nothing I did would ever make that a reality. No one could ever love me, and I could never love them. Not Father, not Victis, not God. And I hated them all for it.

I jerked my hands away from Victis. "I think you should go stand guard outside the door. Just in case."

All the light and joy went out of his face. His body practically deflated, but he stood and followed orders just the same.

That wasn't love. Love didn't follow orders blindly. It didn't mindlessly agree with whatever I said, or give me whatever I wanted just to keep me happy. Real love would be loud, angry. They'd tell me to stop being such a bitch just because life didn't go my way. It would tell me to quit feeling sorry for myself and make something out of myself.

The bathroom door opened and Josiah stepped out, shirtless, an unlit cigarette between his lips. "Where's your pet?"

"Where's yours?"

"She's in her container happily devouring two crickets I believe. You feed yours?" He sat on the bed and hauled his bag up to search it.

My stomach growled as if he'd suddenly reminded it that food existed. When was the last time I'd had actual food instead of drinking my dinner? "No. Probably should though, shouldn't I? I can send him for something."

"Nah," Josiah said and pulled out a plain white tank top. "Might get him in trouble. Those God's Hand assholes were waiting for me in the bar. They're everywhere. Like roaches."

"Holy shit, Josiah. Why didn't you say anything?"

He shrugged and tugged the tank top on. "Dickheads had a point. Apparently, Monahan is up to no good. Wants to be the next King of Hell. If I don't stop him, he'll wipe New York off the map. They could stop him with the snap of their fingers, except for all their damn rules. So, because I'm here, and because my very existence is an affront to their senses, it's apparently my job to do something about it."

He removed the cigarette from his mouth and used it to gesture to me. "But never mind all that. Now that I've proven I haven't forgotten how to shower, let's see that leg, yeah?"

"It's not that bad. I don't even think it needs stitches. It's stopped bleeding."

"Khaleda, I'm not in the mood for any of your Princess of Hell drama." He stood and gestured for me to scoot up the bed. "Get up here and show us the leg."

"Princess of Hell," I muttered and slid up the bed. Though that was technically true, I'd never considered myself any kind of princess. Maybe others did. Father had been grooming me to take his place until I betrayed him and tried to kill him. "Don't call me that."

He didn't acknowledge what I'd said. Just shifted my leg and pulled the stocking off roughly. I grimaced as he poked at the deep cut on the inside of my thigh. He didn't take the hint and thought that meant he should pinch the skin together.

"Ow!" I jerked away. "That fucking hurts! You could at least try to be gentle."

Josiah raised an eyebrow. "Sweetheart, if you want gentle, you're barking up the wrong tree." He sighed and wrinkled his forehead, looking back at the injury. "Well, it's stopped bleeding, but I think we should stitch it up just to be safe. Your call though."

The way he was looking at me, as if he were bored out of his mind, barely there… it was infuriating. Where else did he have to be? For a split second, I wondered what it'd be like to take power from him. He had plenty, more than most. How many times had he said he was more than willing to let me prey on him? I should. Break him. Make him beg on his knees just for a passing glance from me.

No. That was the hunger talking. Wasn't it? But the familiar stir was absent. What the fuck was I thinking? "And if I tell you to go fuck yourself?"

He shrugged. "Then I'm going to smoke this ciggy, call out for a ham and pineapple pizza, eat, probably smoke again, and fall asleep on that small patch of floor there."

I crossed my arms. "You're not going to make me?"

"Christ, what do you take me for?" He rolled his eyes. "You know how that would go? I'd sit on you, and you'd kick like a mule and tear it open more."

I waited for him to somehow relate my injury back to some minor inconvenience for him, but it didn't come. It might've been the first selfless thing he'd ever said to me. "Fine then. Stitch it up."

He retrieved a small black pouch from his bag.

While he laid out a single-use alcohol pad, cotton balls, and the sterile needle and surgical-grade thread, I asked him, "Have you ever done this before?"

"Often enough. Have to when no one else is about to patch me up." He tugged up his shirt and pointed out a faint white line on his stomach. "Were-jaguar. Young couple in Brazil hired me to retrieve their boy after they'd carried him off. No one else would go after him. Paid me a fortune to go into the rainforest. The jags weren't keen on outsiders. Took a swipe at me before I could even introduce myself." He dropped his shirt. "Almost bled out. Spent the night in a cave trying to stitch it closed when I wasn't hallucinating."

"Hallucinating?"

"Jags coat their claws in poison. I didn't get a fatal dose. Just enough to trip. Almost didn't make it back from that one." He gestured to my leg. "If I can do that, I think I can handle this little nick, yeah?"

I nodded. There was no arguing with him anyway. Once he set his mind to doing something, there was no deterring him.

He cleaned the wound and went to work with that same singular determination. I turned away and chewed my lip through the pain. The room felt too hot, the needle icy cold. Each time it went in, a new mix of fire and ice ate at my leg, threatening to push me to tears. I fought it. After everything, I still hadn't cried in front of him, and I wasn't going to break that streak now. Someone like Josiah would never let me live it down if I cried over a few stitches, no matter how bad it hurt.

"One more," he promised. "You doing okay?"

I nodded, closed my eyes, and bit down harder, until blood welled in my mouth and I had to let go.

Josiah's fingers brushed naked skin an inch higher, and my eyes snapped open. He'd finished the last stitch and tied it off and just sat with my legs draped over him, concentrating on his handiwork. He still hadn't lit that cigarette. It drooped from between his lips as if he'd forgotten it was there. "Does it have to be sex?"

"What?"

He tilted his head and removed the cigarette, tucking it behind his ear. "When you feed. Like with fuckwit on the other side of the door there. You fed on him, right? But you didn't—"

I pulled my legs away from him, swinging them over the side of the bed. The one was still sore from the stitches, and moving pulled the thread, but he hadn't done a terrible job. "Are you serious right now? Give it a rest, Josiah."

"Jesus! I swear, I wasn't trying to get laid. For once, it was an honest question!"

"Right." I rolled my eyes and pulled myself up with the help of the headboard. It hurt, but it was bearable if I kept the weight off my injured leg.

"If we're going to be spending this much quality time together, I think I've got a right to know. Next time you've got a cut that needs healing, are you going to suck my sanity out too and turn me into a fucking vegetable?"

I turned around to face him, fists clenched. "I don't know!"

His mouth fell open.

"Oh, no! You're not interrupting me this time. I'm tired of it, Josiah. You promised you'd help me. Instead, we spent all day running around trying to deal with your problems!"

"Khaleda…"

"Shut up! For five seconds, just shut your mouth and listen to me! I don't want to feed on you. I don't want to feed on anyone! I hate it! Everything about who I am, what I am… He used me. Do you understand? I'm what he made me. I wish you'd just left me in Naraka to rot! I wish I'd died there, Josiah!"

"Khaleda, you're bleeding!" He pointed.

I was suddenly aware of warmth on the side of my face. I touched my chin, just below my ear and it came away bloody. Nausea hit me in a sudden wave, forcing me to double over and put a hand over my mouth to keep from vomiting everywhere. In a blind panic, I ran for the bathroom and barely made it to the toilet. Goddammit! When was this going to end?

He was suddenly behind me, filling up the tiny space with his presence. I wanted to tell him to get the fuck out, but my stomach rebelled, and I doubled over again. My insides lit on fire. I felt like

I was dying.

"It's all right," he said and pulled my hair away from the side of my head. "You're all right. Don't fight it. You'll just hurt yourself. Easy. Let's get you off your leg. Here you are." He helped me sit on the edge of the shower.

Exhausted from the fight, the stitches, everything, I gave up trying to stay upright and let myself fall against him. I squeezed my eyes closed and bloody tears fell, staining his shirt. "I fucking hate you," I said and punched him as hard as I could. It was a pathetic attempt.

"No, ya don't." He rubbed my back in small circles while I tried to hit him again and again. "You hate your father, Khaleda. He's the one that hurt you, not me. He's dead. I watched him die."

"You took that away from me!" I landed another punch to his gut, this one hard enough he jerked and grunted. "He was mine to kill! Now what do I have? If I don't have vengeance left, what's the fucking point?"

I took another swing, but this time he grabbed my wrist, stopping my fist short. Another blink and more bloody tears trailed down my cheeks to land on his shirt and spread into a pool of red.

"The point of life is to live." He squeezed my arm. "You want a purpose? There it is. You've seen what happens after. You and me, we're basically fucked just for being born. We didn't choose it, but we've got it. This shit life is the only one we've got today. You've got two choices, Khaleda. You either find some scrap of purpose to get you through to the next shitty hotel, to the bottom of the next bottle, the next pack of cigarettes, or you tell yourself this is the last one. You pick it up, you smoke it, and you put a gun to your head and pull the trigger. Live or die. I can't stop you from dying, and I can't make you live. You've got to make that choice yourself. D'ya hear me?"

I stared at him, not sure how to answer. He was right. Deep down, I knew he was right. This fractured twilight existence might not have been ideal, but it was all I had.

My chin trembled. "I hate you."

"You can't hate me if you're dead."

I wanted to hit him, to make him feel a fraction of the heartbreak and loss I felt inside, but I was too damn weak. *I'm going to get stronger. I'm going to get better just so I can punch that smug grin off your face, asshole.*

For the moment, all I could manage was to stain his shirt with my blood. It would have to be good enough. I threw myself at him, letting go of all the misery, the pain, the anger that had bubbled to the surface in a pitiful sob that left my whole body aching. Josiah hesitantly put an arm around me and took everything I had to offer.

13

JOSIAH

Khaleda passed out not long after her breakdown, and I carried her to the bed. Well, more like dragged. She was a heavy girl. Not fat; it was all muscle, and I was buggered from all the magic I'd tossed around. Part of me wondered if Danny had known about the assassin from God's Hand. Maybe that was why he'd worked me over on the roof.

That lion bastard must've known it'd be hard for me to get off a spell surrounded by all the iron of the elevator shaft and car. It was why he'd cornered us there. Drained, distracted, and cut off from the major flow of magic, it had taken almost everything I had just to summon the Holy Fire to attack him. At least the God Squad in the bar hadn't asked for a fight. I wasn't sure I could've given it to them.

A knock on the door had me jump up from where I sat on the floor. When I went to open it, I found Victis snarling at an acne-ridden pizza delivery boy. The poor kid was white with fear. Interesting. All the pizza places I'd called were closed due to the weather.

"Easy, dog," I said to Victis and addressed the pizza boy. "What's this, then? I didn't even get an order in."

He offered me the flat box and said in an unusually gruff voice for a teenager, "Mr. Monahan sends his regards."

"What good is it having a secret hideout if it's not secret?" I took the box. "I take it I'm not addressing the teenage pizza boy then?"

The pizza boy smiled and tipped his hat. "No charge." He turned without waiting for a tip and strolled to the stairs.

I looked at Victis. "Bark next time, would you?"

He glared at me.

"Come on, then." I kicked open the door and brought the pizza inside.

Khaleda stirred and sat up, rubbing her eyes. "What is it?"

"Don't know." I put the box on the end of the bed.

It was warm to the touch like a pizza, and it smelled like bread and melted cheese, but one could never be too careful. Danny was off his rocker, and madmen could do anything. I put a hand over the box, extending my senses into it. No traps. No spells. Nothing.

"For fuck's sake," Khaleda growled and jerked open the box. "It's just a pizza."

For once, she was right. Steam rose from the surface of a pizza pie topped with cubes of ham, full rings of pineapple, and caramelized red onions. It was almost too good to be true except for the Greenwich Street address scrawled in permanent marker on the inside lid. The message under it read: *I have something you're looking for. How about a midnight rendezvous? Bring the girl if you'd like. Three's a party. Just remember, I don't like to share. D.M.*

Khaleda shook her head. "What's it mean?"

Something I want. My stomach sank, taking with it my appetite. "Nothing good."

"That's Monahan, right?"

I turned away from the box to pace. God, I needed a smoke. I needed five at once. *Fucking hell, Danny. How did I wind up in this mess?* "Why'd you bring me here, Khaleda? Of all the places in the world, why New York?"

She grabbed a piece of the pizza and settled back against the headboard with a shrug. "You didn't have to come. I told you that. I didn't even want you to come."

Her voice raised into a shout as I stormed into the bathroom in search of my cigarettes. Where'd I left the damn things? I'd had them in the bathroom. Maybe they were in my other pants. With a growl, I tore through the pockets in search of them and came up with an empty pack. Fuck, I could've sworn I had at least one left. The expletives slipped out of my head and into the room in a long, exaggerated string.

Khaleda appeared in the doorway. "What's wrong?"

"My ciggies. I swear, I had another somewhere. I just have to find it."

She stepped into the bathroom, and the space shrank as she reached for me. Her fingers slipped behind my ear and came away with a cigarette I must've tucked there earlier.

I drew a hand over my face with another curse.

"I don't know why we came here," she said as I lit it with shaky hands. "It just felt right. Like the place was calling to me. Maybe it was. Do you think that's possible?"

I waited for the first rush of nicotine before answering. My nerves were too raw. It was the lack of sleep, the overuse of magic. That'd done it. "Anything's possible."

What I didn't tell her was that the call she felt might've been her subconscious need to reunite with her soul. Separated from a part of it, the rest would always seek to be reunited. That's what would make the tracking spell I wanted to try work. All it required was tapping into that existing need, teasing it out, making it work on a more physical level.

I have something you want.

Could he mean her soul? And what did he want for it? I saw a sliver of hope for Danny and held onto it. Maybe there was a way to talk him down from this cliff he stood on. He had to know someone would find out and step up to stop him, didn't he?

"We have to go," I said and sank onto the closed toilet. "I don't know how all this is connected, but somehow it has to be. There's no such thing as a coincidence, Khaleda. You were drawn to this city for a reason. Danny's reached out for a reason. Maybe your soul is here. Maybe he wants to be saved." I scratched my scalp. "Or maybe we're all just fucked."

"What about that modified tracking spell you wanted to try?"

I shrugged. "I'm tapped for magic for a bit, but I can still do it if I draw the power from elsewhere."

"Elsewhere?" She tipped her head to the side, exposing more of her neck.

I stared at the exposed skin. In the animal world, exposing your neck was a submissive gesture, an acknowledgment of inferiority to a superior predator. It was both an invitation and a sign of trust. *Here I am, giving you my throat. You can rip it out if you like, but I don't believe you will. I trust you. Don't hurt me.* Humans were animals too, weren't they? But neither she nor I were human.

I sucked down more of the cigarette, making the end glow bright red. "Blood. Life energy from another living thing. Usually enough to kill whatever it is. I'd need a sacrifice, Khaleda."

She hugged herself a moment before she turned and fled the room. A moment later, she returned with Victis. He followed her like a good braindead puppy but set hateful eyes on me. "Tell him what you need."

***

Victis returned smelling like rotting garbage twenty minutes after we sent him out. The plastic bag he held out to me squirmed with two lumps of living, squeaking flesh. I took the bag while Khaleda pinched her nose and rushed her pet off to the shower.

"Hello, uglies," I said, shaking the bag a little.

New York rats were a special breed of strange. Bigger than normal, they were about twice as stubborn as Khaleda. Able to squeeze through gaps of less than an inch wide, survive a forty-foot fall, and tread water for up to three days, the little bastards were about as resilient as they came. Sort of like the rest of the city. In fact, I supposed rats were a perfect representation for your average New Yorker. A little gross, full of spite and the will to survive, able to eat impressive amounts of garbage disguised as food... Yes, the rat was perfect.

While Khaleda coaxed Victis through a bath so we could stand his smell, I deposited the rats in a spelled container that would make them docile. Because I needed the assist, I tried to retrieve a well-fed Milly from her box, but she was in a mood and tried to strike at me. Not surprising, as I'd handled her a lot recently and she'd just eaten.

"Come on, old girl," I said and retracted my hand. "I could use the help."

She backed into the corner. You smell like garbage. And rat. No thanks.

"Oh, I see how it is. You can break out and terrorize my friends anytime you please, but when I actually need you, it's the finger, is it? Drama queen." I closed the container and slid it back into my bag. The only thing more stubborn than a rat was a tarantula with a full belly. Guess I was working without her.

Victis came out of the bathroom looking like a drowned cat. His hair hung in long, ratty clumps around his head. He was naked except for the pair of old, worn-out white undies. Unflattering, to say the least. The rest of him was less so. He was a big man, strong enough to snap my spine in half if you could believe all that muscle. White scars covered his chest and stomach in uneven shapes and lines, leaving his chest hair to grow in uneven. It looked like he'd been hit with shrapnel from an explosion and somehow survived it.

"What happened there, mate?" I said it first in English before I remembered he only spoke Latin.

He looked down at himself as if he didn't do it very often. "IED. Afghanistan. The government left me to die. *Manus Dei* saved me."

"You're American then? What's with the Latin?"

He shrugged and sat on the bed hard enough to nearly bounce me off it. "I don't remember English. I don't remember the war or the time before. Just fire and pain. Praying to die. Then, His light and love filled me, healing me. I swore to serve Him."

I frowned and stood, stripping off the bloody shirt. The ritual would douse me in more blood, and the singlet was a loss, but it was starting to itch. "And you think killing me is the best way to serve your God?"

"In the book of Genesis—"

"The Nephilim were on Earth in those days,

and afterward, when the sons of God came in the daughters of man and they bore children into them. These were the mighty men of old, the men of renown," I quoted. "That's what your book says about me, Victis. It doesn't say anything about me being evil."

"True," he conceded with a nod. "But that section is directly followed by God's decision to destroy the Earth in the Great Flood. The two are textually connected."

I clenched my hands into fists but held back. Khaleda would lose it if I hit her toy. "You want to know what your book doesn't say, Victis? It doesn't tell you what happened to those daughters of man. How it all went down. I don't know if it was an oversight on the author's part or just an outright attempt to gloss over the sins of angels, but it wasn't a love story, mate. Those winged bastards tore into the cities of Sodom and Gomorrah on God's holy orders, slaughtered the men, and took the women by force. They held them in chains for days and took them whenever they wanted. The lucky ones died. You can bet the rest of 'em wished they had when their bellies started to swell with the unwanted spawn of the sons of God. And what does God do about it? He wipes the Earth clean to try to hide his mistake."

I pointed an accusing finger in his face. "That's the God you serve. A selfish, shameful monster who'd rather hide behind his power than face the consequences of his decisions. He's a shit leader who can't control his troops."

Victis jumped to his feet. "I'll not let you take

His name in vain!"

"Let me say it slow so you can understand me clearly." I took a step forward so that we stood toe to toe. "Fuck your God."

He coiled, poised to strike but stopped when Khaleda stepped out of the bathroom, toweling off her hair.

She eyed the two of us, made a disgusted noise, and rolled her eyes. "Stop picking on him, Josiah. He can't fight back. I forbade him to kill you."

"Doesn't stop him from hitting me. Come on, big man. Take your best shot." I took a step back and spread my arms wide. "I'm right here."

Victis ground his teeth and clenched his fists. Anger rolled off him in pulsing waves, flooding the room with raw emotional power. Power that would translate easily into magic if I pulled hard enough.

That's it, Victis. Make yourself useful and get pissed off. See, Milly? I don't need you.

Khaleda grabbed my shoulder and jerked me toward the bathroom. It tipped my balance enough that I almost fell. With another shove, she pushed me behind her and through the bathroom door. "Victis," she growled. "Get dressed!"

"But Teacher, I don't have any clothes."

"Then break into another room and find some. I don't care how you get them, just get them." She spun around and stormed into the bathroom with me, slamming the door shut behind her. "What the fuck?"

I shrugged. "He started it."

She let out a deep, guttural, yet feminine growl of frustration. The small, primitive part of my brain said I wanted to hear her make that sound again, except that I wanted her full breasts crushed against me, fingernails shredding the skin on my back.

"Josiah!" she snapped. "Did you hear anything I just said?"

I hadn't, but I could guess. She wanted me to leave Victis alone. It wasn't his fault. Blah blah blah. "Oh, pull ya head in, will ya? You want me to do this or not?"

"You're an insufferable prick, you know that?"

"So everyone keeps telling me." I sighed. "Grab the rats for me, would ya?"

She narrowed her eyes at me but went to get them anyway.

I performed the sacrifice in the tub, as that would be the easiest place to clean it up. If the maid came in and found the rest of the place drenched in blood, she'd call the coppers, and we'd be behind bars. But in a hotel bathtub, we were almost certain to get away with it. No one ever checked the bathtubs with a blacklight, and if they did, they wouldn't be staying at that dive.

The summoning symbol I used was one I had learned under Danny. It was impossible not to think of him as I drew it on the wall and infused it with a spark of my own blood. Why was it I hadn't thought of him all this time, and now he was everywhere?

Under the symbol, spread out in the bath, I'd placed a street map of New York. Khaleda sat on the floor atop a symbol matching the one I'd just drawn on the wall, another circle I had already closed. Both circles sat inside a larger one, this one simple. The objective, hold the spell in place and keep the power from leaking out to do any damage to the outside world.

With the closing of the second circle, magic buzzed all around, running through me like threads. Other threads hung in the air too. Victis' crimson anger, the buzzing black thread of Khaleda's anxiety and the thin streak of blue thread wrapped around it. I shifted my grip on the razor blade resting between two fingers. What was that?

I gave it a gentle tug and felt the pull in my own chest. Momentary panic gripped me. I'd never seen anything like that before, not attached to me. Did it mean she'd cast some sort of spell over me? No, I'd have noticed. Besides, Khaleda wasn't adept at that sort of magic. I'd have reasoned maybe she'd taken a tiny bite and fed on me, but I knew that wasn't the case. What the fuck *was* it?

"Everything okay?" she asked.

"Of course, it is. I know what I'm doing." *I'll have to sort that out later*. I brought the first rat out of the container and held it squirming in front of me. "I invoke the name of Andromalius, great and mighty earl, master of thirty-six legions. Let that which is hidden be brought to light with this sacrifice." I stabbed the razor blade into the squirming rat while it struggled and screamed.

Behind me, Khaleda gasped, but not because of the rat. An icy arm of magic stabbed through her chest, pushing the swirling, glowing ball of silver, black and red that was her soul to the surface. Not enough power. Dammit.

I seized the second rat and commanded even

louder, "I invoke you, Andromalius. Lend me your
power. Reveal the location of her stolen soul. I
command you!"

A presence reared inside the larger circle,
slithering like a venomous snake into being.
Khaleda arched her back as the presence slid over
her, winding up her body. The serpent head reared
back, fangs poised to sink into her breast. I drew the
razor over the second rat, pressing in deep until
warm, fetid blood ran down my arm.

The demonic snake screamed and threw itself
through the air, slamming into the wall of my circle.
He exploded into a black mist that rained blood on
the bathtub in fat, wet drops. Tap, tap, tap. They
struck the map in five messy globs, one on each
borough. The blood ran, filling every street,
crawling through every neighborhood, testing every
door, and trying every lock. It flowed in every
direction, finding nothing.

Until one crimson smear reached lower
Manhattan. Then, as if called, every drop of blood
squirming on the map turned and sped for SoHo.
No, not SoHo. It'd moved too many blocks west for
that. The blood moved into Tribeca, racing down
Canal Street until it reached Greenwich and made a
hard left.

No.

It coalesced there in a thick puddle, building on
itself until it formed a large, square building made
of brick. An old warehouse that'd been converted
into high-end flats.

"Bugger all." I spat and tossed the rat carcasses
into the trash. I released my hold on the spell and

drew the razor blade over the chalk outline of the largest circle, releasing the magic.

Khaleda collapsed with a gasp. "Where?" she asked, her voice breathless.

I turned on the shower to wash the blood from my body. "Danny Monahan has it."

14

KHALEDA

The address Josiah marked on the map matched the one written on the inside of the pizza box. I stared at the address in silence while he scarfed down another piece of pizza. He'd pulled on another pair of pants, complaining it was his last good pair, and sat on the bed with his back to me, staring at his phone while time ticked away.

Victis stood next to me, a silent statue of solid muscle. "You shouldn't go, Teacher. This is a trap."

I agreed with him. It felt like another setup, but we couldn't just ignore the results of the spell. Daniel Monahan had my soul locked away somewhere in his expensive Manhattan loft, and he was probably going to use it as part of his crazy plan to destroy New York. I didn't give a damn about the city, but I wanted to feel whole again. Ever since I'd come back, there had been something missing, something intangible. I wanted it back. If Josiah wasn't up to the task of killing his friend, I'd claw Danny's eyes out myself to take back what was mine.

"Don't have a choice," Josiah said after finishing up his pizza. He licked his fingers and grabbed another piece. "Danny knows where we are. If we don't go to him, he'll come for us. Besides, I agreed to help your boss stop him from wrecking New York."

Victis crossed his arms. "Decimus isn't my boss."

Josiah ignored him. "Which reminds me. Khaleda, ask your pet to detail the surveillance God's Hand has on the five hundred block of Greenwich."

I clenched my fists on my knees when he referred to Victis as my pet, even if he wasn't wrong. He was only doing it to rub in what I'd done. *Ass. What I did saved your life. Don't forget that.* Just the same, I turned to Victis. "Please, Victis. Do you know what security they have in place there?"

He huffed out a sigh. "There was a recon team in an unmarked van outside. Three days ago, a secondary team attempted to infiltrate the apartment to plant a transmitting device. They were forced to engage Monahan's security team and pulled out before there were casualties."

Josiah twisted to look at Victis. "You sound as if you didn't approve."

Victis shook his head. "They were Commander Decimus' men. He pulled them back too soon. They should have engaged the enemy."

"What if they'd lost?" I asked, tilting my head to him. "Then they'd be dead, your operation exposed, and you'd have nothing to show for it."

He made a fist and struck his chest. "We took an oath to die for the order. I stand by it. Commander Decimus is a coward who'd rather run from a fight than engage."

"Or," said Josiah, standing, "he actually values human life. Wouldn't that be novel? An angel who gives a damn?"

Victis started to say something, but I cut him off by putting a hand on his arm. He couldn't win an argument with Josiah, and I was tired of listening to him serve as a mouthpiece for God's Hand. After spending the day with him, I was starting to believe I wasn't the first person to brainwash him into loving them. God's Hand hadn't even needed magic. All they'd done was pick him up, put him back together, and give him a purpose.

I shivered at that realization. Once, I'd been like him. Blind to everything but a singular purpose. For me, it had been revenge. Stripped of that, I had nothing, or so I thought. Josiah was right. I didn't need blind purpose to keep going, no life goal. Just the unshakable will to keep on living.

Victis uncrossed his arms. "Are you cold, Teacher?"

I shook my head and switched on the television to listen to the weather report. Josiah moved around in the background, gathering things into his bag and searching for a clean shirt. He moved with a solemn purpose, much like a soldier preparing for battle. In place of guns and knives, Josiah armed himself with magic pendants, a length of silver chain wrapped through his belt loops, and five simple bands of gold for his fingers.

I tried to ignore him, but he wasn't an easy person to ignore, especially when he got into that mode. Despite being a tall, thin man with average looks, he had a way of calling attention to himself whenever he entered a room.

Victis' cold stare followed him around the room as he worked, a predator watching another predator prepare for the hunt. Memory flashed behind his eyes. What had his pre-deployment ritual been? Prayer and fasting? Did he know when he broke into that apartment in Brooklyn that he might face a fate worse than death?

The weatherman was calling for eight to twelve more inches of snow and winds in excess of forty miles per hour, creating whiteout conditions. Despite assurances that the plows and salt trucks were working in full force around the clock, there was talk of canceling the Macy's Thanksgiving Day Parade, though one interviewee seemed to think the idea was crazy. He called the parade an American Institution and spent three minutes pretending to be offended by the suggestion.

Never mind all those paradegoers might be dead in a few days' time. He didn't know that. How could he? Sometimes, I envied the average person whose biggest concerns amounted to a snowstorm, a parade, and which drive-thru to hit for dinner.

At eleven, the three of us got up to retrieve our coats. Mine still held splashes of blood from earlier in the day, so I spent five minutes dabbing hydrogen peroxide on the troublesome spots. It didn't take them all out, but hopefully, no one would notice in the dark. My leg ached, but I had less trouble walking on it now that I'd had a few pain killers. Just the same, I sent Victis to pull the cab up.

"What are you going to do if this is a trap?" I asked Josiah, pulling my coat closer. The wind vomited a new assault of white flakes down the street.

He patted his trusty bag. "Got everything I need in here. God's Hand wants me to kill him, you know. I think he can be reasoned with."

I turned to give him a questioning look, but the icy wind stung my eyes, so I quickly shifted my gaze forward. "I thought you said he was crazy."

"Oh, he's mad as a cut snake in every sense. But he wouldn't be inviting us if he didn't want something. He'll be offering a trade for your soul."

"A trade?" I considered what Danny might want. As little as I knew about him, I knew Danny and Josiah had history. "Your soul for mine?"

Josiah smiled. "That'd be the easy way out, wouldn't it?"

Victis came around the corner at a snail's crawl, his taxi a yellow beacon in a sea of white.

"And what about his plan to destroy all of New York? Think you can talk him down from that?"

He shrugged. "Have to see. Trust me, Khaleda. Just let me handle him, and we'll be headed our separate ways in no time."

The cab pulled up. Josiah jumped forward and opened the door for me. I hesitated just long enough to make sure it wasn't a trick before climbing in.

15

JOSIAH

Howling wind pushed the curtain of white down the streets. Mounds of dirty white snow, freshly plowed, buried parked cars in front of a flat, six-story shrine of brick and glass. Black canopies rustled against the onslaught of early winter. A yellow moon rose behind sharp silver clouds, casting milky light on everything.

I stopped on the sidewalk across the street to look up at the top floor. Danny was in Penthouse One, waiting for me. Waiting to kill me maybe, or maybe just ten million strangers. Maybe both.

The surveillance van for God's Hand sat up the block, facing away from the building. It was a white windowless van with a plumbing logo flaking off the side. Bastards had to be freezing in this cold. The temptation to turn on the van had to be overwhelming. Let the heat run and warm those achy old bones. Just for a minute. No one'll notice the exhaust. But the van sat behind another mound of snow with frost crawling up the windshield in fractal patterns. Gotta hand it to the bastards. They were stronger than me. I'd never had the patience for stakeouts.

Khaleda stopped next to me, her limp barely noticeable. Victis stood next to her in a sweatshirt that was too tight across the chest and arms. I had voted to leave him behind, but Khaleda wouldn't have it. She'd let her guilt make a decision for her again. Hopefully, it wouldn't get us killed.

We crossed the street as one.

No doorman waited inside to open the door, and the lobby was deserted at that hour of everyone but the night watchman. He looked at us and saw trouble, but was smart enough not to get involved directly. His eyes tracked us to the elevator and narrowed as I tapped the button. Plastic rattled. The faint hum of a dial tone as he picked up the phone, no doubt to announce our arrival to Monahan's security upstairs.

I got into the elevator and pressed the button. As the car carried us up, I wondered if I could do it. Could I kill Danny Monahan in cold blood? God's Hand would back off if I did. Some might even call me a hero, but New York would never know. Every night from this one forward, I'd fall asleep with a friend's blood on my hands.

Not that I was innocent by any means. I'd left plenty of corpses cooling behind me in my day, but most were nameless, faceless thugs. Criminals who'd be rotting behind bars otherwise. Killers.

Had Danny killed? It was hard to imagine. Between the two of us, I'd always been the violent one. Danny was a bookworm with a gentle soul who loved theory and knowledge. I'd once seen him cry over a dead cat in the street. How could that boy grow into such a monstrous man? I had to hear it from his lips, this plan to kill millions. Until I heard him say it, I couldn't believe it.

The elevator stopped, and the doors opened with a ding. Two thick men in black suits and turtlenecks were waiting for us. Ball caps, sunglasses, earpieces with white wires crawling down their collars, military-grade weapons in hand… It was like walking onto an army base and not a residential floor.

"Mr. Quinn," said the on the right. He nodded to Khaleda. "Ms. Morningstar. You're expected." He frowned at Victis. "No one said anything about a third party."

"This is Victis." Khaleda gestured to her pet. "He's my personal attaché. He goes where I go."

Bodyguard One looked to Bodyguard Two. "Have to clear it with the boss."

He stepped away and tapped the communication device in his ear. The other guard moved just enough to allow us to step off the elevator, placing himself between us and the door down the hall.

"You got any ciggies, mate?" I asked as we waited.

He scowled at me. "No smoking in the building."

I sighed. "Well, that's going to make for a long

night. What d'ya do on your breaks then?"

"None of your business."

"You should switch to vaping," said a heavily accented female voice.

She strolled forward, blonde curls, tiny black sleeveless dress, sparkling diamond necklace... I hadn't seen her in the hallway when we first emptied the elevator, but she was there now filling it completely with her presence. She walked up to me, a small device in her hand. It was too big to be a pen. One of those things that wished it was a cigarette. I'd always thought they were for trendy city kids, the ones more concerned with being relevant than catching the buzz.

The blonde puckered her lips, slid the contraption between them and inhaled. Interest flashed in her ice-blue eyes as she pulled the machine away and blew out a perfect circle.

I smiled. "Well, if I could look as good as you, maybe I would."

She giggled and offered me her hand. "Noelle Islana. And you are?"

"Josiah Quinn." Her fingers were like ice.

"You're Daniel's friend." She gave me a once over, eyes rolling over me like a snowplow over ice.

"And how do you know Mr. Monahan?" Khaleda crossed her arms. There was an edge to her voice that said she didn't like being upstaged.

Noelle's smile didn't waver. "Oh, I'm just his neighbor. I live in Penthouse Two through there. We're old friends, though. Moved in about the same time. Daniel has the most interesting things to say. Intelligent. Dark past. Dangerous." She eyed me again and licked her lips.

"Poor girl," I said. "Hate to break your heart, but you're not exactly Danny's type."

She puffed on her vape whatchamacallit and blew sweet-smelling smoke in my face. "Oh, I know. It's too bad, really. It gets so lonely up here, you know?"

Bodyguard One returned with the all-clear and eyed Noelle with a curt nod. "Ms. Islana."

She nodded back. "See you soon," she called as the guards led us forward.

Something about the way she said it made me shiver.

The two guards escorted us to an oversized metal door that looked like it'd be more at home as the entry to a meat-packing plant than a flat. Iron. The bricks around it were laced with some heavy-duty spell that was currently inert. Since it was shut down, I couldn't tell what it did, but I had to assume it would make for an unpleasant evening if activated. They opened the latch and stepped aside.

The door opened on an impressive space of several thousand feet. Exposed brick and beams heralded back to the loft's previous life as a warehouse. Huge picture windows with tasteful evergreen colored drapes lined the far wall. Furniture, all dark wood and deep velvet colors, sat in crowded clumps around the room. Sofas in front of a fireplace, chairs in a reading nook full of leather-bound books, a mahogany table with comfortable, modern chairs. Another set of iron doors, these with frosted glass panels, were open on the right. An oversized skylight cast snowy shadows over another library.

Danny came down the floating wooden staircase, buttoning his suit jacket. He flashed a warm grin and opened his arms wide. "Joey! Welcome! It's good to see you again!" He grabbed my hand in a firm shake, still grinning like a fool. "Glad you could make it. I know it's late and the weather's awful. You want something to drink? I was just about to have an Irish coffee."

"Leave the coffee and cream out of it, mate. Just the whiskey, if you would?"

Danny snapped his fingers without turning, and another suit I hadn't noticed darted off for the kitchen. "And you, my dear?" He took Khaleda's hand and kissed it. "I have a very nice Sauvignon."

Khaleda's smile grew tight. "Just some hot tea, chai if you have it."

"Excellent, and you, sir?"

"Nothing." Victis kept his voice neutral.

While the suit went about making up our drinks, Danny escorted us to the sofas near the fireplace and fussed about, making sure we were comfortable. He was stalling, playing the gracious host. Suppose that was more familiar to him than what would come next.

The suit came over with a silver tray full of drinks and several dishes of cheese.

Danny's Irish coffee was more cream and sugar than coffee. He picked it up and leaned back. "Not to ruin the mood, but I have to ask. My security team retrieved a body from an elevator at the building this afternoon. You wouldn't know anything about that?"

I tapped my fingers on the untouched whiskey I held in my hand. "Let's cut the shit, Danny. God's Hand cornered me in a bar this arvo with a wild story about you."

"And what wild story would that be?" He sipped at his coffee.

"That you were hellbent on cashing in the souls of New York, possibly for a shot at the Devil mantle."

"I see." He was silent for a long moment before leaning forward and placing the unfinished coffee on the table. Danny's gaze focused on Khaleda, calculating, before he turned back to me. "You always were a man of few words, weren't you, Josiah? Always business. I'd almost forgotten how single-minded you could be when it suited you."

Khaleda blew some steam from her teacup. "Is it true?"

"Yes," said Danny. "But I'm not the monster they're making me out to be. I called you here to explain things, hoping that we could come to an understanding."

I placed my drink back on the tray and stood. "There's no understanding to be had, Danny. I'm not going to let you murder ten million people for power. Come on, Khaleda, Victis. I didn't come here to drink with a madman." I turned and found two of his security goons in my way. "Danny, call off your dogs before I turn them into stains on your expensive floor."

"Afraid I can't do that, Josiah."

Fine then. Danny wants to play rough, we can play rough. I extended a hand and reached for my power only to find an empty void. Fear stabbed at my chest and I tried again, but it was no use. The magic was there, but lurking somewhere beyond my reach.

The floor creaked as Danny stood. "It's no use. I've had every inch of this place hermetically sealed against all magical energies. You couldn't spark a flame in here, let alone call down the wrath of Heaven."

I turned back to Danny, feeling queasy. We'd always talked about it, sealing off a space so magic couldn't flow through it, but it was impossible. You'd have to go over every square inch, seal it on one side and then pull the power through the other, storing it in something else. The circle would have to be perfect, the mage working it immensely powerful with perfect concentration. More than that, he'd have to devise an apparatus to sit in the entry that would somehow shed any magic coming through. Shit, the spell at the doorway. It wasn't inert; it was only meant to seem that way. He'd done it. The genius bastard had done the impossible.

Danny smiled. It was a good-natured, boyish smile. "There's no need for violence, Joey. We're friends here, aren't we?"

"Friends don't keep friends from leaving with guns and muscle, mate."

He came to put his arm around me, leading me away from the seating area. "Don't think of it as me keeping you here. Think of it as me keeping you safe. Out there, in the snow and cold, the city is a dangerous place. Anything could happen. In here, you're protected. No spell can breach my walls, no power can touch you. Not yours, not mine, not God's Hand. In fact, you're safer here than you've ever been." He turned and placed his hands on my shoulders, still grinning. "You can let your guard down here, Joey."

I frowned. "What d'ya want? Really?"

"I told you. I want you. I want you with me like old times." He moved his hands to my face.

I pushed him away. "We can't go back to the way things were, Danny. Things have changed. I've changed. The whole damn world has changed. We're not boys anymore."

His face hardened, and his jaw flexed. Something dark and sinister moved behind his eyes, promising fire, brimstone and vengeance. The same look he'd given me just before I defeated him on that rooftop eighteen years ago. *That's it, Danny-boy. Take a swing. Let's work this out with our fists instead of magic. Come on.*

But he didn't. He walked away, collected his drink, and went to the window. When he spoke again, his voice was cold and purged of all emotion. "This storm is going to clear earlier than expected, just in time to allow the parade to go on as planned. Then, tomorrow while the rest of the city is glued to their televisions with their turkeys in the oven and thankful prayers on their lips, I will activate the spell and wipe New York from existence."

I sighed. "Danny…"

He put his back to the window and looked to Khaleda, addressing her rather than me. "You have until ten tomorrow morning to support my bid publicly. Once you do, I will return the portion of your soul that was taken from you."

"Hold on." Khaleda put her tea down. "Wait just a minute."

Danny cut her off. "Refuse, and both of you will be executed as sacrifices to fuel my spell. Until then, you may have the use of these facilities as if they were your own, but you may not leave. You may not make outside calls. Any attempt at violence will be met with deadly force. Do we understand each other? Good." He looked at both of us and swept from the main room through a set of double doors that led to the rest of the flat.

Khaleda met my eyes, her face marked by fear and confusion. He had us right where he wanted us, and we had less than ten hours to stop him, or we'd be as dead as the rest of New York.

16

JOSIAH

"Danny! C'mon, mate. Talk to me." I followed him into the rear of the flat, passing another seating area. Past that, two small bedrooms stood off to the left while another, longer hallway led to a master bedroom. That's where I found him, pouting on the end of his bed.

He glared at me, his gaze glacial. "What else is there to say?"

"I don't know." I spread my arms and shrugged. "Explain it to me. Why the fuck would you want to be the Devil? Why New York? Why any of this?"

He laughed, but his eyes sparkled with the promise of tears. "Of course you wouldn't understand. Not you. It was always so easy for you, wasn't it? The power. You know, I remember the day Christian brought you back. You were a skinny, dirty kid with a dream and barely two dimes to rub together. You knew a handful of tricks, but we all knew you had promise. A year later, you rivaled Christian in raw power while I hit a plateau."

"I know it looks like I had it easy, Danny, but I promise you I paid for it."

"You lost Evette!" he shouted. "One person! I lost everything!"

Evette… I shook the memory away. Danny wasn't going to listen to reason, but maybe I could appeal to his emotion.

I sighed and sat down on the end of the bed next to him. "It wasn't fair what happened to you. If you want to hurt me, then hurt me. It's got nothing to do with all these people. These ten million idiots are nothing to you."

He chuckled and shook his head. "They're a means to an end. It doesn't have to be New York. It could be Seattle. Chicago. Los Angeles. They're just cities, and cities rise and fall. What's one wrecked city in the grand scheme of things?"

A chill slithered down my spine at the casual way he mentioned murdering millions.

Danny looked away, focusing on the fire escapes winding down the next building. "You want to know why I want to be the Devil? Why not? What else am I supposed to be?"

"Anything you want, Danny. You're a free man now. Do what you like."

He swallowed, his throat working with the weight of what I'd said. "Thing is, I have. I've done a lot since then. When I heard the news about Christian, I thought everyone was dead. I wanted to die too. I was tired. Tired of being used, lied to, tired of trading blow jobs in back alleys for food, of sleeping in tents and thinking that was all there ever was. I was tired of being powerless."

I put a hand on his back and leaned forward. "But you're not. Look at what you've done with yourself. You've got your own bloody company. You're a millionaire, Danny-boy."

He stood and went to the window, leaning his forehead against it. "I made a deal, Josiah. A new life, money, nice apartment on the other side of the country. Everything I thought I wanted. I was even married for a little while. To a woman. Can you imagine? God, that was awful. But I thought if I could just be someone else, I'd be better. I sold my soul for it."

So, there it was. Danny'd hit rock bottom and cut a deal, his soul for a new lease on life. Everything he had, he owed to some smug bastard in Hell.

He shook his head. "But no matter how rich I became, or how much I owned, it meant nothing to me. I want more. I can't be fulfilled. This thing inside me, this hunger, it can't be ignored. It has to be sated, do you understand? And I don't know how. I just want it to stop. You say I'm free, but I'm not. I'm still a slave." He struck the glass with a fist before pushing away. "But if I were the King of Hell, every soul would be mine. Every dark, twisted, and monstrous shadow could be mine. I'd have everything. I'd be a god!"

Danny stopped in front of me and took my hand. "Imagine my surprise when I found out that not only were you alive, but you were coming to New York with Khaleda Morningstar. I knew what I had to do. With her support, and you by my side, nothing can stop me. I could finally have everything."

I didn't know what to say to that. What was there to say? Danny was stuck in a moment eighteen years ago, a moment that had made him feel powerless and pushed him to make a stupid deal.

I took a deep breath, closed my eyes, and tried to imagine it. The gentle, slightly eccentric genius with all the good looks and none of the sense, shivering in the dark. Alone. Forgotten. I hadn't even looked for him. No one had. No one cared.

Maybe it didn't happen overnight. It didn't happen when his family disowned him and threw him out, or in the years Christian spent torturing him, or his first nights on the street for a second time. It must've taken years, but slowly the light behind his eyes went out. The Danny Monahan I had known broke under the weight of the world.

"Steel is forged in fire," Christian had said to me the night after he exiled Danny. In the memory, Christian put an arm around my neck and led me down from the rooftop for a congratulatory drink. "You're steel, Josiah. Danny was more like wood. You burned through him. You don't need him anymore. From now on, Danny is dead, do you understand? He's dead to you."

The words had stung. I hadn't wanted Danny to go, but his leaving was also a relief. With Danny gone, I could move on, pretend that what'd happened between us wasn't real. Too much to drink, too many drugs. I didn't like boys. I was into girls. I loved Evette and not Danny. The idea that I could've ever had both was dismissed as teenage lust, and I boxed myself up nice and neat to be like all the other boys I knew.

That box had long ago burned to ash. Still, the one part of me I thought I had figured out was the sex. Then the ghost of Danny Monahan walked into my life and reminded me of a time when the lines blurred into non-existence.

The bed shifted as Danny sat down next to me again. I opened my eyes, suddenly acutely aware of his leg against mine.

"Danny," I started, turning to him.

Danny put a finger on my lips. "Don't say anything. Not yet." He leaned in.

Warning bells went off in my head and the bottom dropped out of my stomach, the instinctual alarm that something terrible was about to happen. A train wreck in motion I couldn't turn away from, even if I had wanted to. And I wasn't convinced I did. I wasn't convinced of anything.

Soft lips grazed mine, so light I doubted it ever happened. Something lit a fire in my chest and made it burn. Silence weighed down the air, the only sounds his breath and the fire burning quickly through the rest of me. My brain screamed for me to stop, but the rest... The rest of me didn't care. All the rest knew was that someone was touching me, and I liked it.

A smile touched the corner of Danny's eyes that never quite made it to his lips. He kissed me again, and this time, there was no pretending it didn't happen.

Eighteen years lifted, and we were back in the small room we shared with the four other boys, pressed against each other as if we knew what we were doing. Except this time, there was no need to whisper, to clamp hands over each other's mouths to muffle moans or to retreat to separate beds and fall asleep alone and confused. No one there would dare point and laugh or snicker.

But ten million people would die.

I snapped back to the present and pulled away from Danny. "Call off the spell," I said, suddenly breathless. Why was I breathless? It was only a kiss. But dammit if a part of me didn't want it to be something more.

"I can't." He tried to kiss me again.

I turned my head aside, though it didn't stop him. He simply redirected his affections, teasing the sensitive skin where my jaw met my ear with his tongue. I almost caved. We could talk about this after.

No.

I closed my eyes. "You said you wanted me. Prove it. Call off the spell, and I'll stay."

He made a small, exasperated sound and leaned back. "Joey, I just explained this to you. I need this."

"Then find some other way, mate. I'll help you. You want to be King of Hell? Fine. Let's do it, but not like this."

His face changed. Danny pushed away and stood. "I knew you wouldn't understand. What is it?

You're with her?"

I blinked and almost burst out laughing. "Khaleda? Not even close."

"You always did like the girls better. Acted like I was nothing to you. Always fawning after Evette while I was just a convenient fuck when you couldn't get to her." He started pacing, stomping so hard whoever was below us was likely to come knocking.

"That's not what this is." I tried to reassure him several times, but Danny wouldn't have it.

He planted his feet and pointed to the door. "Get out! Get the fuck out of my room! Guards!"

"I'm going! Christ, Danny." I hurried out of the room and shut the door behind me only to run into his security in the hall.

Hadn't met those two yet. Maybe there'd been a change in shift. They scowled down at me.

I gave them my best smile, despite the pounding in my head. "Hey, fellas. Either of you got a ciggy?"

17

KHALEDA

They locked us in one of the guest rooms. The three of us. Together. Five thousand square feet, four bedrooms and two living rooms and they shoved us in the same room to wait out the night. It was as if they knew it was a punishment.

Josiah lay on the bed, staring at the ceiling. He'd finally stopped whining about not having any cigarettes and resorted to massaging his temples in silence. Victis leaned against the opposite wall, next to the room's only window, arms crossed.

I reached the wall and turned around to pace the length of the room again. "They can't do this. We need to tell somebody. Don't you have a phone or something in that bag? Maybe a spell to notify someone?"

"Spells don't work here," Victis reminded me.

Josiah groaned. "Khaleda, sweetheart, would

you mind not pacing or talking? In fact, don't do anything that makes noise."

I spun around, ready to kick him. "It's only been two, maybe three hours since your last smoke, asshole. It can't be that bad yet."

He groaned and put the pillow over his face. "Thanks for reminding me."

I almost laughed at him. Reduced to a puddle over a cigarette. At least I knew how to get to him.

"Wait a minute." Josiah flung the pillow aside and sat up, jabbing a thumb toward Victis. "If magic doesn't work here, why's he still mush for brains?"

I started to answer him but stopped because he'd made a good point. "Victis," I said, lacing my voice with a seductive command, "raise one arm above your head."

He did as I asked.

Josiah blinked. "Can you do anything else, Khaleda? Anything at all with your powers besides creating love slaves?"

That was it. If I was going to die tomorrow, I was going to hurt him before I went down. I stomped toward the bed.

"Excuse me," said Victis.

I stopped. Josiah shifted to face him, head cocked to the side.

He gestured to the window. "This is just glass. We could break it."

"We're six stories up, mate. Unless one of you can fly, that's a bad idea."

"No need to fly," Victis said with a shrug. "All we have to do is get into the floor below us. There's a large enough ledge outside to hang from. I could kick in the window on the floor below us. Then you two just drop down. I'll catch you and pull you inside. We make a run for it. Their response time is likely to be fast enough we'll encounter them in the stairway, but it's only this floor that's sealed against magic, right?"

Josiah looked at me, surprised. I smiled at him. *That's right, prick. Mine's more useful than yours. Let's see your stupid spider get us out of here.* Of course, they'd taken Josiah's bag and everything inside it, including Milly.

No time to be smug. We were on the clock with less than nine hours to go. "Say we do get out of here alive. Then what? How do we stop him?"

Josiah moved to the end of the bed, resting his elbows on his knees. "We know what he's going to do and why. What we don't know is how. I need to do some research. See a guy about some surveillance."

I didn't miss the part where he left out any mention of retrieving my soul. Danny had it somewhere in that apartment. "And the missing piece of my soul?"

Josiah shook his head. "Without those souls he's planning on claiming, Danny has no basis to a claim. He's got no power. He's just your average everyday wizard with a god complex. He'll release it once he realizes he's failed."

"And if he doesn't?"

A mask fell over Josiah's face. "Then we find it. We take it by force. Let's hope it doesn't come to that. Danny will be a tough one to put down."

We rearranged the room as quickly as we could, bracing the bed against the door. The building likely had an alarm, and once we broke into the next floor, it would go off. The door wouldn't hold for long against two goons with guns, even with the bed against it, which is why I'd elected to take care of them. I unplugged the lamp and ripped the cord out, winding it around my right hand. They may have taken my knife, but they hadn't left me unarmed.

Cold flooded the room when Victis opened the window. Snow blew in and melted once it hit the floor, forming tiny puddles. He looked back at me. "Ready?"

I nodded.

He gripped the window sill and dropped as if he'd done it a hundred times. Glass shattered. Alarm bells screeched on the floor below.

Josiah went to the window. He was supposed to dangle himself until Victis grabbed his legs and pulled him through, but he paused to look back at me instead. "I'll be waiting for you. Don't make me wait too long?"

Pounding began on the door as they tried to open it and found too much resistance. I barely heard it. *I'll be waiting for you.* The words sparked something in my chest that I quickly dismissed. He wouldn't wait, not for me. He'd run the second he got clear, which meant I had to make short work of the assholes about to come through the door.

"Go, you idiot," I snapped.

Josiah dropped.

Gunfire erupted, ripping apart the door. I spun

to my left, avoiding it and pressing my back flat against the wall. I let the heavy end of the cord dangle from my hand, gripping the section I'd ripped out of the lamp. Hands hidden in tactical leather gloves tore apart what was left of the door, clearing enough space for one of them to stick his head in. I snapped the cord up like a makeshift whip, the metal prongs striking him just below the eye. He fell back through the door with a curse. Bullets ripped through the room, peppering the walls in erratic patterns from the other side.

I threw myself to the floor and eyed the open window just as Josiah's fingers disappeared from the ledge. Victis had gotten him inside. If I ran for it while they were still firing, I was dead. Had to wait for the reload.

They didn't. While one of them fired at the wall I'd just been leaning against, another kicked the door hard enough it moved the mattress, pushing it between me and the window. Dammit! The gunfire halted, and both forced their way into the room. They raised their guns.

With a shout, I shoved the mattress back at them. It collided with the one in front, knocking him back into the other. I pushed myself up and ran for the window, dropping to a crouch just as they opened fire again. Something cold impacted my shoulder hard enough to push me out the window.

Before I could process what was happening, the icy sidewalk was suddenly rushing up to greet me.

Pressure closed around my ankles and I jerked to a stop.

"Gotcha," Josiah grunted. "Pull us up, mate."

I slid backward and crashed to a wood floor in
another apartment. My shoulder hit something
hard—a wall, I think—and pain exploded, radiating
in every direction.

"She's bleeding!" Victis shouted.

Josiah pulled me to my feet. "No time. You
good?"

I nodded, and we stumbled forward, working
our way through an empty apartment in a hurry.
Victis jerked open the iron door, and we ran into a
hallway matching the one above. The other tenants
poked their heads out of their apartments to stare at
us. Someone shouted they'd already called the
police. That would explain the sirens closing in.

"How are we getting out of this?" I shouted at
Josiah as we made it to the elevator. The cab was
too far away to make it.

He tapped the down button frantically. "I'm
still working that out!"

"Well, work it out quicker!"

The elevator doors opened, revealing four
armed guards in formation. They raised their guns.

Victis threw himself into the elevator with a
battle cry, tackling the two gunmen in the front. The
two in the back shifted their aim on instinct,
focusing on him. Except they couldn't shoot him,
not without hitting one of their own.

Josiah barked out a word that made the lights in
the ceiling flash and spark and then darted in,
twisted a rifle from the hands of the closest guard
still on his feet, and slammed the butt into the other
man's face.

One of the men Victis had tackled slipped away

and raised his gun to fire. I kicked him in the face, which made the shot go wide. Bullets dented the ceiling. With a loud creaking snap, the elevator shifted downward. He must've hit something important. Another kick to the face and he slumped over, blood leaking from the corner of his eye. The gun fell to the floor.

I picked the gun up and pointed it at the soldier Victis was still wrestling with. "Surrender or die, asshole."

He raised his hands.

I squeezed the trigger anyway and took him out with a perfect headshot. Then I turned and put two in the one I'd taken the gun from. I was about to shoot the last one when Josiah kicked him in the groin and he went down.

"Stop killing people!" Josiah shouted and slammed the button for the lobby.

I lowered the gun. "That's two less to fight later."

"Yeah, and two more reasons for the police to call in the FBI or Homeland Security!" He pressed two fingers to the last man's temples. A short blast of magic filled the elevator car as it crept down, and the man slumped over.

I put a hand on my shoulder and pulled it away covered in blood. Every movement ached. I could feel the bullet inside, just a few inches deep in the meat of my upper arm. It had gone in at a weird angle, stopping just short of penetrating to the bone. All I had to do was dig it out and bandage it up.

Josiah stopped the elevator once we reached the second floor and pressed the button to open the doors. "We go out the back way. Victis, you head straight for the cab."

He turned his head to look down the hallway as Victis helped me into the elevator. With a curse, Josiah grabbed me by the injured arm and shoved me hard into the elevator car just in time to avoid being hit with a ball of icy blue magic. He threw himself against the wall, only barely managing to escape it himself.

"Get her out of here," Josiah snarled at Victis and reached in to tap the Door Close button.

"Josiah!" I shouted and tried to push myself up, but my shoulder was too badly hurt. I went down with a curse. "What about you?"

"Don't worry about me," was all he said and turned away. The doors slid closed, sealing Josiah in the hall with whoever had attacked him.

18

JOSIAH

I waited until I was sure the elevator was well on its way before I stepped away from the doors, adjusting my jacket.

Danny stood at the far end of the hallway, his once-kind eyes wild and full of rage. In front of him stood the lovely blonde I'd met in the hallway before. Noelle. Her dress sparkled like black ice as she took another step forward, full lips quirked into a deadly smirk. She extended her hand and sheets of sharp, blue ice crawled down her elbow to coalesce into a swirling ball of steaming cold in her palm. The spell complete, she parted her lips and let out of a contented sigh before quirking an eyebrow at me. "Leaving so soon?"

"On the contrary." I dusted a bit of ice from my shoulder. That last spell had come a bit too close for comfort. "Thought I'd stay and hold you off so my injured friend could escape. You wouldn't happen to have a light on you, would you?"

Noelle laughed, dark and sultry, a promise deep in her throat of forbidden pleasures that made my spine tingle. "Afraid fire's not my specialty." She raised her spell, ready to hurl it at me.

"Stop." Danny put a hand on Noelle's shoulder and stepped past her. "Go and take care of the others."

Murder flashed in Noelle's ice-blue eyes. "We had a deal, Monahan. If you die—"

His fingers squeezed tight on her shoulder. "I said, go!"

She cast one threatening glance back at me before blowing a kiss and retreating in search of the stairs.

"Still rude to pretty girls, I see." I unbuttoned my sleeves and rolled them up, pacing to the center of the hallway. "Worried she'll upstage your magic, Danny-boy?"

He flashed pure white shark teeth and mimicked my movements, stepping to the side. "Always have something smart to say, don't you, Joey Josiah?"

I had no choice but to sidestep as well or else risk letting him get the upper hand. The two of us circled in the narrow hallway, sizing each other up. He'd shown me only a fraction of what he was capable of on the rooftop earlier. Of that, I was certain. Anyone who could manage to craft such an intricate spell as the one laid on the floor above was not someone who would go down easily.

But it wasn't just anyone, was it? This was

Danny Monahan, my teacher, my friend. I had loved him once. Now, I'd have to kill him. He wouldn't listen to reason. No, Danny was too far gone for that.

The first spell whipped out of Danny in a streak of electric blue. I jumped to the side and let it slam into the wall at the end of the hallway. Brick exploded. The building quaked. People screeched and ran, panicked into the hallway, pushing past me on their way to the stairs. The presence of all the innocent Normals didn't slow Danny down one bit. He twisted his fingers in the air as if braiding a rope before making a fist and pulling empty air back toward himself.

The wall behind me collapsed, throwing bricks, wooden beams, and live wires to lash out at me. I put my arms up over my head as a heavy beam crashed to the floor off to my right. He was literally tearing the building apart to get to me. Well, two could play at that game.

"You can't win, Josiah," Danny shouted through the dust rising from the rubble. "Why are you fighting me? We should be working together, not fighting each other!"

"If you think this is my sort of gig, you don't know me half as well as I thought you did." Let's see. A building this big, with that much magic soaked into the bricks above, I'd need a doozy of a spell. Blood would be the easiest fuel, and unless I wanted to grab one of the passersby fleeing the scene, I'd need to collect it from either me or Danny. I searched the ground for something, anything sharp that I could use.

A fireball careened through the air. I gathered my will into a thick wall of blue magic and raised my hands, stretching it between them. Danny's fireball struck the shield, the strength of the impact forcing back a step. Another slammed into my shield, followed by another. The attacks were unrelenting, and only growing stronger, the more desperate he became.

Danny's silhouette appeared at the edge of the darkness and dust, hands raised, another, larger fireball spinning between his palms. "Dammit, Joey." His voice broke under the strain of emotion, cracking as if he were a teenage boy again. "We could've been something. We could've been great. Why? Why'd you do this to me? I could've given you everything, yet you throw me away like trash. After all these years, it's still all about you, isn't it? What Josiah wants." He stepped through the cloud of dust, close enough that the dark circles under his eyes were visible.

Now was my chance to strike, but I'd have to drop my shield to do so. The second I did, he'd hurl that fireball at me, and that thing was too big to dodge. Once it hit the floor, the whole building would go up, and us with it. Better than letting him kill everyone in New York.

Danny had taught me a lot back in the old days, but his spells relied on his understanding of the elements. Science, the elements, the very knowledge of how electrons spun around the nucleus of every atom, that was how Danny understood magic. He'd married science, reason, and the arcane to craft spells that could tear the world apart with enough will. Such an understanding gave him control and accuracy that were unmatched.

But that wasn't how I understood magic. Magic had a cost. Like fire, it needed fuel, something to burn in exchange for the power it gave. Blood and sacrifice were the easiest way to fuel a spell, but they weren't the only way. Raw emotion, while unpredictable, could feed some of the angriest, most powerful spells in any wizard's arsenal, though tapping that power was dangerous. Feed too much into the spell, and it could easily careen out of control.

I dropped the shield and tapped into the boyhood memory of what I'd felt for Danny. The love and lust, yes, but also the anger that he had walked away. The shame I had used to build a wall around those memories, keeping them locked away, so I'd never feel that again. The silent tears shed alone in a bed I had earned by betraying the one person who understood me best. Hope, rage, loss, betrayal, all balled into one explosive force that tore out of me in a bolt of raw power. It slashed open the side of Danny's face and sent him spinning to the ground. A few inches lower and the blow would have sliced his throat wide open. This could've all been over.

No time to think about that now, not with his fireball flying toward me. I had one option to survive, and it wasn't a good one. Danny had forced my hand.

I barked two syllables and made a fist, drawing on the well of power that sat deep within, nearly untouched. It woke at my call and rose, stretching like a lazy cat waking on a warm summer afternoon. My heart beat once, pushing fire into my veins that burned to the surface, threatening to devour me. Blinding light consumed the world around me while a high-pitched buzzing vibrated my eardrums until they burst. I opened my mouth to scream, but all that came out was more flame.

In the presence of Holy Fire, Danny's fireball fizzled to nothing. I had survived his spell. Now all I had to do was survive my own summoning.

The earth quaked under my feet, trembling in the presence of its creator's power. Brick and glass melted. Support beams snapped and tumbled. I called to the cool of the night, to the snow I knew was falling through the cracks all around me. A choir of terrible voices called to me, all chanting the same thing: Abomination. Unclean. Sinner. I reached for them, for the promise and power that was mine by right. Save me.

But no angel grasped my hand to pull me from the flames of Hell nipping at my heels. They turned their backs on me and let me fall into perdition with all the rest of the souls trapped in the flat that night.

19

KHALEDA

The elevator doors opened, and Victis grabbed my hand to drag me out. I hesitated, pulling back. "We have to go back for him."

Victis' face hardened. "Teacher, that man is a menace. We need to escape this place while we still can."

My jaw trembled. I had felt the magic rolling off of those two at the end of the hall. Josiah was powerful, frighteningly so, but I didn't know if he could take them both on. Not by himself. He'd barely gotten this far without my help.

Victis' fingers squeezed my hand, threatening to crush it. "I won't let you die for him."

My head snapped up. "It's not your place to decide what I live and die for."

His eyes widened, and his face jerked as if I had slapped him. Dammit, he was right, though.

Injured as I was, I was no good in a fight. Josiah stood a better chance of getting away if I wasn't there to slow him down.

He let go of my hand. "Please, Teacher. He told us to go. You're hurt. You need medical attention."

Well, Victis was right about that. My shoulder ached like it was broken and burned at the same time. The fresh stitches Josiah had put in my leg were sore too, and exhaustion had finally hit me. I wouldn't be upright for long at this rate.

Victis didn't wait for an answer. He grabbed my hand, and we raced for the rear stairs. He threw the door open and frigid night air washed over me. I instantly regretted not bringing my coat. The stairs were icy, difficult to navigate in heels even if I wasn't weak from bleeding and exhaustion. Victis had to help me down. Even then, I stumbled into his arms.

"Easy there," he said and helped me get back to my feet. There was no affection in his tone. No comfort. The way he handled me, it was just something he needed to do. An order to follow. He may have claimed to love me, but Victis couldn't love anyone. Never again.

Something rumbled behind us. The building shook, forcing me to stumble away from it. The walls trembled, pushing bricks out to crash to the ground below. Victis pulled me back to a safe distance as I stared in horror, watching whole sections of the building cave in.

No!

Josiah was in there.

Ice water pumped through my veins. Maybe

he'd gotten out. He was right behind us, wasn't he? And Josiah was a Nephilim. He was tougher than most. Maybe he was okay.

I waited in silence, listening to the police and fire truck sirens drawing closer. The dust began to settle, replaced by wild, driving snow. My heart sank into the churning of my stomach and died there. He wasn't coming. He'd pulled the building down on himself and gotten crushed, the idiot.

Why should I care? He wasn't anything to me. Just someone I knew. The only someone I knew. The only person I knew I could trust with my life. Yes, Josiah was a narcissistic bastard, but he wouldn't shove me in front of a bus, not as long as he thought he could get something from me. And if he was gone, I'd be all alone. Nowhere to go. No hope of taking on Danny Monahan myself to get my soul back. Maybe there was a tiny, microscopic part of me that would miss having him around to torment.

Nephilim or not, there was no way he could've survived having hundreds of tons of brick dumped on top of him.

Victis put a hand on my shoulder. "We need to go before the police find us."

I nodded and wiped melted snow from my cheeks. Victis put his hand on my upper back and guided me away from the fallen debris. I felt numb. Josiah, gone. I really was all alone. Victis would try to help, but he was too broken to do anything more than whatever I ordered of him. Where would I go? What would I do?

Without my soul, I couldn't even feed properly.

Every time I tried, I got sick. I wouldn't have even tried if it weren't for Josiah pushing me. He was a bastard, but he was just the kind of bastard I needed to push me through when I didn't want to. I'd survived this long, if for nothing other than to spite him. Without that, I didn't know if I could go on.

Weak. I could hear my father's voice in my head as he lashed out at me. Pathetic. What kind of succubus are you? You're not unable to feed. That's an excuse. Only the weak need excuses, Khaleda. I didn't raise you to be weak.

I squeezed my eyes shut, fighting back tears. My breath caught in my throat. He wasn't real. The scene wasn't even a memory. Lucifer Morningstar was dead, and he couldn't hurt me anymore. Yet there he was in my mind, invading my thoughts, hurting me every time I closed my eyes.

Stop whining, chided my father's voice in my mind. You have a ready and willing food supply right next to you.

I looked over at Victis, who was holding me up. That close, it was impossible not to feel the emptiness of his mind. No, not emptiness. His mind was scrambled. Memories of who he had been before I destroyed him floated inside blank space, jumbled, senseless without an identity to attach to. He knew about the things he'd done, the kind of person he had been, but that was gone now. On occasion, parts of that identity would surface, but only so much. He could never again swear loyalty to another, never bow before his God in true worship, something that had once brought him joy and peace. I'd taken that from him.

Bricks tumbled from a pile loudly behind us. I let go of Victis' arm and turned. If Danny fought his way out of the rubble now, we stood no chance. He'd kill us both. I couldn't even run with as much pain as I was in.

A shadow appeared in the settling dust and falling snow. Light sparked, illuminating a dark face with sharp, bony features.

Josiah?

Blood trickled down from a gash in his head, but he paid it no mind as he lit the cigarette, drew in a deep breath, and then pulled it away, coughing. He climbed from the rubble and limped toward us, waving wildly.

"Oi," he called and pointed to the bent cigarette between his fingers. "Lookie what I found!"

The pain and doubt I'd held onto faded, replaced by a swollen ball of anger. That bastard! I was going to murder him.

20

JOSIAH

Khaleda was pissed, but she knew better than to take a swing at me with her arm injured. Victis turned and started away from the fallen building. Khaleda and I fell into step behind him, limping along. Fine pair we were, me bleeding and bruised, and her shot to hell. At least when the building came down, one of the central support beams bent over me, holding up most of the mess and creating a clear way out. I hadn't meant to topple the building, but it served them right. Damn thing was coming down anyway. Calling down the power of Heaven only assisted it in its downward journey.

Khaleda slid on a patch of black ice. I caught her and held her up, despite the sudden screaming pain in my side. My lungs suddenly felt tight, and the pressure built the more I leaned to the side. Shit, must've cracked a rib.

"Almost there," I promised her. "Round the corner, up the street, and we're there."

We came around the corner and nearly bumped right into Victis' back. He stood in the center of the narrow alley, feet planted wide in a challenge.

At the other end of the alley, a sleek, feminine shape blocked out the light. Heels clicked as she walked toward us, passing through a dying pool of yellow light. Noelle, and still in that sleek black number, despite the cold. Sparks flew and metal ground against brick as she closed the distance. Christ, I'd nearly forgotten about that icy bitch.

Noelle stopped a dozen paces in front of us. Metal flashed on either side of her as two ice blue blades appeared in her hands. "Evening, boys. Josiah. I see you found yourself a cigarette."

I let go of Khaleda. "Two swords? Isn't that overkill? We're not even armed."

She shrugged. "I've always been a fan of finishing first. But then, it's no fun to finish alone." She tossed one of the swords in the snow.

"Afraid I'm no good with swords," I said and nudged it back toward her with my foot.

A sinister yet somehow sensual smile touched her lips. "That's not what Danny said. You really should make it your policy to kiss and tell, Josiah. I do love a good tragic romance."

"Fuck this," Khaleda growled and leaned over to pick up the sword. She extended her hand and cursed. Crimson drops appeared in the snow.

I pulled her back. "You've got a bullet in your arm, fuckwit."

"Well, well." Noelle pushed some hair out of

her face. "You two are a mess. What about you, big guy? Any fight left in you, or did she fuck it all out of you?" She gestured to Victis with her chin.

Victis glared at her a moment before reaching for the sword.

I put a hand on his shoulder. "Pick it up, and you're a dead man." I turned back to Noelle. "Not just a friendly neighbor, then, are ya? You're working for Danny?"

Noelle laughed. It was a deep, velvety sound laced with venom. "Come on now. You know better than that. You knew that when we first met, didn't you?"

She held her hand out, catching some of the falling snow before smearing it over her arm. A cold blast of magic shocked the alley, forcing the temperature to plunge so low I couldn't keep my teeth from chattering. Glittering frost crawled over her skin, building into glowing gauntlets, vambraces, and then a full suit of form-hugging armor. Snow swirled around her head, pulling it into an out of the way knot. More snowflakes gathered at her back, creating a cape of pure white. Gone was the soft seductress; a hard warrior stood in her place.

"What the hell are you?" Khaleda asked, gripping my arm.

"Does it matter? Now, if you want to escape, one of you will have to fight me. Let's make it interesting. When I kill my opponent, and I will, you other two will go straight back to apologize to Danny and maybe he won't slit your throats to fuel his spell right now."

"And if we win?" I puffed on the cigarette, wishing it would warm me. My fingers, toes, and nose had all gone numb. It had to be below freezing in that alley, and none of us had our coats.

Noelle licked her lips. "If you win, it won't matter. I'll be dead. Now, pick up the sword."

Victis held out the keys to his taxi. "Go."

"Victis," Khaleda said, "she's wearing armor, and she has magic."

He picked up the sword without looking at her. "The only other option is to go back where the police will arrest you, or Monahan will kill you. I'll keep her busy. Go!"

She tried to protest again, but I grabbed her arm and pulled her away. "Better him than us."

While Khaleda squirmed, Victis stepped forward and shifted his stance as if he knew what he was doing. Noelle's smile widened, and she brought her sword up, wholly focused on him. The two remained as they were, frozen in place for a long moment, and then she *moved*, her body blurring and reappearing to Victis' right for a slash at his head.

Victis somehow blocked the sword and pushed her back. Noelle slammed into the brick wall and spun to the left, narrowly avoiding Victis' powerful strike aimed at her chest. His sword hit the wall and sparked blue magic, sending a vine of ice climbing toward the roof.

Noelle slashed at his exposed left side and Victis lifted an arm on instinct, moving as if he'd had a shield. But he didn't and the sword bit into his forearm, grazing the outside. It was a deep cut, but not fatal. He hissed in pain and fell back, cradling his arm and watching in horror as it froze solid.

Khaleda squeezed my arm. "Help him."

I shook my head. Even if I'd wanted to, I was tapped out completely now. Just staying on my feet took almost more energy than I had, and we had to make a run for it.

Victis looked back at us, his body trembling. Sweat froze on his forehead. He met my eyes with a fierce glare, the message clear. *Stop staring and get her out of here.* Once he was sure I'd gotten the message, he surged back into the fight with an animalistic growl, slashing and slicing at Noelle with no reprieve, pushing her back. He backed her into a dumpster, clearing the way for us.

I grabbed Khaleda, and we limped down the alley as fast as we were able. The parking garage loomed in sight. Just another few seconds and we'd be inside. Then we just had to get to the third level, find the taxi and—

Behind us, Noelle let out a frustrated scream. Something crashed with a wet thud. Magic surged and swept toward us in an icy torrent. I pulled Khaleda out of the mouth of the alley just in time to avoid being hit by the spell. It swirled by, sucking all the warmth out of the air and freezing everything—including droplets of moisture in the air—into a solid mass. If that'd hit us, we would've died instantly.

Our path to the garage was cut off. She'd hit us if we sprinted back for the opening, and inside the narrow walkways, we'd be easy targets. I scanned the street in a panic, settling on a small, circular area where the snow had refused to stick. A manhole cover. Perfect.

I ran to it and grunted, trying to pull it up. Damn thing was heavier than it looked. Khaleda ran to help me, and we finally got it free. The stench from below made me gag, but the smell was still preferable to dying. I motioned for her to go. "You first."

Khaleda pinched her nose. "You."

"Pearls before swine, sweetheart."

She flipped me off, but she finally started to lower herself into the tunnel.

Noelle tore around the corner and spun on us, her cape and armor steaming and splashed with crimson. Blood dripped from her sword to paint the snow. Khaleda was still half in the tunnel and she wasn't going to make it down before Noelle repeated her spell, which meant I certainly wasn't.

Magic swelled. The temperature plunged around me.

No choice. I gritted my teeth and slapped a hand over the gash in my head, pulling on what little power remained in the blood and feeding back into myself, urging it into my muscles for an extra burst of strength. It wouldn't last but more than a few seconds, and it'd leave me without any magic for at least a few hours, but at least I wouldn't be dead. With a shout of effort, I lifted the manhole cover, spun around once and let it fly like a frisbee straight at her head.

Noelle extended her hand and caught it.

Bugger.

Steam rose from where her flesh gripped the metal manhole cover. Her eyes widened as her gauntlet disintegrated and red welts sprang up on her hand, spreading like wildfire. She screamed in agony and let go of the manhole cover just as I dropped into the sewer.

***

It felt like we'd walked for hours in silence. I didn't particularly know my way around the New York City sewers, but most of the turn-offs were marked. Once our noses adjusted to the smell, it wasn't so bad.

Khaleda walked with her head down, hugging herself, speaking only when spoken to. She didn't seem to care where we went or how we got there after the initial flight through the tunnels. It took us several minutes before we realized Noelle hadn't come down after us. Smart girl. Between the sewers and subways, there were enough underground tunnels in New York to form another city.

White, painted lettering ahead pointed us toward the Jay Street Metro station. We must've crossed under the East River at some point. No wonder it felt like we'd been walking forever. I followed the arrow.

Khaleda suddenly looked up. "She was fae, wasn't she?"

I started to shrug and stopped. My shoulder was sore. "Didn't care for the iron content of the manhole cover. That's for certain."

I hadn't had many dealings with the Fair Folk in my line of work. They tended to avoid angels and demons on principle since the Angelic Host had robbed them of significant power in the olden days. To find a Winter fae working with someone trying to become the next King of Hell was troubling, but not out of the question. To secure his position, Danny-boy would need the backing of powerful entities outside of Hell. He'd hoped to bully Khaleda into giving her support, but she couldn't have been his only supporter. Winter was backing him, too. Only question was, what did they have to gain?

We reached a small maintenance door that connected the sewers to the subway tunnel. A rusted padlock kept it closed, but as tired as we were, it was enough of a deterrent. I stared at it and considered just waiting out the end there. At least down there, God's Hand, the fae, and demons would leave us alone.

I sighed and decided I didn't want to die in a sewer. Three good kicks and the lock broke. I tore it away from the latch and forced the creaking door open. "Found the A-line. If we can get to the station down the way, I think we can get to where we need to be."

"I felt him die."

I turned away from the opening, resting one arm on my knee. Her whole left side was wet and sticky with blood. She trembled, either from the cold, shock, or both. Putting her on a subway line in that state, even in the middle of the night, would be akin to cruel and unusual punishment. Poor girl was suffering, and she was stuck with a bastard like me.

"Khaleda, keep it together just a little while longer. We're almost there."

Her chin quivered, and she gripped her throat. "She cut off his head, Josiah. He was so afraid. I felt his last breath, his mind reached for mine. He wanted me to feel."

"No, he didn't."

"Of course he did. I destroyed him, and he wanted me to die with him."

I stood and put my hands on her shoulders. She didn't respond, even when I shook her. "Fuck what he wanted! He tried to kill us, Khaleda. Or did you forget that part? Victis was a zealot and a murderer who would've killed anyone, anywhere, just because God's Hand told him to."

She looked at me, her chestnut eyes big and wet. "I would've done the same for my Father."

The realization struck like lightning to my chest. She'd seen herself in him and thought she could save him somehow, even though he was doomed from the start. She'd tried, and she'd failed. Even under her control, he couldn't shake the brainwashing. What if she couldn't either? It didn't matter that her father was dead and couldn't order her to do terrible things anymore. That wasn't it at all. It was the possibility that haunted her. Lucifer was torturing his daughter from beyond the grave.

Hot, fiery rage bubbled in my chest. It wasn't my fight, had never been my fight, but if it were in my power, I would've brought him back so she could kill him herself. It was that closure that was missing for her. She hadn't seen him die. What if he hadn't? What if he was coming back for her? No matter how many times I told her he was gone, she couldn't stop thinking about it.

I cupped the side of her face. "You're stronger than him. Stronger than Victis, than your father.

Khaleda, you're stronger than me. Hell, maybe half the men in this city. Danny Monahan is afraid of you."

She sniffled. "Why? I'm nobody. I'm nothing without him."

"Look at me." I held her face in my hands until she did. "I'm terrified of you. Not because you're the deadliest person I know—even though you are. Not because you're Lucifer's daughter. I've seen what you can do with a knife. Trust me when I say that tongue is twice as sharp. You don't need to be Khaleda Morningstar, Lucifer's daughter anymore. You be who you want. No one but you is in control of where you go, what you do, and how you live your life. You're free of all that. Say it."

Her lips parted, but no sound came out. She blinked. Tears trailed down her cheeks and fell, wet and warm, onto the back of my hands.

"Say it, Khaleda."

"I'm free of my father." The words came out as a whisper of disbelief.

"Say it again. That didn't convince me. Why should it convince you?"

Khaleda sucked in a shaky breath. "I'm free of my father. He's dead. He's never going to hurt me again."

I smiled. "There's my girl. What'll you do to any asshole who tries to hurt you from now on?"

In a blur of motion, Khaleda pushed my hands away, grabbed one of my arms, and twisted me, raising the arm at a painful angle behind my back.

"Christ! I didn't mean me, Khaleda!"

She let me go, and I almost fell flat on my face.

"Prick."

That was it. After everything, that was how she was going to be? Oh, it was on. I rolled my shoulder and turned around to find her smiling at me like it was all a big joke. But the sparkle was back in her eyes, which made it hard to stay mad at her, despite the sore arm.

"Bitch." I said it with a smile and a wink before crawling through the next opening.

The maintenance hatch opened onto a narrow ledge that stretched a quarter-mile to the next station. It was empty except for a collection of bums huddled under sleeping bags in one corner of the station. A flashing sign announced the last train of the evening would be arriving in two minutes. We had great timing.

Our luck held, and we got onto a car that was eerily empty. Just to be safe, we found a seat in the corner where she could keep her bloody shoulder mostly hidden. It felt good to sit, even if it was on the most uncomfortable metro seats ever.

"How's the shoulder?" I asked as the train screamed through a tunnel.

"Aches." Khaleda shut her eyes and swayed. She had to be exhausted. "Bullet's still in there."

"We'll get it out once we get where we're goin'," I promised.

She yawned. "Which is where exactly?"

We couldn't go back to the hotel. Not only did Danny know where that was, but God's Hand would be getting desperate soon. They'd assume I'd accepted Danny's offer and come to kill us as soon as they knew we were back. It wouldn't be long before they spotted us on the metro either, but that couldn't be helped. I'd lose them once we got off the train.

I spread my arms over the back of both seats and leaned back. "I don't have many contacts here, but I do know someone. He won't be happy to see us. Once we explain things though, he'll help. His place isn't the Hilton, but might be able to get a little rest before we have to go save the city again."

Khaleda leaned to the side. I thought she was falling until her head landed against my shoulder. I froze, muscles still coiled tight from the urge to jump up and catch her. Was it an accident? She was normally as cuddly as a croc, with fierce teeth to match. But she scooted closer, pressing her body against mine.

"Thank you," she whispered.

"What for?"

"For not dying back there. For not leaving me when I told you to. For making me live."

"No worries there, Khaleda. You just get some rest, yeah?" I leaned my head back and sighed. I'd never figure that woman out.

21

JOSIAH

Legend has it that in November of 1948, a subway station opened up just over the border between Brooklyn and Queens. The line supposedly ran along Pennsylvania and Pitkin Avenues to 76th Street. As the story went, there were all kinds of problems with the line's construction due to shortages during the Second World War. Parts of it were completed under dubious management by non-union employees who'd done sub-par work. Some rumors claimed the line was unfinished or unsafe, depending on who you talked to. This, of course, led to significant controversy and the station was shut down after just a month of operation. A concrete wall sealed the 76th Street Station and the connecting lines in an underground tomb, forgotten by all but the most intrepid urban explorers.

Explorers like my old friend, Reggie Wold.

Access to the mythical station was difficult, to say the least. We got off the A-line at the Shepherd Avenue station and followed the tracks into the darkness, due east until we came to a bit of tile wall on the left. There, hidden behind an illusion spell, was a maintenance door.

The tunnel inside was hot, cramped, and completely dark, yet we found our way. I walked along, holding the third pipe down from the ceiling, the only cool one of the bunch, and clutching Khaleda's hand, guiding her along behind me. An old security door marked the other end of the maintenance tunnel, the latch broken long ago. I fumbled to find the handle.

The door creaked open on a grimy concrete platform. Rusty old tracks trailed off into darkness to the right. Blue light emanated from the other end of the platform where a wall of computer monitors bathed a lumpy humanoid form in light. Stubby fingers worked their way over a keyboard at a breakneck pace, pausing only to pick up a soda can and pop the tab on it.

Keys stopped clacking when I took a step forward. The chair spun around. "No!" growled the gray-skinned man sitting in the chair. His oversized nostrils flared, and he pushed greasy black hair away from beady eyes. "No, no, no! Not you! Get out, Josiah! Get. OUT!"

Khaleda braced for an attack as Reggie stood to tower over us. "I thought you said he was a friend."

"Friend is such a loose term." I raised my hands. "Easy, Reggie. This is an offer you'll want to hear."

"Oh, right. Like that time you offered me a bag of gold for my magic die? That gold turned to lead, by the way. I knew I should've checked it."

I shrugged. "It was gold when the last guy gave it to me. I swear, Reggie! Besides, that's not worthless to you, is it? You can still trade lead."

He grimaced, showing yellow teeth. "Or how about that time you gave me that talking plant?"

"What's wrong with the plant?"

"It bit me!" Reggie's fists became boulders. Literally. "I still have the rash! So, no, I won't be hearing you out this time. Get. The hell. OUT!"

"Fine," I said, taking a step back. "But before I go, you should know that if you don't help us, everyone in New York will be dead by noon tomorrow."

Reggie blinked and halted his advance. He released his fists and glanced at Khaleda once before turning back to me, his face hardening. "What did you do, Josiah?"

***

Reggie made us tea while I summarized everything that'd happened so far and helped Khaleda to the bed he had tucked into a corner of the platform. It stood behind a set of heavy blackout drapes on a metal frame. Simple, but homey.

After he put the tea on the overturned crate that served a nightstand, he went to retrieve one of the medical kits he kept on hand. Reggie wasn't much to look at, but in a pinch, he was a good friend to have. Hoarders always are.

He placed the medical kit next to the untouched tea. "So, what do you want me to do? I mean, besides be your safe harbor and probably die when you fail."

I opened the medical kit and eyed what he'd brought me. Reggie bumped my arm with a jug of sterile water. I took it and did a quick wash before pulling on the blue surgical gloves. "You're tapped into the city's mainframe, right, Reggie?"

"I can control every stoplight in the city and about ninety percent of the power grid from here to Hoboken, as well as some other odds and ends." Reggie crossed his arms. "Why?"

"Need you to find a way to cancel the parade tomorrow, mate."

"The Macy's Parade?" He uncrossed his arms and shook his head. "I don't think I can. I can't exactly hack a parade, Josiah."

"Then I'm going to need a map of the route. I also need that big brain of yours to help me figure out what he's using as the catalyst for the spell. It'd have to be something every New Yorker has, something that creates a sealed circle over a five-mile radius. Could be he had some cables laid. Rail lines." I picked up the scalpel and looked to Khaleda. "You ready?"

Her eyebrows knitted together. "Are you sure you know how to do this, Josiah? These aren't the most sterile conditions, you know."

"Won't be the first bullet I dug out of someone while sitting in an abandoned subway tunnel." I pushed on the swollen lump in her arm, under which the bullet was probably resting in fragments.

She pulled away with a curse. "That hurts, asshole!"

"Just proving I know where it is. One quick cut, a little digging and a quick check from Reggie here and we'll get all the pieces out."

Khaleda looked at Reggie, questioning.

He shrugged. "All trolls have an element they're attuned to. Mine happens to be lead. I can find it anywhere. He might be an asshole, and a con man, but he wouldn't let another woman suffer under the knife."

I hesitated, the flash of memory biting at the back of my brain with his words. Dark hair in a sweaty halo. Pained whimpers, growing weaker by the second. Insides splayed out all over the pillowtop mattress like a dissected animal. Blood everywhere. Evette.

I blinked, and she was gone, but the tightness of loss in my chest remained.

I leaned in toward Khaleda, resting the scalpel gently against the swollen lump. "You're in my light, Reggie. Go make yourself useful and get that map, yeah?"

"Fuck you, Josiah," the troll spat and stomped off.

Pulling out a bullet wasn't easy. Damn things tended to fracture on impact, even in soft tissue. This one had gone in at a lucky angle, missing bone and staying shallow enough the largest part was easily accessible. All the tissue around it was angry and inflamed. A small bit of fluid encased it under the skin, making it easy enough to identify. The big piece came out in a matter of minutes, but I spied two more small pieces while I was in there.

Khaleda whimpered as I dabbed up some of the

blood.

"You doing okay? Need a break?" I asked.

She bit her lip and shook her head. "Just get it out."

"As you wish."

I had the second one out inside fifteen minutes, but the third piece was a bleeder. Every time I nudged it, I had to stop and mop up the mess just to see what I was doing. All the while, I ignored the tears streaming down Khaleda's face. Reggie came back to offer painkillers a second time, but she refused them like the stubborn woman she was.

After the third piece came out, Reggie sniffed the wound and declared it lead-free. I washed it out with a bit of saline, put in three stitches, and smeared the whole thing with antibiotic ointment. It wasn't ideal, and the likelihood it'd get infected was still higher than normal given the conditions, but it was the best I could do.

"Who was she?" Khaleda asked as I started wrapping gauze around her shoulder.

"Who was who?"

"The woman Reggie mentioned. He said you'd never let another woman suffer again. I assume that means someone did before. Was it in this cult you and Danny were part of?"

I considered not telling her. What business was it of hers, anyway? If we survived this, she'd get her papers from God's Hand, and we'd go our separate ways. Then again, she'd taken a bullet for me. She'd killed to save me, and she'd lost a small part of herself when Victis died. I owed her more than I could repay. A name and a story wouldn't hurt anyone who didn't deserve the pain.

I rolled the gauze over her arm one more time. "Her name was Evette. She, Danny, and I were at the top of the class. Best of the best of Christian's soldiers. Inseparable, the three of us. But there could only be one successor to Christian's madness. After Danny was exiled, I…" The words caught in my throat as I touched the scar of a memory I'd sealed away long ago. "Christian murdered her. Used her pain and suffering to gain power. Power he then offered to me. I rejected it, and then I burned him and the rest of his cultists alive."

"Holy shit. Josiah, I'm sorry."

I shook my head and forced myself to smile. "It's in the past. Everyone has regrets. If this mess proves anything, it's that you can't run from that. The past always catches you, no matter how fast and how far you try to fly away from it. It's not something you escape. It's always there, in the mirror, staring back at you. How d'ya think I got this ugly? Wasn't for trying."

She lifted her other hand, reaching as if to touch me.

I pushed away from the bed and out of reach, pulling off my gloves. "Now, if you don't mind, I had part of a building fall on me. I'd really like a lie down about now."

Khaleda blinked as if she'd just come out of a trance. "Oh, right," she said, pushing off the bed. "I'll help Reggie get that information you wanted, I guess. And listen to the weather report. I heard they were talking about canceling the parade tomorrow because of the weather. Maybe we'll get lucky and the snow will hold."

I almost laughed at her hopeful optimism. "Right, and maybe snakes will sprout legs."

"Josiah? Thank you."

I nodded without looking at her.

She waited a moment, as if she were expecting me to say something else, then rose and stepped through the curtains.

I spent about thirty more seconds tidying up before I lost patience with it and eased onto the bed. The thin mattress felt like heaven on my aching body, lulling me toward sleep.

Can't sleep yet, Josiah. I rolled onto my back with a groan and a muffled hiss of pain as my rib reminded me it was there. All work and no play makes for a bad day. Christ, I hope the next place I visit is tropical. I'm thinking nude beach. Tahiti sounds nice.

The clock ticking on the wall stopped.

"Tahiti, Josiah? Really?"

My eyes snapped open and I shot up. The voice had come from the foot of the bed where a skinny, dark-skinned creature with no discernable gender stood. A squiggly shock of blue hair twisted like the top of an ice cream cone on their forehead. Sparkles dusted their cheeks, forehead, and the exposed skin of their upper arms. Feathery, gray wings folded behind their back.

"Ira." The name escaped my mouth like a curse. It'd been some time since I'd had a heart-to-heart with my guardian angel. Most of the time, Heaven didn't want anything to do with me, but they'd been unusually interested of late.

The angel's eyes glowed blue briefly. Wings twitched. "It's Irabriel. You know I prefer the long form."

"And I prefer to be left alone." I collapsed flat on my back again. "Go away."

"That's it? I save you from certain death in a collapsing building, and this is the thanks I get? A collapse you caused, Josiah."

"Not on purpose." I closed my eyes, shifted my leg, and winced at the pain. Something there was definitely off.

Ira appeared standing over me, arms crossed over their flat chest. "Three people died in that collapse. One of them was an old woman who had nothing to do with your fight with Daniel Monahan."

"Old lady, you say? Old enough to have had a good life then." I cracked open an eye. "Why're you here, Ira?"

Ira frowned down at me. The blue sheen passed over Ira's eyes. "You have a bruised femur, which is why your leg hurts so bad. Painful, but not fatal. It's the cracked rib I'm worried about. You keep going at the rate you're going—and we both know you will—and it'll snap. It will pierce your lung. Thanks to your smoking habit, it'll kill you in short order."

I put a hand over the aching spot on my rib. It throbbed painfully in response. "I can't just lie here until it knits itself back together. Your side hired me to stop Danny from wrecking New York, remember?"

"Why do you think I'm here?"

Ah, so someone higher up than Decimus had taken note of what was happening and wanted to put a stop to it. It'd have to be someone with lots of clout if they were ordering Ira about.

Ira smiled, a warm, loving smile. "Brace yourself."

I tried to move out of the way, but even I wasn't faster than an angel. Ira thrust their hands into my chest as if the skin and bone weren't there. Hot fingers brushed against my insides, singeing them, burning them to ash. I choked on the agony and gritted my teeth as Ira traced burning fingers over bone and muscle, feeling for the crack.

"Stay with me, Josiah," Ira urged, a smile evident in the tone. "This is no fun if you pass out from the pain."

Get fucked, you winged cunt. I couldn't say it out loud, but I didn't have to. One of Ira's gifts was the ability to read minds. All I had to do was think it.

Just when I thought I was adjusting, Ira's fingers probed an even more sensitive spot. "There you are."

I kicked on instinct, my primitive nervous system working on overdrive to try and propel me away from the unbearable, searing pain as Ira mended my bones. My lungs seized, refusing to draw in air. Tears touched the corners of my eyes, and I choked on a scream.

When Ira had finished with my ribs, they moved on to correcting the bruise on my femur.

"I thought you said that wasn't fatal," I ground out through clenched teeth.

Ira smiled. "It's not. I just like watching you suffer. You know, you're lucky I'm doing this at all. There's still a standing kill order. If I didn't like your father so much, I'd have ripped your heart and brought it upstairs instead. Gift wrapped. Let me take care of your head, too."

There were only so many ways to describe pain, and I was all out, but Ira wasn't. Ira had a whole language based on pain and made sure to teach it to me.

When Ira was done, they withdrew their hand and shook it. "There. All done. Don't you feel better?"

I couldn't respond. Everything ached. My insides felt like they'd been put through a blender and funneled back in where they were set on fire. My skin felt chilled, though I knew it had to be stuffy and warm as far down as we were.

"Your magic will return within the hour. Your father sends his regards, by the way." Ira toweled blood from their hands. "Said his offer is still open."

I fought the exhaustion to raise two middle fingers.

Ira sighed. "I told him you'd say that. I also told him he'd do good to visit your mother. Is she still in that private hospital in Melbourne?"

"If he goes near her, I will flay him living. Understand me?"

"Temper, temper." Ira patted my chest. "All that smoking's got your blood pressure up. I'd give it up if I were you. You know that leads to performance issues. Wouldn't want your little succubus friend to be disappointed."

I took a swing only to find Ira gone.

The clock on the wall started ticking again, and I collapsed onto the bed, holding my head. If I never saw my guardian angel again, it'd be too soon.

22

KHALEDA

"So how do you know Josiah?" I asked the troll.

He'd been ignoring me in favor of staring at the wall of computer monitors. I peeked over his shoulder to see what could possibly be so interesting. Each screen had been divided into four sections showing snowy streets. Some were empty while brave drivers still crawled over others like little bugs, all scurrying home. Only one screen wasn't focused on a street, and it played a continuous news station with the sound turned off.

Reggie's fingers stopped moving over the keyboard just long enough to tell me he paused to think. "He saved my life once. Feels like another life, honestly. Another world. I barely go up to the surface anymore. I like it down here. There are no bridges here."

I looked around the grimy platform. It could use a good power wash, but it wasn't too bad for an underground lair. Still, I'd never choose to live there. "I thought trolls liked bridges?"

"Some trolls." He stopped typing and turned his chair around to face me. "Did you know there are over two thousand bridges in New York City? More than enough for every troll to have one. Except that's not how it works. Some trolls own two or three. Some have none. I was one of the ones who didn't have a bridge to call his own. I tried, but…" Reggie sighed. "I don't really like bridges. It was never important to me, you know? I just like *things*. According to some, that means I'm not a very good troll. Bridges are very important in troll society, you know." He rolled his eyes.

I shrugged. "What kinds of things do you like if not bridges?"

Reggie's eyes lit up. He stood and stomped excitedly over to another curtained-off area. "My collection," he announced proudly and pulled the curtain aside.

Shelves lined the tiny alcove beyond, each one stuffed to bursting with trinkets. Tools, books, plastic containers, cutlery, picture frames… Common, everyday items that didn't seem in any way connected to one another.

Reggie picked up a baseball. "I know it might look like junk to you, but that's the beauty of it. They don't look like much, but each one of these things is magical." He let go of the baseball, but it remained suspended in the air as if he were still holding it.

I put my hand under it, and it fell into my palm just like a normal baseball. "So you collect magical odds and ends?"

"Things nobody else wants." He gestured to the shelves. "Most of these things don't do much. The baseball, for example, just floats. Good if you need to work on your swing, I suppose. Useless for anything else. I have books whose pages turn blank once you've read them, self-cleaning coffee cups, a spool of thread that never knots... This plate turns blue if you put anything with peanuts on it."

I frowned. "How is that useful?"

"It's life and death for someone with a peanut allergy." He shrugged and put the plate back to pull out a length of yellow rope. "This rope is made of Korrigan hair. Do you know what a Korrigan is, Khaleda?"

I started to say that I didn't, but he charged on ahead, too excited not to explain.

"In Lower Brittany, they're a sort of a cross between a fairy and a siren. All female, with hair and clothes made of gold. In most stories, they lead travelers off their path, never to be seen again. In truth, they prefer wizards. They lure them off, and drain anything magical of its powers. The hair, once they get it wrapped around you, effectively shuts off all magic until it's removed. Nasty pieces of work, the Korrigans." He held the rope out to me. "Here. Do yourself a favor. Once this city is saved, go tie Josiah to a post and leave him there with this. You can thank me later."

I took the rope in my hand. Magic lashed out and bit into my skin, tasting, searching for something. The hunger inside me rose to meet it only to back away and dissipate into nothing. I stared at the rope and tried to awaken the hunger on my own. *Come and feed, you monster*. It stirred but refused to surface.

"Is everything okay?"

I draped the rope over a pipe sticking out of the wall and smiled. "Of course. You have an interesting collection, Reggie. It's just... You said Josiah saved you, yet you don't seem to like him much."

Reggie shrugged. "He saved my body from certain death, but he ruined my life." He ushered me away from his collection and closed the curtain behind us before returning to his chair. "I was going to jump from the Brooklyn Bridge. Would've been easy, except they put up those huge panes of safety glass. No problem for a big strong guy like me, right? But standing there, realizing I had to break the glass just to do it, I stopped to think. Then he strolls up. 'Oi, ugly,' he says, 'You gonna jump or what? Yer blockin' the walkway an' I got places to be.' Bastard."

I nodded. "Sounds just like him."

"When I didn't answer him, he offered me a cigarette and stood there and talked to me." Reggie shook his head. "I don't know why he listened. Or why I talked. It was weird. No one had ever cared. Humans all think I was disfigured in a fire or something. They run away. And the other trolls, they laughed at me. Pushed me around because I didn't want a stupid bridge. No one listened. But Josiah did. Listened for the better part of an hour

and told me I was being a fuckwit. Wasting my
time. Jumping off that bridge wouldn't have done
anything but made a mess for someone else to clean
up. I'd just be another problem for someone else.
But, if I lived, maybe I could be useful. Maybe I
could find something that'd make me happy, even if
it wasn't a dumb bridge."

That sounded like him too. Josiah had a way of
changing how you looked at your problems. He was
mean, he was rude, and he was the biggest asshole
I'd ever met, but he cared in his own way.

Reggie cleared his throat. "Anyway, a bunch of
punk kids showed up and took a cell phone video of
him putting the broken glass back together with his
magic after I'd broken it. Put it up on the internet as
proof that trolls and magic were real. Started talking
all about things no one is supposed to know about.
Supernatural things that could get normal people
hurt. Every troll in New York was pissed at me, and
so were the fae, and everybody else. I spent eight
months cleaning up that mess on the net.

"Lucky me, I found out I was pretty good with
computers and finding things. So that's what I do
now." He gestured to the wall of monitors. "I scrub
security footage all around the country of
supernatural happenings and keep magical creatures
out of the news. I sit here, and I stare at screens all
day. Every once in a while, some asshole threatens
to cut me into little pieces because I missed
something, and I wonder how the hell I got into this
mess. The answer is always the same: Josiah
fucking Quinn."

"He is a walking disaster, isn't he?" I

suppressed a chuckle and leaned in for a closer look at the monitors. "Any luck finding that connection he was looking for?"

His chair spun around. "Not yet. A circle that big would run out into the Atlantic, and there's nothing out there. Saltwater notoriously breaks up magic energies too. Whatever he's using to mark out the area of effect for the spell, it isn't a circle."

"What else could it be?"

Reggie shrugged. "Something atmospheric maybe? Radio waves. A television broadcast?"

None of those fit. With what little I knew about magic, even I knew that. People might be glued to their televisions while the parade was on, but not everyone. Enough people would either be there, physically at the parade to watch, or have their TV off that the spell couldn't cover enough area.

I pointed to the map he had on one monitor. "What about the parade itself?"

Reggie enlarged the map with a click, spreading it over all the screens to show the highlighted parade route. "I ran the numbers, and there wouldn't be enough people along the route either, even if the parade was packed. If he's shooting for ten million souls, he'd need something to hit every home in New York City, all five boroughs and beyond. Nothing I can find would do that."

I glanced at the clock on the wall. Almost four. We had just over six hours to figure this out, or we were all screwed. Staring at the screens and trying to figure out how Danny was going to launch his attack so we could stop it was pointless, especially without Josiah. But he was beat and needed rest if he was going to be any good in the upcoming fight. Which reminded me…

"Hey, Reggie, could you do me a favor? Find me everything there is to know about a Noelle Islana."

Reggie's eyes got big. He gulped in a mouthful of air. "Noelle? What the hell are you two doing tangling with the Winter Knight?"

The Winter Knight? Well, at least that confirmed who she was. I knew a thing or two about fae knights, even if I didn't know this one. Father had cut deals with most of the courts at one time or another, but we'd never had any dealings with Winter. Explained why I didn't know her. It also told me her weaknesses.

The fae knights inherited their powers from their title, which was much more than just a position of honor. The Winter Knight would be expected to guard her kingdom against intruders, protect her queen's interests and holdings, and secure alliances that would enhance Winter's standing. As such, the queen would confer the mantle of knighthood on her chosen knight, granting them special powers associated with the office. Winter was a season of cold, harsh weather. Ice and snow would be her power, iron and flame her weaknesses. And I had seen her fight. She was good, at least as good as me. Fighting Noelle would be a challenge.

I glanced at the curtained-off bedroom and rubbed my injured shoulder. I'd need to heal first. With stitches in my leg and arm, I was worthless even if I had an appropriate weapon, which I didn't.

With only a few hours left on the clock, the chances that I would heal enough to present an obstacle for the Winter Knight, let alone a challenge, were non-existent.

Unless I fed the Hunger.

I turned back to the troll. "Reggie, do you have any weapons in your collection? A sword, maybe?"

He shrugged. "Probably, but I'd have to go up the line to the bigger storage unit. I don't keep things like that here."

I flashed him my best, most seductive smile, satisfied when his pupils dilated and his throat worked to swallow. "Could you please go and find one or two for me?"

Poor Reggie couldn't get out of his chair fast enough.

23

JOSIAH

With my bag missing, I felt naked. The worst part wasn't the missing bag, though. It was knowing Milly was out there all alone. She hadn't been crushed by the rubble when the building fell; I'd have felt that. Milly and I were psychically bonded to be able to sense each other with the tiniest spark of magic. The old girl was more than just a pet. She was as close as someone like me could get to a familiar spirit, though that term didn't quite fit either. Milly was a magic spider, crossed over from a world where magic was more common than tech. More than that, she was a friend.

And friends don't abandon friends.

Laying in Reggie's bed, my body aching from Ira's healing, the magic slowly seeped back into my body, a sparking live wire that struck nerve endings with renewed pain. I let it fill me until I was itching

with it and then closed my eyes to reach for her
across town.

The first time I touched her spider mind, I'd
recoiled and vomited. The shock of crawling into
another creature's brain was too much, and hers too
different. Though she was intelligent and powerful
for her size, Milly was still a spider in all the ways
that counted, and spiders didn't think like humans.
Now, it was second nature. I needed only to close
my eyes and hover on the edge of a dream in the
place where distance and reason didn't exist, the
birthplace of both magic and madness. They were,
after all, two faces cut from the same stone.

I let myself fall into that state of waking sleep
and called to her. *Milly, where are you?*

Empty night flew by, fat snowflakes spinning
out of control toward the silent streets. I flew on the
wind, propelled toward some far off destination.
Over sleepy neighborhoods, closed shops, across
the East River, twisting through tall buildings
toward SoHo. Red and blue lights flashed against
dark windows as if speaking some advanced form
of binary code, red for danger and blue for calm.
Tired faces huddled near the open rear doors of
ambulances, blankets pulled tight around hunched
shoulders.

Not here.

Past the police cars and up the block lay a
broken heap of brick. The once-proud building full
of upscale flats had toppled on the southern side,
leaving the guts of the building exposed to snowfall.
The top floor was mostly intact, but Danny's
penthouse hadn't survived the fall. Everything from

the kitchen forward was gone, crashed into the floors below as if it'd never existed. I let my consciousness hover over the rubble a moment, hoping to catch the familiar pull of Milly's mind.

She'd already moved on.

Over here. Her voice called me down the alley we'd fled into. A tiny shape crawled briskly through the darkness, making the rats scurry away from their garbage feast.

There you are. The pull of her magic drew me in, and I surrendered to it.

Darkness makes for good hunting, but there's not much worth hunting in this alley. The crickets have all gone away because of the cold, and the rats have taken their young into the deep nests underground. The city is awash in dark magic. It tickles the hair on my legs with every step.

I want to go back into my burrow where it's warm and be away from this spell. The human and I have done lots of magic together, dark magic. Blood magic. He's a good student. But this is not our spell. This is the magic of a breath held. Like a cricket caught in my web, the city struggles in its grip, feeling but not understanding that the end is nigh.

A hot spot appears in my vision ahead, a pool of cooling orange against a sea of ice blue. Lighter, colder orange wafts from it. Blood. A larger predator has been here. I should keep to the shadows.

Voices drift on the frigid wind from around the corner. Josiah wants me to listen to them and see what I can learn. I crawl onto the wall, going high to see from above. There are three of them, two human males and a female fae. At the sight of her, I'm frozen. The blood in the alley isn't hers, but she is part of it. I have found the predator.

"Relax," says the predator female to one of the males. I glean Josiah's mind and come up with a name: Noelle. "This doesn't have to change anything. The spell is still primed for use at any time."

"Yes," growls the smaller of two males. Josiah says this is Danny. "But if we wait, we risk losing access to the souls. It has to be tomorrow. Without the circle in my solarium, I'll need direct power to get a circle up and running. Divine blood, and we're painfully short on that type of sacrifice, Noelle. You shouldn't have killed him."

Noelle smiles. "How many do you need? Just one? Then bleed Josiah when he comes back."

Danny moves into striking range of the predator, challenging. "What if he doesn't come back?"

"Danny, Danny, Danny." She adjusts his shirt, picking off invisible lint. "That's not my problem. I've fulfilled the terms of our agreement by blanketing the city in snow. Once you've collected your souls, we stand prepared to support your claim, but until then you must prove yourself worthy of the title. What kind of Devil would you be if you can't even secure a proper sacrifice?"

Danny turns to the other male. "Is the body secure?"

"Yes, sir."

"Take it to the office. Then I want you to

contact God's Hand. Tell them we're calling a truce and instruct them they can collect him, and my surrender, from the rooftop tomorrow morning at nine sharp." Danny flashes his flat teeth at Noelle. "Will one of them do?"

"Perfect," says Noelle. She turns her head, eyes gleaming red. She's seen me.

In a panic, I skitter up the wall and over the building. Where are you, Josiah? I don't like this city or that fae. She wants to squish me.

She'll do worse than that if she gets you. We're at the 76 station about ten miles east. How long'll it be, then?

I have eight eyes and roll all of them. It's a human gesture I've picked up just for him. **Two hours if I hurry, but I'll be tired.**

No worries. Did ya happen to see my bag? Danny has it.

He says nothing, but I feel the hesitant fear. It's more than just a fear that Danny will uncover some secret buried in the depths of that bottomless pit. He's worried he's just returned a gift.

Really, Josiah? This is hardly the time for human cultural protocol. Besides, Danny is hardly a suitable mate. He didn't even dance for you.

Tarantulas can't laugh, but if I could, I would laugh at his exasperated insistence that I stick to advising him about magic. **D'ya know how he's doing it, then?**

I tap my feet in a smug rhythm. Of course. You should, too. He all but admitted it openly.

Not only did Danny not know how to dance, but he also didn't know how to keep a secret. A bad mate, indeed. But then, Josiah was no catch. Good thing humans didn't mate for life.

Now's not the time to be smug, Milly. Out with it.

I should tell him. He's clearly exhausted. Whispers of pain have trickled from him into me. But he didn't listen to me when I told him not to call on Ira's power. I told him it might cause extensive damage to the structure. He also didn't listen to me when I told him not to go into that bar. In fact, Josiah hasn't been listening to me since we left New Orleans. Plus, he's kept me locked up in that tiny box, and wouldn't let me make the succubus scream whenever I wanted. He would never learn if I gave him all the answers.

I'll tell you everything I know if you haven't figured it out by the time I arrive.

Milly!

Josiah prepares to scold me as usual except something distracts him suddenly. He is on alert. Pulse and respiration up. There's a new danger in the room. I run faster and push myself through a small hole into the ground. **Josiah? What's wrong?**

All he says is, **I'll call you back**, and abruptly disconnects.

Someone else was in the room. No, not someone. Some*thing*. It looked human, sheathed in Khaleda's skin and wearing her shocking blonde hair, but it wasn't her looking at me. The thing peering out of her eyes was dark and primal, a hunter with one purpose: devour the living.

I stayed, unmoving on the bed, pretending to sleep, my hands folded over my chest to feel my pulse racing. Was it fear pumping so fast through my veins or something else? All I knew was my mouth was dry as the Gobi Desert. I'd have killed for a drink, a smoke…anything to drown in.

She pulled the curtain tight behind her. With slow, hushed movements, she stalked to the side of the bed. I couldn't see her with my eyes closed, but I tracked the subtle rustle of fabric as she moved. Bedsprings creaked. Weight shifted, pulling me down at first before settling on top, straddling my hips.

"I know you're awake, Josiah."

"Am I?" I opened one eye. "I'm not so sure."

Soft, warm fingers crawled under my shirt, tracing gently over the sore skin of my chest. "How are the ribs?"

"See for yourself."

Khaleda made a sound deep in her throat, something caught between a growl and a purr, gripped two handfuls of my t-shirt and ripped it open. The fabric tore slowly, the sound drawn out against the heartbeat drumming in my ears. I could feel my neck thumping along with the beat in a building tempo. I'd never had a woman rip off my clothes before, nor had I considered it, but now that I had…

Her fingers moved over my ribs, tracing the lines and circles tattooed there without regard for the bone underneath. She'd forgotten already she was supposed to be checking for an injury. Good thing Ira'd popped by. The winged asshole had finally done me a favor.

She leaned forward and brushed her full lips gently over the pulse in my neck. Not a kiss, not even the promise of a kiss, but just enough to remind me of one. "I sent Reggie to get some things out of his storage. He won't be back for a while."

"Sly move." I slid my hands up her back, feeling through the thin fabric of her borrowed t-shirt. In my mind, we'd moved past this part of the dance. I'd already pushed her to the bed and pulled her pants around her ankles. But that wouldn't do. Rushing in like a fool may've worked in every other aspect of life, but this... This took time.

And turnabout was fair play.

I grabbed firm fistfuls of fabric and jerked them in opposite directions. Her shirt didn't tear slowly; it ripped in one quick explosion of force.

She let out a small surprised gasp and froze.

I turned my head to whisper into her ear. "Your move."

Khaleda smiled, leaned back, and shrugged off the destroyed shirt. Her hands went behind her back and unhooked the white bra. Satin straps slid loose on her shoulders. I helped her get it off, so it didn't bump the injury I'd just sewn up. It was the nice thing to do, after all. It fluttered to the floor.

An instinctual alarm pricked my spine, reminding me that the thing looking down at me with those burning eyes wasn't human. What I was doing could kill me. But isn't that how every man wants to die? Better with her than in whatever fiery apocalypse Danny had planned for me. Ecstasy over energy any day, right?

Khaleda leaned forward, hands reaching for the pipe running through the wall behind the bed. Full, round breasts hovered over my face, practically begging to be tasted and teased. I took full advantage until she pushed my shoulders flat against the bed. A braided golden rope was draped between her hands, curling around one arm like a tame snake. Thin tassels hung from one end.

I raised an eyebrow. "Should I be thinking of a safe word then?"

"It's not for you." Khaleda shifted her weight lower, pinning my legs in place. "It's for me. Well, mostly for me. When I tell you, you have to wrap this around my wrists. Can you do that?"

That was a surprise. Not at all what I'd been imagining. "Whatever you say."

She moved the rope, letting the delicate fabric tassels brush over my chest and stomach. The familiar buzz of magic bit at my skin, gentle, tempting nibbles, all spark and no flame.

"If you don't, you'll get hurt," she said. "You still might. This is dangerous, Josiah. Only way to stay safe for certain is to back out now. Tell me to leave, and I will."

She took a breath, waiting for me to tell her to go. But I didn't want her to go. By magic, by a runaway bus, a downed plane, or a succubus, I was dying eventually. Everything was a risk. The greater the risk, the more coveted the reward, and there was no higher price a man could pay than to give his life. No way in Heaven, Hell, or any other plane of existence would I pass on this.

"Stay," I said and pulled her down to kiss me.

Teeth snapped, biting down on my bottom lip while hands groped, alternating between tearing away more troublesome clothing and feeling for more tender, exposed flesh. Nothing about the exchange was gentle, loving, or full of any purpose beyond carnal lust, a thirst to be slaked. She pushed. I pushed back. It didn't take much to push her over, onto her back.

She shouted a curse at me and swung to hit me.

I caught her fist. "Does that mean stop?"

Khaleda gritted her teeth, her chest rising and falling with the effort of breath. A dark, dangerous fire burned deep in her eyes. "Did I say stop? Either fuck me or don't, but don't waste my time." She swung with her other fist.

I took both and pinned them over her head. Didn't stop her from bucking like a wild horse to try and throw me off. She'd never looked so hot as she did fighting me. At full power, she was stronger than me. Even now, if she'd wanted, she could've pushed me away. Could've snapped every bone in my body if she'd wanted, but that wasn't what she was after. Just to be sure, I held her with only one hand, pressing her wrists to the bed with little effort. The other hand groped her breast, pinching the delicate, dark bud between two fingers.

She gasped. Her body tensed. Smooth legs stopped kicking and hooked around me, pulling me lower to grind against me. Selfish bitch, even when it came to sex. Two could play that game.

It took some effort, but I pried one leg loose and moved lower to kiss the stitches I'd put in her leg. She hissed in pain, but that sentiment quickly

died as I traced my tongue up the inside of her leg
and pool my efforts against the slick wetness
between her thighs. Fingers curled in my hair, first
threatening to rip it out by the roots, then pressing
in.

"Bastard!" Khaleda gasped.

I don't know what she was complaining about.
I was the one doing all the work.

Magic snapped at my mind, tugging on an
invisible thread implanted in my brain and flowing
into her. I felt the energy move like a bolt of
lightning in slow motion, burning up from my core,
stopping only when I forced myself to pull away.

The deep gash in her leg knitted itself back
together. Christ, that was a handy power to have.

Her slap came out of nowhere, sharp like glass.
It snapped me out of the momentary stupor and
brought me back to the inexplicably infuriated
woman in the bed.

The infuriated naked and willing woman.

Don't waste my time, she'd said. *It's
dangerous*. Well, time to test that theory out.

I grabbed her and flipped her onto her stomach
as roughly as I could. Khaleda tried to move away,
but I pulled her to me, shifting so that her back was
pressed against my chest, hips tilted slightly so that
I was pressed against her opening. I expected more
of a fight. More anger and feigned resistance, but
instead, she became more pliant, almost relaxing
against me.

I smiled against her ear. "Admit it. You want
this."

"Fuck you." There she was, the angry, spiteful,

spoiled woman who could melt the flesh from my bones and turn my soul to ash.

"That's the idea."

"Fuck you," she repeated, "you narcissistic, entitled—"

I took it as an invitation.

She stopped fighting.

Magic clawed at me, mind and body, trying to pull me away. I snarled at it, a deep animal sound that broke into something more vulnerable. That same primal fear from before bit into my spine, a warning that was lost on my lust-hazed brain. The only thing that mattered was the moment, the pleasure, getting more, giving more, ending. For the first time in ages, I had a purpose. There was a goal to rush toward, something attainable, and it was within reach.

Claws of a different type dug into my neck. My name escaped her lips once as a murmur, and then a second time more desperate. "Josiah, the rope!"

Right. Best not get too into it yet.

I pawed at the rope hanging from the pipe only to find it wrapped around. There was no pulling it down without breaking things up, which I wasn't keen to do. Easier to just tie her to the pipe. My hands shook through the whole process, partly because the alarm bells were ringing louder in my head, and partly because she never stopped moving, pushing back against me. Her movements had become faster, more desperate, and there I was still fumbling with the damn rope. This was not well thought out, but then, hindsight was twenty-twenty, right?

I pulled the rope tight.

Her wrists shot up, suspended. Her body jerked away from me, moved by the sheer force of the rope. She whimpered and panted, "Need more."

I was happy to oblige, pulling her hips back to me and meeting her soft, heated need with my own. She let out more desperate cries that built to a quivering crescendo. I expected the magic to lash out at me like a whip, but it stayed contained. Part of me wished for it, the sweet bliss of absolute simple pleasure and powerful magic. I wanted it to break free and consume me more than I'd wanted anything in the world, a need she tried to draw out of me against my will.

Even tied to a wall and completely helpless, she wasn't mine, and I was poorer for it. At that moment, Khaleda was the most beautiful creature I had ever laid eyes on, and I still wanted to bathe in her magic more than I could ever want her. It was all I wanted until the fire of that need burned my mind and body to ash.

24

KHALEDA

Josiah's mind was an endless empty hallway of locked doors, and I had the key. A ceiling of stars hung above. Tangerine clouds clashed against a sapphire sky, an angry swirl of dizzy color.

My footsteps echoed through the hall as I moved, fingers running over the unlabeled doors until one creaked open under my touch. I stepped into the room and found myself inside a memory caught on replay.

It was a bedroom in an upscale apartment not so unlike the one Danny had trapped us in. Blood soaked the white sheets made of Egyptian cotton. The bed had strangely been moved to the center of the room, away from the headboard. A circle of vaguely familiar faces stood around it, holding hands, chanting. I took a breath and breathed in blood and magic.

The body of a woman lay on the bed opened from ribcage to pelvis. Wet, slippery strings of her spread around her body like a bloody aura illuminating pale skin. Empty eyes stared in frozen horror at the face of a monster. Tall and muscular, dark hair curled down over his shoulders. He spread his hands wide and black wings sprang into being behind his head.

A sudden cry made me look down to find a squirming child in my arms. She was covered in blood and so was I, up to my elbows. Nauseating pain settled in my gut. It lasted a moment, just a flash in the pan before the pain erupted into rage. No, rage wasn't even a strong enough word. Loss, pain, anger, and betrayal all wrapped into one burst of murderous intent that ripped out of me to become a living thing. It shot through the room, devouring the nameless human shapes in a fire so hot, it burned the air away.

Still, it wasn't enough. If I'd had the power, I would've resurrected every one of them and burned them away again and again. Instead, I burned their ashes to nothing.

Another presence filled the room, one I couldn't see or hear, but that was impossible not to feel. Josiah was suddenly there, pushing me out of the memory and back into the hall. The door slammed shut in my face. Chains snapped into place, held by two padlocks. An iron grate crashed to the floor over the door and bricks laid themselves, sealing it beyond reach.

Another door opened behind me. I walked into a dark room, another bedroom. Sleeping bags covered the floor between two sets of bunk beds, leaving only a narrow space to walk. The memory led me to one of the lower bunks where a younger version of Josiah lay on his back. A younger version of Danny Monahan curled up against him, one arm thrown over Josiah's bare chest, eyes closed, resting peacefully. Josiah lay awake, staring at the bunk above, running his fingers gently over the side of Danny's face as if he were comforting him.

"We should leave," Danny murmured into Josiah's chest. "You and me, Joey. Just go."

"And where would we go?" Josiah swallowed and shook his head. "Christian is right. The rest of the world doesn't get it. They don't get us. There's nowhere we can go together, Danny. Nowhere but here."

Danny shifted, sitting up just enough he could look at Josiah. He touched Josiah's chin. "You don't want to leave Evette. You love her."

Josiah was quiet for a moment. "Do you think someone can love more than one person at the same time? Or is that too greedy? To want it all?"

He leaned in to kiss Josiah, long and passionate. When they parted, Danny whispered, "I'd give you the world if you wanted it. I can't give you Evette, but I can give you me. Everything I am, everything I have. For as long as you want me." His kisses trailed down Josiah's body before Danny disappeared under the blanket.

Josiah drew in a breath and closed his eyes. "I want everything."

Sadness hit me, regret as heavy as the building Josiah had dropped on himself.

Stop it. I reached for the memory and found a wall blocking me. You don't have to hurt anymore. It's not your fault.

I could take the memory, steal his pain, and make it mine. It would forever be gone from his mind, a burden for me to bear instead. A gift from me to him.

But if I did, he would have to relive it one more time, the entire memory in all its sensory detail. It would break him, heart and mind to lose it. Even through the wall, I could feel that this was it, the memory that sat at the center of his being, the one that had formed him more than any other. When he woke, this was what made him get out of bed. This pain was so inextricably a part of who he was that he couldn't exist without it. I could no sooner take it away from him than I could rip out his beating heart.

The ground quaked and rolled, pushing me back out of the room. Thunder shook the walls, and lightning cut the sky in two. Foreign magic rained from the sky and yanked me from his mind.

And then suddenly I was back in my body, my power simmering around me in invisible waves of heat. Strange and unfamiliar magic surged around me, icy and sharp against the smooth heat of my own. The two powers snapped at each other like snakes, striking, intertwining, wrestling for superiority.

I strained my wrists against the magic rope binding me, limiting my strength. My heart was pounding so hard it hurt. We had to stop. I was losing control, even with the rope. If he pushed me over the edge now… The beast woke again, and she beat against the cage, rattling the bars and roaring to be set free. I couldn't fight her and him at the same time.

"Josiah… No, don't!"

But it was too late. We'd already passed the point of no return.

Climax broke over me in a flood of pain and ecstasy. Muscles tensed and released, unable to do anything but quiver uselessly. Hot kisses coated my back, the slick softness of his tongue darting out to lick up the sweat. His icy magic slipped through rough, calloused fingers to caress my neck. It should've hurt, the prick of a foreign power so cold, but I was so lost in the haze of satisfied lust that every touch was just more pleasure.

I couldn't move. I couldn't fight. Helpless. He could do whatever he wanted, and I couldn't stop him. That should've been terrifying, but instead it was freeing.

Teeth grazed my shoulder, then sank in, just short of breaking the skin. A sound vibrated out of his chest, morphing into a desperate curse. His fingers squeezed tight, one on my hip and the other gripping my breast so hard it might've left a bruise. I cried out, my skin still on fire from the touch of whatever magic burned around him, and he gave up his fight. The sudden spill of heat against all the cold inside left me shocked and breathless.

We stayed like that for a long moment, just catching our breath, willing muscles to stop trembling. Then he kissed my jaw, almost tender.

This had to end. If it didn't end here and now, I

might start to like him, and it couldn't become that. I could never have that.

I turned my head toward him. "You going to untie me?"

"I'll consider it." He kissed my shoulder.

I shrugged his face away. "Untie me, asshole. Now."

Josiah made a frustrated sound. "You're a real bitch, you know that?" He tugged on one dangling end of the rope, and it released.

I twisted and pushed his weight off me so I could climb out of bed before I changed my mind. "And you're still a prick."

The ruined remains of my clothing lay around the room. I picked the pieces up one by one and infused them with a small spark of power, willing the threads back together enough to cover the essentials. The rest, I'd take care of when he wasn't staring at my ass.

"Is it so awful to admit you enjoyed it?" He reclined on the bed, arms folded behind his head and that smug expression on his face like he'd won some major victory. "Just say it."

"You want me to thank you?" I gagged. "Do you hear yourself? I've met some narcissists in my day, but you… You're something else entirely." *Come on, Josiah. Let it go. Let's just go back to trading jabs and icy, hateful stares. I can't do this.*

The memory of the way his magic touched me made me shiver. I'd never felt anything like that before, and he certainly wasn't the first person with magic I'd ever slept with. What the hell was that? Did he even know he'd done it?

"Well, that'd be a start, wouldn't it? 'Thanks for putting up with all my shit, Josiah. And for the sex. You're amazing, by the way.' Pass me my jeans, would you? Might have another ciggy in there."

I picked up his jeans, waded them into a ball and threw them at his face as hard as I can. "You smoked all your damn cigarettes, ass! And I hope you never find another one in your life! In fact, I hope I never see you again after this mess is over."

He grinned and winked at me. "You weren't so bad yourself, Princess."

It was all I could do not to pick up the nearest heavy object and club him to death. I had to get the hell out of there. With a furious growl, I ripped aside the curtain and stormed back into the main section of the station.

Reggie stood on the platform halfway between the entrance and his chair, an oversized hoodie hiding most of his body. If he'd pulled up the hood, he would've looked like any other overweight New Yorker out for a trip to the corner store. Two leather-wrapped wooden handles peeked up from behind his back. He had them secured there with a leather baldric. A plastic bag hung from his fingers, and he held a box of doughnuts in his hands. His face was frozen in shocked horror.

I stormed over to him, jerked the plastic bag away and overturned it. Two packs of Marlboros tumbled to the cement floor, along with a brand new lighter. I picked up the lighter and held it to the corner of each container until it lit up.

"What the hell are you doing, woman?" Josiah

tore out of the makeshift bedroom, still pulling on his pants, and rushed to try to stomp out the fire.

I stepped back and tossed the lighter in between the rusty tracks. "Smoke on that, asshole."

"Vindictive bitch!" Josiah picked up the surviving pack and dusted away some ash.

Reggie frowned. "Did I miss something?"

"No!" Both of us snapped at once.

"Uh…You're bleeding." Reggie pointed to my face.

I touched the skin under my nose, and it came away red. Heavy blood tears trailed down my cheeks, and nausea struck. Goddammit! Not again. I ran for the bucket that served as his toilet and vomited blood until nothing else would come up.

Reggie shrugged and put the box of doughnuts down on a long sheet of plywood suspended between two crates. A makeshift table. He unbuckled the baldric and placed both weapons on the table. "I brought what you asked for. I didn't think I had one, but you were in luck, it seems."

"Swords?" Josiah scoffed and held a water bottle out to me. "What'd you need those for?"

"Not technically a sword." I spat and took the water to clean out my mouth and wash my face. That done, I shoved the empty bottle back at him and paced to the makeshift table. My stomach was still upset, but it would settle itself once I got my mind on something else. I closed my fingers over the grip of one weapon.

Nineteen and a half inches of smooth, sharpened steel whispered free of the wooden scabbard. The flat side sloped into a gentle curve about two inches in, drawing to a harsh point. The blade itself held much more of a full-bodied curve almost like a machete but with the added benefit of a guard that would keep my fingers safe. Longer than a traditional knife and too short to be a sword by most accounts, they were technically classified as bolo knives. The correct term was "*talibong*," and they were weapons native to the Philippines. Adapted during the Spanish occupation from a farming tool used to clear grass into a deadly weapon for filleting humans like meat. The shape lent itself toward chopping rather than stabbing, but it would do in either case.

I drew the blade over the inside of my arm, letting the blood awaken the spell buzzing inside the blade. Fire sparked, racing down the edge, hungry to devour every trace of life. "This," I said, holding the flaming knife up for them to see, "is Amihan. That one's Perlas. They're going to rip that fae bitch apart."

Josiah and Reggie exchanged a terrified glance.

"Right then," Josiah said, clearing his throat. "Any luck with those maps, Reggie?"

The troll shook his head. "Can't find anything. It can't be a circle because anything that wide would run into—"

"The saltwater, yeah." Josiah put a cigarette in his mouth and patted himself down, looking for a lighter. When he didn't find one, he scowled at me and snapped his fingers to call up a blue flame to light it instead. "Hold on. What's that?" He pointed to the news report in the corner of Reggie's screen.

"Just the weather. They've been going on about

it since Tuesday. They'd been calling for a light dusting of snow until then, then suddenly it swelled into the Snowpocalypse. They even gave the storm a name."

"Artemisia," Josiah whispered.

Reggie cocked his head to the side. "Yeah, how'd you know?"

"It was the name of one of those rock bands out of Europe that me and Danny used to like. Lots of screaming. Occult symbolism. Aside from the magic, it was about the only thing we ever had in common. Would've been easy for someone with his power and influence to name it. Bastard probably couldn't resist."

I lowered Amihan. "It's a love letter."

"It's a bloody cry for help is what it is." Josiah shook his head. "Danny's off his nut. Turn it up, would you?"

Reggie expanded the news coverage to fill all the screens and turned up the volume.

The meteorologist, a heavyset man in a suit, paced, all smiles in front of a map with cartoon clouds. "…A rather chilly morning out there, especially this time of year, but at least the snow is dying down. Winter storm Artemisia, in a pattern fairly atypical among nor'easters, sat on all five boroughs for about twelve hours, just dumping snow. Nine inches in The Bronx, eight in Queens and Brooklyn, six in Staten Island with Manhattan taking the most at twelve. Oddly enough, not much going on outside the city. Artemisia seems to have worn herself out hitting us, but good news. Sunshine is on its way, just in time for the Macy's

Parade, so bundle up and get out there and enjoy the show."

Josiah removed the bent cigarette from his lips. "Christ. It's not a circle. It's the snow! He's working with that Winter bitch. The snow's the catalyst for the magic. All he has to do is provide the spark and this city is fucked."

That was bad. A circle we might've been able to deal with, break it apart or just dump enough salt in the right place to render it useless. But the snow was everywhere, and it was too cold to melt it. There was no way we could move thousands of tons of snow out of the city either.

I stepped up behind Reggie. "How do we stop him then?"

Even as I asked, I knew there was only one way to end this. The way Josiah feared most.

Josiah stared at the screen, his face a mask of memory. "I have to kill him."

25

JOSIAH

We prepared to surface in silence. Khaleda practiced with her new toys while I doused myself in Reggie's makeshift shower. He let me borrow a shirt from his collection, a white button-down with an anti-stain spell woven into it. It was a size too big, but it fit better than anything from his closet would've.

Milly found us about the time it would've been dawn above. I scooped her up before Khaleda could see and carried her to a corner for a little advice. "I can't beat him," I whispered. "He's better than me."

She sank into my hand, exhausted. Even with all that skill, he's still just a human. His body is still mortal. Stab him. Shoot him. Take your pick.

I tried to imagine stabbing Danny and couldn't. "He'll want to fight with magic."

Of course, he will, Milly said, cleaning her

fangs. That's where he's strongest. And he knows most of the spells you do. He'll have studied you. That's probably what the rooftop exchange was. He wanted to see how good you were after all that time.

"Even if I can get inside his defenses, I don't know if I can do it."

Why not? You seem healed and capable.

I sighed. "It's not a question of being capable. It's…" How could I make a spider understand? If Milly ever decided to mate, the poor male stood to lose his head if he didn't get away quick enough. They didn't form the types of bonds primates did. "Danny was my friend once."

I see. It would cause you emotional pain to hurt him. Milly perked up and crawled forward in my palm. Which thing do you want more? To save your friend or to save ten million people?

My heart dropped into my stomach. "Danny can't be saved."

Then the choice is simple. Kill your friend.

I tried to swallow the lump growing in my throat. "Milly, the thing is, Danny's more than a friend. Or was. I… It's like watching Evette die again, except I get to play the part of Christian this time. I have to kill the person I—" I stopped myself before I could say it out loud. In eighteen years, I'd never said it aloud. Not even when we were together. I'd never told him. It didn't seem fair to tell Milly and not Danny.

I shook my head. "Never mind. Is there a way to neutralize the snow? In case I fail?"

Well, if you had enough power, you could warm part of the city enough to melt some of the

snow, but it wouldn't be enough to save everyone.
Your best bet would be rain.

"Rain?"

That's what I said. Pull rain from the lower
atmosphere. Make it fall fast enough, and you'll
create enough friction to keep it from freezing until
it hits the ground. Make enough of it, and it'll be
just warm enough to melt the snow into ice. What it
doesn't melt, it will disrupt. This close to the ocean,
there might be enough saltwater in the atmosphere
to drown it completely.

"Vinè." I snapped my fingers.

I sensed Milly didn't approve of my choice
even before she spoke. He's a serious contender for
the Devil mantle, Josiah. Are you sure you want to
draw his attention and force him into service?

I shrugged. "D'ya know any other powerful
storm demons, Milly? What's the summoning?
Walk me through it."

The summoning she described was terrifyingly
simple. Most were. Your average kitchen witch
could call up an earl of Hell with a kitchen knife
and a trip to the pet store. Unfortunately, the bigger
the demon you called on, the more blood they
wanted. A few rats wouldn't be sufficient for Vinè.
I needed a living human.

As the plan began to form itself in my mind, I
realized Khaleda was right about me. I was an utter
bastard who didn't deserve to draw breath.
Despicable as I was, I looked for another option and
came up empty. Sometimes the only way to save the
world was to be the bad guy.

Once I decided on a course of action, I went to

Reggie at his computer station.

"Any idea where he'll be?" Reggie asked.

I studied the street map on the monitors. *Let's see. If I were a maniac on a power trip, where would I go to murder a whole city of innocent people?* It could be anywhere. In a city the size of New York, the possibilities were endless. Snowfall in Manhattan was heaviest, and Manhattan would be where the parade went through. He wouldn't pick a place on the parade route, though, because it'd be heavily patrolled by police. Knowing Danny, he'd go for a rooftop, as high up as he could find. Somewhere with access to lots of people.

"What's the tallest residential skyscraper in Manhattan, Reggie?"

He tapped a few keys and brought up search results. "432 Park Avenue."

"He'll be there on the rooftop." I tapped the screen, only to have Reggie push my hand away.

"What makes you so sure?"

I shrugged. "Danny likes to be high up, it's out of the way of the parade route, and lots of ready souls just below him." I turned to Khaleda. "We can expect the God Squad to make an appearance. Danny needs a higher lifeform sacrifice. I think he's gearing up to kill an angel."

She swiped through the air with her knife. Sword. Whatever. "Can he do that?"

"We have to presume so." All I'd heard through Milly on her walkabout seemed to suggest that was his plan, though I didn't know how he'd do it. Only a handful of things in existence—outside of someone like me—could kill an angel. I could do it.

One of the advantages of being half-angel myself, and probably why they didn't want me to live. Danny, however, didn't stand a chance. Once he acted directly against God's Hand, they'd be free to defend themselves. The contract of neutrality would be broken, and they'd smite the hell out of him.

I watched Khaleda move the blades, weaving them flawlessly through the air as if they were extensions of her body. "Noelle will be protecting Danny. I'll need you to keep her busy while I deal with him. You don't have to kill her, but that would be a plus."

"For once, we agree." She took a step back and repeated the drill.

"Noelle has two full-length broadswords, Princess. What're you going to do with those little knives against that?"

Steel flashed, faster than I could track. "She can't hold two swords if she's only got one hand." A spin, a kick. "And she can't stand on broken legs. All I have to do is get inside her reach and bleed her if nothing else. These are iron. She's fae. You see, Josiah, it's true what they say. It's not the size of the tool. It's how you use it." She winked at me.

My heart was somehow convinced I was in the middle of running a marathon. "Size and skill can go hand in hand, you know."

"Give it a rest, you two," Reggie said, spinning around in his chair. "If you leave now, you should be able to get there early enough. Subway will be crowded headed into Manhattan."

He was right, but I didn't want to go. Going meant it was real, unavoidable. Though it was already inescapable. Danny and I had been on a collision path for eighteen years. In a sense, he was a monster I had made.

I should've run away with him when I had the chance. How would our lives be different now if I had? Could we have been happy? Maybe at least one of us could have been. No sense in focusing on what could've been.

"Get your coat." I tapped the back of Reggie's chair so he'd know I was talking to him.

"Me?" His rocky nose twitched. "Why? I'm not a fighter."

"There's something I need you to do while I'm taking care of this. An errand I need ran by someone who knows how to get around unnoticed. Think you can do that, Reggie?"

He glanced at Khaleda, a worry line appearing on his forehead.

I spread my arms wide. "C'mon, Reg. It'll be easy, and the whole city will owe you."

"Okay." He sighed and rubbed his forehead. "What do you need?"

26

JOSIAH

The subway train rattled by in the dark, grim faces flashing by in an instant, each one a life with hopes, fears, dreams, and love. Their faces existed in my life a moment, less than a fraction of a second before the tunnel swallowed them. Brakes screamed. Steam rose from the tracks like ghosts. All around us, bodies shifted. A wave of red-eyed families surged toward the train. Children, excited at the prospect of the parade and a holiday meal, pulled on tired hands. Strollers folded. Anxious parents grasped tiny hands and held tight.

I flowed into the subway train with the New Yorkers, a single cell transitioning from tissue into the fast-moving bloodstream. We weren't supposed to be there. This city wasn't ours. The two of us, we were foreign invaders, antibodies sent to search and destroy an even worse disease.

The car dinged, announcing the imminent closing of the doors. More people pressed in at the last second, displacing breathable air. Everything felt stilted, stale. Every breath was stolen. Or maybe that was just the need for another cigarette squeezing my lungs.

I closed my hand around the cold metal pole and braced for the sudden jerk forward, but it didn't come. The train moved, but the acceleration was slow and smooth. Nothing about the day felt right.

My skin prickled, warning that I was being watched. I turned my head and met the disapproving stare of an elderly woman in her seat. She stared at me a second before giving Khaleda a longer, more worrisome look. It was as if she could sense how much we didn't belong. We could dress like them, move like them, even adjust our manner of speaking, but we would never be part of them. It wasn't just the city either. It was humanity. Half-human wasn't human enough.

Khaleda's hand shifted up, bumping against mine. More people were staring at her than me. While I looked vaguely threatening, she was beautiful and dangerous. The promise of violence surrounded her like an aura. Gone was the broken, half-drunken succubus from just a few days ago. She died with Victis. Now, she was a vicious killer, a living weapon with a target. I didn't fully understand the transformation she'd undergone, or what it was that had changed her, but I was glad to see it.

Pain pinched my chest as I realized that meant our time together was almost at an end. Once I completed this job, Decimus would get me her papers, and she'd be free to go where she pleased. She wouldn't need me anymore. I'd be alone again.

Good riddance, I forced myself to say. I've been working alone for eighteen years. No need to change that now. Besides, she complicates everything. All of this would've been easier if I didn't have her to worry about.

She caught me looking at her and narrowed her eyes into a warning glare.

I smirked and winked at her. I would miss our verbal sparring matches.

Since it was a holiday, the subway ran on a modified schedule. That meant less frequent stops and bigger crowds. The city had issued something called a gridlock travel advisory, which I took to mean the roads were impassably crowded. With the heavy snowfall discouraging travel the previous two days, an unprecedented number of people were out and about. Cabin fever, they called it. The parade would be more of a welcome escape than normal for the weary people of New York who'd been cooped up in their apartments for two days.

We shuffled from one train to the next in silence like the rest of them. The more changes we went through, the more crowded the trains became until we got off in Manhattan. Most passengers would go on, getting as close as they could to Central Park before disembarking. Several stations in midtown were apparently closed due to parade preparations, so they'd go on foot, herded by police and signs.

Our ideal stop would've been on 57th, but that

station was closed, so we wound up going all the way to 59th Street, putting us about half a kilometer from our destination. We came up from the subway station onto a street lined with luxury fashion and beauty shops. Throngs of people crowded the sidewalk at the crossing, waiting for the light to change. Breath pooled in a white halo above their heads. Laughter cut through the cold air, sharp and stilted, falling into a sudden stop as the light changed and people surged forward.

Khaleda and I crossed the other way, moving away from the crowd.

I stopped on the other side of the street to light one last cigarette. Once I went into the apartment building, there'd be no more, not unless I was lucky enough to walk away from this one. Khaleda waited, eyes, scanning the street and all the faces that passed us by.

My lighter made a cold metallic click as I flipped the top closed. "You know, you don't have to go."

She looked at me like I was a moron. "If I don't, Noelle will cut you into tiny pieces."

"She might still do that anyway. Point is, there's still time for you to get clear of this. You could go back to New Orleans. Someone there would help you."

Her fingers brushed the oversized knives hidden by the hem of her shirt. "She made it personal when she killed Victis. He belonged to me. Besides, her form is sloppy. She lets her ego and temper trump technique. It's an insult to women blade fighters everywhere."

"Right." I pocketed the lighter, and we started down the street again.

The Park Avenue apartment building was a dizzying structure of ninety-three stories. Unlike most high-rise apartment buildings, this one was a small, universally square structure, like they'd just stacked a bunch of cubes. Most buildings of that size had to be wider at the bottom than the top to prevent swaying in the high winds. This one seemed to just be reinforced on the inside. Every six floors, two floors sat empty and open, allowing the wind to pass through. I supposed that was one way to do it. I saw the building as a testament to modern New York itself: cramped, stubbornly defiant, and smugly materialistic. It was the perfect place for me to face Danny. I hoped I was right about him being there.

As if it were some sort of sign, a black car pulled up on the street. The passenger door opened and Decimus stepped out, still wearing August Jessup's face. He adjusted the collar of his coat and came to meet us.

"Here to make sure I follow through on our deal?" I dropped the cigarette butt and ground my shoe into it.

He pressed his thin lips together and wrinkled his nose. "Contrary to what you may believe, the world doesn't revolve around you, Josiah."

Khaleda crossed her arms and shrugged. "That's what I keep telling him, but he doesn't listen."

Decimus frowned at her. "You must be Khaleda Morningstar. I didn't know the two of you would be here. I assumed you'd already failed when Monahan's apartment building came down. I was hoping one of the two unidentified bodies was yours, Josiah. Seems God isn't done with you yet."

"If ya didn't know we'd be here, why're you here?"

His eyes trailed up the building toward the top floor.

I grimaced. "Hell, Deci. Tell me you didn't send a whole squad up after him."

"Last radio cut out four minutes ago."

Of course, they had. I'd assumed they'd be smarter about it, but then I'd forgotten I was talking to a lower angel. Common soldiers acted according to pre-set rules of engagement and if-then principles. If you knew where the enemy was, and the clock is ticking, then eliminate him with a holy death squad. Never mind that Danny likely leaked his location on purpose.

"Come on," I said, grabbing Khaleda and pulling her toward the entrance. "This moron likely gave Danny the sacrifice he needed. We've got to get to him before he can finish the spell!"

The door flew open when we were just short of reaching it. One of Danny's private security goons leveled a sub-machine gun at us and opened fire. Screams erupted on the street behind us. There was nowhere to go, nothing to duck behind, and I didn't have time to put together any kind of spell to stop bullets. We were fucked until Decimus pushed us aside and squatted behind a glowing, curved shield that came out of nowhere. It was big enough to shield him from head to foot, just like one of those old Roman shields. Guess all the Latin wasn't just for show then.

Khaleda cursed and pushed herself up from the ground, drawing her knives. The gunman turned his attention from Decimus to her just in time for one of her knives to slash at him. The first one missed, but the second didn't. She took his arm just above the wrist, severing muscle, tendon, and bone. The hand remained attached only by a small string of stubborn muscle. Before he could even process what'd happened to him, she twisted one leg around his and took him to the ground, using his own falling momentum to drive the first blade into his chest.

"Clear," she shouted and sliced through the strap that held the machine gun to the dying man. "Get to the elevator."

Didn't have to tell me twice. I ran for it, pushing through the glass doors into a lobby full of frightened people. They huddled behind stone columns, padded chairs, and desks, phones pressed to their ears. "Get out!" I shouted. That shook them from their frozen terror, and they ran screaming from the lobby.

Khaleda sheathed her blades and picked up the gun.

Decimus stormed into the lobby, teeth bared. "So much for handling this covertly. All of New York is about to bear down on this building. I hope you two idiots have a plan!"

Police sirens wailed. Tires screeched as the police cars pulled up to create a barricade. NYPD response time was good today.

I walked to the nearest fire alarm and pulled it. Alarm bells screeched, alerting anyone still left in the building that they should get the hell out. Having civilians streaming out the door would also make the coppers think twice about shooting at us. The elevators behind me hummed to life. Activating the alarm would've called them all to the lobby floor.

Khaleda stepped up beside me, gun pointed at the elevator in front of us. "How much do you want to bet one of these comes down with a surprise?"

I cracked my neck. "Hopefully there's more than one, or it'll be boring."

The numbers ticked down. People began to stumble into the lobby from the stairs and stream out the side entrances. Someone screamed at the sight of the body.

Khaleda squeezed a few shots into the marble floor. "Hurry up and get out!"

Didn't have many stragglers after that.

The elevator doors on all three cars opened at once, but only one had passengers. Two more armed guards. Khaleda opened fire, bullets raining on the two guards in a relentless spray from left to right. The men in the elevators jerked, pushed back by the sheer force of being hit with a barrage of bullets. It blew bloody holes in their bodies, and still, they didn't go down.

Great. Demons. Killing the meat suit wouldn't make them go down. That'd take a little something more.

I glanced to Decimus. "You feel like helping or is that against your rules too?"

His magic shield flashed into being in front of him. "God helps those who help themselves, Josiah."

"Fucking figures." I rolled up my sleeves.

Khaleda finally stopped firing into the elevator. The demons stumbled forward, sadistic grins painted on their faces. Grins that faded once Khaleda stepped aside, leaving me to deal with them.

"G'day, fuckwits."

They tried to get their guns up, but their bodies were too riddled with holes to move quickly. I slapped a hand over each of their faces, covering mouths, noses, and eyes, and summoned the bright blue angel fire that was my birthright. With a blast of willpower and a verbal command, I forced the fire in through every opening under my hands and burned their black souls from the inside out. They screamed, shook, and flailed under my hands, but the power held them tight until it finished its work.

Two empty carcasses toppled to the floor, the eyes and tongues burned out of their heads.

"Jesus," Khaleda whispered. "This is what you do?"

I turned around to answer her but stopped. Decimus was gone. The door to the stairway snapped closed on the other side of the room, but not before I saw his backside rushing through it. Damn coward.

"Come on." I kicked the bodies out of the way and stepped into the elevator.

Khaleda followed.

The cars were on lockdown thanks to the

impromptu fire drill, but I had an ace up my sleeve. I pulled a burner phone from my pocket, a gift from Reggie, and sent a quick text. Twenty seconds later, the elevator whirred back to life from lockdown. The doors slid closed and the number pad lit up.

"Good on ya, Reg," I said and hit the button for the highest floor on the menu. It wouldn't take us to the top. We'd have to switch elevators to get that far, and when we did, there'd be trouble waiting for us there too.

Khaleda stopped messing with the gun and glanced over at me. "So you could do that the whole time? Why didn't you just blast the demons out of Danny's goons back at his apartment so we could make our escape? Would've been better than blowing up half the building."

I turned on her and held up one finger. "First of all, it wasn't half the building. It was only about a quarter, a third at most. Second, we were cut off from magic there, remember? And even if I wasn't, I wouldn't have. Every time I use that power, I become a blip on the map for the God Squad, and there're higher-ups that want me dead."

She raised an eyebrow. "So, it's not because it would kill the human host too?"

"S'pose that figures into it a little too."

She laughed and shook her head.

"What's so damn funny?"

"You, Josiah. You want people to think you're this big, tough asshole, but inside you're just a softie. A protector of the innocent and the ignorant. You're a good person, like it or not."

I looked away. "I'm no hero. I'm just the idiot

who keeps getting stuck cleaning up other people's messes."

The elevator stopped, and the doors slid open.

Noelle was waiting for us, her ugly e-cigarette resting between two fingers. She blew out a mouthful of smoke and put it down gently on the lobby table next to her before drawing her two swords. "About time you two showed up. I was starting to think the demons would get to have all the fun."

She spun the swords and offered one to Khaleda.

"No thanks," Khaleda spat and shoved the gun at me so she could draw her knives. "I brought my own."

I swallowed a ball of ice and opened my mouth to object. I should've stopped her. No matter how good Khaleda was, she was no match for a Winter Knight. Noelle's magic would freeze her, and she had no defense against it. I had walked her to her death.

"Khaleda..." I put a hand on her shoulder.

She turned her head to look at me but didn't back away from Noelle. "Go finish this, Josiah."

If I stayed to help, Danny could finish his spell. I wouldn't be able to stop him, and we'd all be dead anyway. There was no choice but to leave her and hope for the best. I felt like I should say something, but the words were caught in my throat.

I stepped out of the elevator and ran.

Noelle sliced her swords through the air after me but found Khaleda's smaller blades blocking her. The last thing I saw before the next elevator opened was Noelle's wicked smile.

27

KHALEDA

I kicked the bitch back and worked Amihan and Perlas in a perfect single weave, pressing her back before she could fully recover. The small swords in my hands flew, knocking aside a messy lunge. Every time she stepped back, I had to take two steps forward.

Broadswords were made with reach and armor in mind, their wielders trained to make larger movements in circular patterns. Targets were necks, heads, limbs, and joints. Cleave, thrust, stab. These were broadsword words, short, cutting words, the killing power of a broadsword reflected in language.

Dance, deflect, slash. Those were my words, seduction my art. Any exposed body part became a target. Fingers, wrists, eyes, nose. A slice to the back of the leg was as valuable as one to the arm. Two light, dancing steps for every one of hers.

Noelle feigned an attack on the right. I blocked

with an upward swing of Amihan and brought Perlas down to block the true attack on the left aimed at my hip. For a moment, we were both wide open but unable to take advantage since our blades were locked against each other. She smiled and stepped in, taking away the leverage I had on both swords in one move. The swords slid behind me, and her leg came up for a kick. I slashed at it, expecting to meet muscle and bone. Instead, the blade glanced off, impacting the hard shell of armor I couldn't see. Shit, a mistake.

I dropped, ducking away from the swing at my head. She meant to smash the cross guard onto my temple. Her second sword came at me from below, slicing up in an angry arc. It missed only because I balanced on my heels and leaned back. The next chop would come from above. Her feet were right in front of me, a perfect place to stab, but there was no time to mount an offense. If I stayed, she'd cleave me in two. I leaned back further and let my body roll in reverse. The momentum carried my feet up into a kick that impacted her hand just below the elbow. If she hadn't been wearing armor, she'd be nursing a broken arm. As it was, all I managed was to kick her sword arm away. Her sword struck the wall and bounced back.

Rather than pursue me, Noelle took a step in reverse. "Interesting fighting style. You're very flexible. I bet the men love you."

I stood, gripping my blades. "Do you plan on fighting me or fucking me?"

She smirked and spun her blades. "Depends. How do you feel about double penetration?" With a

shout, she swung both blades at me as if the two
were one.

I caught them with my own. She kicked my leg,
and it folded under me. I tried to pull it in, but it
locked and refused to obey. Her sword sailed down
in a perfectly executed chop that should've taken
my leg, but I spun Perlas in a wide arc, knocking
the blade aside. Icy-cold metal bit into my calf just
below the knee, a glancing blow, but no less
damaging. Still, she'd over-extended herself. I
brought Amihan up on the inside of her elbow
where the armor would be weak. I felt Amihan slide
against the armor and catch on something, a sharp
edge. A joint. With all my strength, I pushed the
blade forward into the opening.

Noelle screamed and pulled away, taking
Amihan with her. My knife stuck out of the inside
of her arm. The fingers of her right hand uncurled
and one broadsword clattered to the floor, her
fingers twitching uselessly as blood ran down them.
I'd severed a tendon, making it impossible for her to
hold two weapons.

"You!" she snarled and gripped Amihan's
handle. Rather than pull it out, she infused the
weapon with a blast of sub-zero cold and shattered
the blade. Even once it was gone, her arm didn't
heal itself. Black veins appeared around the hole, a
sure sign of iron still in the wound.

Noelle renewed her attack with her one
remaining sword, hammering it down toward my
head in an enraged fury, all the icy power of Winter
behind it. I blocked it just as I'd done before, except
this time I sent flame racing down the blade to meet

her ice. The two magics collided in an explosion of metal, fire, and shards of ice.

The sheer force of the explosion knocked me onto my back and sent Noelle flying to dent the elevator doors. I lay in a deaf daze for a moment, trying to remember how to breathe. When I finally did, it wasn't air that filled my lungs, but an intense icy cold that froze the blood in my veins.

More cold wrapped around my neck and Noelle jerked me up to my feet. Black spots riddled her once-perfect face, at the center of each a tiny piece of Perlas. Blood streamed from the corners of her eyes and from cuts on her lips.

"Do you think I don't know who you are?" Noelle snarled as her fingers tightened around my throat. "Lucifer Morningstar's bitch little girl. You think just because your daddy was King of Hell that you have a right to that title?"

I didn't want anything to do with Hell ever again, not even if they begged me to come and take his place. But I couldn't tell her that. I couldn't breathe. Blackness closed in at the edges of my vision. I clawed at her hands, raking off skin and leaving bloody tracks behind. Still, she held.

Noelle bared her teeth. "You want to know what the funny thing is? I don't give two fucks who sits on the throne in Hell. You can. Danny can. I don't care if a two-headed flying pig runs things down there. All I care about is getting what I want. And I want my bloody crown!"

She slammed my back into something hard. It might've been a wall, or it could've been the floor. I wasn't coherent enough in the moment to know. My head bounced off whatever it was, and the world swam. Noelle pulled me away and slammed me into it again and again until my insides burned from the impact and bones rattled.

Another hit and whatever it was she'd been slamming me into split open. The room tilted, and suddenly I was on my back looking up at bent elevator doors. I gasped in a breath but couldn't force it out without choking. Somewhere nearby, Noelle stalked. I could feel the vibrations of her shoes on the floor. Metal scraped against marble.

Noelle returned with the shattered edge of her broadsword in her hand, a piece just barely large enough to fit in her hand. It was still plenty sharp enough for the job. She fell onto me, letting the full force of her body impact my hip. A new lance of pain shot up my spine. Something inside cracked. She pulled herself up to straddle me, breathing hard.

"I wonder," she panted, "when you die with only part of a soul, how long it takes to break it down in Hell. A month? A year? Whatever torture you endured before will be nothing compared to what's in store for you this time, sweetheart." She caressed my face and raised the broken blade. "See you in Hell."

"After you, bitch." I lifted my hips off the ground, threw my legs up, and strained my back to lift her weight. She struggled and tried to get away, but I lifted her too fast. She fell forward, tumbling over my head into the elevator shaft and down fifty stories. The momentum forced me to flip in after her, holding onto the ledge. My head swam. Nausea surged as the world turned upside down. My fingers slipped and, for a moment, I floated in dead air before I came down again and caught the ledge.

My heart pounded in my chest as I scrambled to pull myself up and out of the elevator shaft to safety.

The stairway door burst open, and two men in black body armor came through. Red dots danced on my forehead. "Get on the ground! Hands on the back of your head!"

I tried to comply but didn't move fast enough. They pushed me down, flat on my face, and held me there at gunpoint until a woman in white stopped, her white heels an inch in front of my face. I glanced up at her and spied the red hand pinned to her suit jacket. God's Hand.

She smiled. "Hello, Ms. Morningstar. I have a proposition for you."

28

JOSIAH

I pressed my back against the wall and glanced up at the reflective lens in the corner. A camera sat behind it, recording everything I did, but I wasn't concerned about human security. Too late for that. Aside from the mess in the lobby, and whatever was happening on the fiftieth floor between Khaleda and Noelle, I'd had to take out two more demons when the elevator stalled on the eighty-seventh floor. After that, I decided to take my chances with the stairs for the last six stories. I'd ditched the gun and climbed the stairs.

Two demons stood guard at the roof access door, one on either side. The lens distorted their faces, but they were on alert. I could take them out the same way I had the last few. Call on the heavenly light in my blood, melt them from the inside out. Yet if I did, I didn't know how much I'd have left to throw at Danny. I was knackered from the four demons I'd already taken out.

I could use Milly's help right about now. But she'd been too tired to be of any assistance, so I'd sent her with Reggie. Once I texted that I was clear of the elevators, they should've left the control center to go run my special errand.

Focus, Josiah. Milly and Reggie's errand should be the least of your concerns right now. I had demons to deal with. As much as I wanted to destroy them, I had to save my strength.

I pushed off the wall and walked around the corner, my hands raised in surrender.

The demons lifted their guns and pointed them at me.

"Easy, fellas. D'ya know who I am?"

"You're a dead man," the one on the right growled.

"Maybe, but I'm pretty sure Danny-boy'll be mad as a cut snake if you do the honors yourself. See, he wants me for his sacrifice."

They exchanged glances. "This is a trick."

"What if it is? Would you rather let me trick you or kill you? Today's ladies' choice, fellas. I'll let you decide."

They stared at me a moment before the one on the left bared his teeth. "We'll let Monahan decide what to do with you."

I didn't fight them as they grabbed me, or as one zip-tied my hands behind my back. The other gave me a pat-down and declared me clean. I felt like a trussed-up turkey by the time they jerked open the roof door and pushed me through.

Cold wind bit my face and pushed hair away

from my face. After the climb, my face was damp with sweat, making the cold a welcome change at first. That quickly changed as I adjusted to the freezing temperatures.

Huge metal fans sat inside giant rectangular exhaust ports. Snow piled around them as if it had been pushed there. Plastic snow shovels were piled in one corner where several guards milled around. Their eyes burned against my skin.

Danny stood at the opposite end of the roof, a stone's throw from the edge. He'd put on a suit and tie for the occasion. Red tie. Always did look good in red. He held Decimus against him, a knife to the angel's throat. The bastard looked like he'd put up a good fight though. Someone had carved up his face, slicing a sealing spell on his forehead. Decimus couldn't leave his body so long as the sigil was intact, and he wouldn't be calling down any heavenly powers either. He was sealed inside, unable to act. Which meant the poor bastard he was holding a knife to wasn't Decimus at all, but August Jessup. The fool had no idea what was going on. He was crying.

"That's far enough," Danny shouted.

The demons grabbed my shoulders, halting my advance.

I tilted my head to the side. "Danny, what're you doing, mate? You know you can't just slit his throat."

Danny stared at me. The look on his face... It was the same look he gave me when I followed him down to the street after our duel eighteen years ago. Betrayal. Hurt. I'd let him down. "Aren't you going to tell me there's still time to stop this madness? Try to talk me down?"

"Tried that once. Didn't work out so well for either of us, now did it?"

"No, I suppose not." He had a hint of sadness in his voice, as if he were expecting me to try again. He thought I'd given up on him.

Don't worry, Danny-boy. We're in this together until the end now, no matter what happens. "I know what you did. The deal with Winter, the snow, all of it. All you need is the divine power to kickstart it all, and since you don't have any yourself, you think you can borrow a bit from Decimus. If that's your plan, you know that knife isn't going to do you much good."

"That's right." Danny shifted the knife against Decimus' neck and walked him forward several paces before pushing him to his knees. "Only the divine can kill another divine."

"Please!" shouted August in a strained voice. "Please don't kill me!"

I shook my head. "Sorry, mate. I don't think there's a version of this where you walk away, no matter how this goes down."

Danny spun the knife so the handle was toward me. "One more chance, Josiah. You've had your fun. You've run all over this city and seen the shit it's got to offer. After all your hard work, no one gives a damn about you. In fact, even if you succeed in stopping me, you won't walk out of this building a free man. The police have us surrounded, and you're a wanted terrorist now."

My eyebrows shot up. "Terrorist, is it? When

did I get that upgrade?"

"When you destroyed an occupied building. My building." Something dark flashed in Danny's eyes. "I made some calls. Gave some damning testimony to the police this morning about a deranged Australian who'd been radicalized by a recent trip to the Middle East. It's easy to spin that tale here these days. Paranoid bunch, New Yorkers. Your life is over. You can either rot in an FBI torture prison, or you can reinvent yourself. Be who you were always meant to be." He put a foot on Decimus' back, forcing him onto his face. "Come on, Josiah. Heaven's spat on you your entire life. Help me, and we can make them pay for it."

I turned to look at the guards on my left and right. The wind picked up, chilling the side of my face until it was numb. *Here goes nothing.* "Why?"

Danny lowered his hand slightly. "Excuse me?"

"I said, why? Why would I help you when I could *be* you?" I raised my voice to make sure I was heard over the wind. "I've already proven myself, more than you have. I've killed more demons and angels than you. I've survived your assassins, your Winter Knight. And the succubus you were so desperate to get to support you? She's mine."

Danny's eyes widened. His arm sank to his side, his face going slack. "What?"

I took a step forward. "That's right. She's in my corner now, Danny-boy. I have her full support to do what I please. I don't even need you. I know how your spell works, and you need me to make it work unless you intend to kill me, which you haven't got the balls to do. Otherwise, you'd have done it already. Look at you." I shook my head. "Lovesick. Broken. Pining for a romance that never was. You wanted so bad for it to be true, you set all this up. You're not fit to rule Hell. You're not even fit to run the demons of Manhattan. I'm more fit than you'll ever be."

He stood there, the shock evident on his face and in the tightly coiled muscles of his shoulders, the loose grip he had on the knife.

Come on, Danny. Take the bait.

His breathing quickened, and his eyes darted back and forth. I braced myself as he screamed in rage and drew the blade of his knife over Decimus' neck. Blood spurted, and the body fell over, but Decimus wouldn't be dead. Just out of the game for a minute or two. Danny pushed Decimus aside and charged me with the knife.

I dodged to the right and backed away, weaving left when he slashed at me again. "A knife, Danny? Come on! What's the matter? Still know you can't beat me with magic?"

"I'll kill you!" he screamed and slashed again.

I lunged to the right again only to have some of his goons grab me and push me back. The cold metal of Danny's knife bit into my side and sank deep. I tried to gasp in a breath, but the cold seized my lungs, and I couldn't get any air.

Danny looked down at his hand on the knife, watching as my blood spilled onto his hands. "Shit!" He jerked the knife out.

I tried to take a step but wound up falling to my knees. Bastard must've hit something important. I couldn't get a good breath to save my life.

Danny grabbed a gun from the nearest goon, pointed it at the one that had shoved me into him and pulled the trigger, putting two rounds in his head. The body dropped, and he kicked the head so hard bone snapped. "This is my fight! The next one of you assholes who interferes gets it worse! Do you hear me? Don't you fucking touch him!" He spun around with the gun, pointing it at all the demons gathered on the rooftop.

They lowered their guns and took a step back.

When he was sure they weren't going to get involved, he came back to me and knelt in front of me. "Shit, shit, shit! Dammit, it wasn't supposed to be like this!" He jerked my shirt up and put a hand over the bleeding wound.

I was losing enough blood to be dizzy, but I forced myself not to fall over. It'd stop soon enough. "How'd you think this would end, Danny?"

He put the back of his hand against his nose, staining it with my blood. Danny's eyes were red. "I don't know. Not like this."

"Doesn't have to." I gasped for another breath. It stabbed my lungs and pushed more blood out my side. "Cut me loose. Put away the knives and the guns. Let's finish this…the way we should've eighteen years ago."

He considered it and shook his head but said nothing.

"C'mon, mate. Easy terms. Last man breathing wins. I win, New York lives to rot another day. You win, we'll be together in Hell this time tomorrow."

His throat worked. "No tricks?"

"No tricks, Danny. Just magic."

Danny looked around the rooftop as if he just realized where he was and the enormity of what was happening. Fear touched his face. There was a time I'd have stood by him and said fuck the angels. Fuck Heaven, Hell, and everything in between. We deserved a chance to be happy. But life wasn't about getting what you deserved. Otherwise, I wouldn't be on that rooftop trying to save the ungrateful assholes of New York from the man I used to love.

He sniffled. His voice was small and raw as he choked out, "Yeah. Okay."

Danny slid the knife between my wrists, sawing through the plastic zip tie. Then he helped me to my feet. "Ready the circles."

One of the demons stepped forward. "Sir—"

"I said ready the damn circles! Am I your king, or aren't I?"

The demon glanced from Danny to me, his expression uncertain. Then he turned and walked to the other side of the roof where two silver hoops had been propped up against another exhaust port. Danny had come prepared. That just further re-enforced my theory that he cared more about a rematch than winning. Poor man was stuck on that rooftop eighteen years ago, unable to move forward. He was willing to destroy the whole city for his chance to try again.

The demon placed one circle on the ground in one corner and walked across the roof to drop the other one there. "Ready."

Danny walked me to the first circle the demon had placed. Even if I hadn't been dizzy from blood

loss, I would've felt queasy that close to the edge.
Ninety-three stories was a far drop. I closed my
eyes and held them closed until I was facing away
from the edge.

He left me there in the circle and walked back
to his own. "Josiah Quinn!" he shouted over the
wind as it whipped his coat around him. "Are you
ready?"

My heart sank into my toes as I realized he'd
recreated the scene almost exactly. The silver
circles, the audience… He'd even used the same
words Christian used.

I lowered my hand away from my bloody side
and flexed my fingers. "I'm ready."

Danny's face lit up as if he were two decades
younger and still invincible. "Then let's begin."

29

JOSIAH

According to Christian, a duel between equally matched wizards had rules. Always stay inside your circle. Face your opponent and stick to magic. No outside weapons allowed.

Danny handed his knife off to one of his henchmen and shrugged off his coat, tossing it aside. He swept his hands in a circle, moving with the determined grace Danny'd always had when he used his power. A grid of thick, white magic appeared in a dome before him, the shield I would have to get through to score a hit. He'd been working on it since our last bout. This one was more solid, stronger. I could feel the buzz of it from where I stood.

Don't hold back, Danny had said on the rooftop before. *I can take it*. He had to know I'd never go all out against him. How much did he know about what I could really do?

Time for a demonstration, Danny. I pulled my bloody hand away from the wound in my side and swiped three fingers through the air, drawing a diamond shape. Blood flowed out of me, answering the call and filling in the space I'd just marked out. With a push of will, the disc of blood expanded, creating a point in the center.

Danny raised his chin. "A blood shield?"

I forced myself to smile. "Christian did always say my power was in my blood. It only took me another five years after I killed him to learn he meant it literally."

The problem was, the more blood I drew out of myself, the weaker my body became. I couldn't hold it, not if the wound sealed, and I couldn't use it if I wasn't bleeding. In a way, Danny'd done me a favor, stabbing me. I was probably a dead man walking, but I was going to do my damnedest to take him with me.

Danny made a fist. Light pulsed inside his closed fingers once, twice, then shot out in an electric blue beam of energy no wider than a pencil. The spell slammed into my blood shield and vibrated down my arms. I gritted my teeth and held the spell as he added another needle of magic. Then another. With each new lance of power, my shield shuddered and caved. The edges shrank as the spell compensated, pulling blood from the edge to fill the holes Danny was making.

"You can't hold it," Danny shouted, adding yet another lance. "Fight me, Josiah!"

He pulled back the smaller beams of power and formed them into one focused blast. It hit me with enough force to make the whole shield disintegrate and knock me onto my back. My head hit the edge of the circle and bounced off. Christ, that hurt. I was still wincing in pain when the next spell hit me, a graceful arc of red-hot power that encased my body and bit into every nerve ending. The magic clawed at my skin, peeling it away and crawling inside to stab like a thousand needles at my insides. If I thought I knew pain before that moment, I'd been wrong.

I fought the agony coursing through me long enough to slam my palm to the rooftop just outside the circle. Sticky blood cooled, a stranger's blood. Human blood. The power in me recoiled at the impurity of it, revulsed by the very idea of mixing, but I forced it, infusing the human blood with my own.

August's dead eyes stared back at me from just a few feet away. The blue sheen of Decimus' soul flickered inside, awoken by the power. *Come on, you angel bastard. Heal. Get up.*

Danny sent another, stronger pulse of pain magic into me. "Get up and fight!"

My body spasmed, pulling my hand away. On instinct, I unleashed a blast of blue angel fire to strike Danny's shield. It wasn't enough to break it, but it did force him to redirect his energy into holding and repairing the shield.

I tried to stand, but the stabbing pain in my side was so intense, I couldn't rise past my knees. I fell forward, pressing my bloody palms against the concrete and pushed with my power. A wave of concussive energy flew from the front of the circle, tearing up the rooftop as it moved toward Danny. He snarled and swept a hand aside, deflecting the blow. He was so busy doing that, he didn't see the second one right behind the first. It tore his circle from the ground and pulled his feet into the air. His head landed on the edge of the building and he lay there, covered in chunks of rooftop concrete and twisted hunks of his silver circle.

A beat of time passed before he groaned and shifted. I'd dealt a serious blow, but he wasn't dead yet. In a moment, he'd be back on his feet and ready to hit me with everything he had. I had to move fast.

I dipped my fingers into the blood flowing down my chest. My whole side was wet with it. "I call upon Vinè, prince of Hell, master of the deepest pit, sire of all storms. With this sacrifice, hear my words and lend me your power."

"You…" Danny pushed the largest chunk of cement off his chest and fought to stand. He was bleeding from a cut over his eye and a split lip. Dust coated another bleeding wound at his hairline near his ear, and the rest of him was covered in superficial scratches. His tie hung loose, fluttering in the wind. "I made you. Taught you everything I knew. Gave you everything and you threw me away the minute I was no longer useful! You used me!"

I closed my eyes and focused on finishing the invocation. "Hear me, Vinè! Hear me and appear."

"And now ten million people are going to pay for your mistake, Josiah." Metal scraped against concrete. Uneven footsteps shuffled toward me. The circle around me broke as Danny passed through it and pressed the knife to my throat. "Your blood will buy me my crown."

I opened my eyes and looked up at the gray storm clouds gathering. Lightning flashed, and thunder roared. "Unfortunately for you, my blood is already spoken for."

A bolt of lightning shot down from the sky. Concrete exploded, and pain washed over me in a blinding bright light. The air smelled of singed hair and electrical fire. When I opened my eyes again, small, orange flames dotted the rooftop all around.

Kneeling in the center of the rooftop was a deformed creature with scaly red skin. A mane of black hair raced down the demon's back, which ended in a spiny tail. Black horns curled on either side of his head where ears should've been, and more spines jutted from his elbows, chin, and knees. He lifted his head and smiled at me, showing pointed yellow teeth.

The first raindrop struck my head, fat, wet, and warm. More fell, turning the pale gray concrete of the roof black. The pile of snow in the corner steamed and began to shrink as the rain picked up speed.

"No!" Danny gripped my hair and pulled my head back, further exposing my throat. "What did you do?"

"Danny, meet Vinè. One of your rivals for the Devil mantle. Vinè, Danny. For the measly price of my soul, he's come to stop you."

Vinè unfurled his huge form. He had to be at least three meters tall.

The knife relaxed in Danny's hand as he beheld the behemoth demon and his murderous grin.

I grabbed his wrist and twisted the knife away. Before Danny could move, I turned on him and jammed the blade into his chest. I'll never forget the sound he made, a horrible, strained gasp. Danny looked down at the knife in his chest. I flinched as his hand shot out, but it wasn't a strike. He gripped the side of my face and stared into my eyes, his face locked in a terrified expression.

Time stopped. Memories fled by, flashes of moments without meaning or connection. I remembered the first time we'd met, but not the whole thing. Just the awful music playing in the background at the party. We'd both hated it. I remembered the way he used to sleep all curled up with his chin tucked. How he hated the way his beard grew in fiery red instead of dark. The way he'd sometimes snort just a little when he laughed hard enough.

With a shout, I twisted the knife and felt something meaty inside shift.

Sound fled the rooftop. Danny teetered and collapsed. Something in me panicked and reached out to catch him before he could hit his head. He landed awkwardly over my lap, still making that awful sound every time he tried to breathe. Danny coughed, and dark blood stained his chin. His hands flailed, searching for something, anything to hold onto. "Joey... it hurts."

I pulled him closer and gripped his hands tight. They were freezing. "Shh, it won't take long. It'll be over soon."

"I...I don't want it to be over."

It suddenly felt like the knife was in my chest

and not his. "I know. I'm sorry, Danny."

His breathing became shallow, more desperate, and full of wet sounds. His whole upper body stiffened as he stretched out to draw in one more breath. "You said…"

I squeezed his hand. "I didn't mean it. I did need you. We should've left that night, shouldn't we? Maybe in the next life, mate."

"Don't…" He blinked rain out of his eyes and stared at nothing. "Don't call me that…unless you…mean it."

His last breath escaped in a cold fog. Rain pooled in the corners of his eyes, dripping down his face like tears. I lowered Danny's body to the rooftop, barely noticing the pain in my side.

"It's time," Vinè snarled behind me. "Pay for what you bought, Josiah Quinn. Your soul belongs to me now."

"Oh, about that." I glanced over my shoulder at the demon squatting behind me. "You may want to get in line."

"What?" Vinè's eyes glowed red. He spun around just in time to take the full force of Decimus' shield in the face.

A sword appeared in Decimus' hand and he swung it. Vinè lifted an arm to protect his face. Decimus' sword sliced through the demon's flesh like a hot knife in butter and Vinè's arm tumbled to the rooftop.

The demon grabbed his stub and backed away as Decimus squared up for another go. "Bastard! We had a deal!"

"Sorry to rain on your parade, Vinè, but you

don't have the authority to claim my soul. Not without permission." I stood. My legs were numb, and my head swam. It was cold enough that the rain was freezing into slush in some places, including on my skin. I didn't even feel it. That couldn't be good.

He squeezed his oozing arm. "Impossible. Only Lucifer rivaled me in power. I am the strongest among the Fallen, and I will have what is mine! You can't go back on your bargain!"

Decimus touched two fingers to his throat, sealing the bleeding wound there. "Josiah's soul is not his to bargain with. He traded it already some time ago. If you want it, you'll have to go through me first."

"Fine," the demon growled. "Kill him."

The lesser demons on the rooftop opened fire. Decimus turned, ready to defend against the hail of bullets. Stupid angel. His meat suit was already gone. But he was a good soldier. Well trained. He responded as he'd been drilled to and addressed the more immediate threat.

Vinè grabbed him from behind, wrapping his one remaining hand over Decimus' head. The gunfire died. He looked at me. "I'm going to enjoy torturing you, Josiah," he said and squeezed.

Decimus' head popped like a grape, blood and brains spewing through the cracks in Vinè's fist.

I staggered away from the demon. Bugger, was I fucked.

Vinè cast what was left of Decimus aside and stomped toward me. "You know, I've never been a fan of this whole 'only divine beings can harm divine beings' shit. Angels fighting demons…

Everyone knows the Fallen will win every time. Angels just aren't smart enough. They don't think dirty, so they don't win. It's as simple as that." He extended his hand and grinned. "If you come willingly, I promise not to let your father have you first."

I looked around, searching for a way out and finding none. *Any time, Reggie. Any time!* If he and Milly hadn't found my bag in the wreckage, then this was it. At least if I went with Vinè, I wouldn't have to deal with dear old dad. That was plus. Always an upside to everything, even when trading your soul to a demon for a little rain.

The cell phone vibrated and began playing the opening guitar riff of Metallica's For Whom the Bell Tolls.

Vinè's grin faded. "What the hell is that?"

"It's called music."

He ground his teeth. "Why is it playing now?"

"Oh, that." I reached into my pocket and pulled the phone out, flipping it around so that he could see the caller ID. "That's just the signal I've been waiting on."

The wind picked up, blowing across the rooftop heavily charged with magic. Above, the storm clouds parted in a perfect circle and the golden light of Heaven poured onto the rooftop. A tone, high and painful, vibrated through the air, shaking my bones. Vinè lifted a hand over his face and tried to back away, but the light just grew more intense until it swallowed him whole.

Black wings sprouted, barely visible at the center of the light. A white blade flashed followed by a blast of pure blue fire. The sheer power of the explosion knocked me back onto my ass. I landed over Danny's body and rolled onto my stomach to shield my face from the flame. It licked at my back, singeing my hair and threatening to burn me to ash. The whole thing lasted ten seconds, maybe twenty, and then it was over.

Shaking, I pushed away from Danny and chanced a look back at where Vinè had been standing.

Vinè was no more. There wasn't even any ash to suggest he'd ever been, just a dark stain on the rooftop. More dark stains painted the edges of the roof, right where all the lesser demons had been waiting. Kneeling in the center of the massacre was a blonde angel in shining silver armor. A blue halo of light surrounded his head and filled his hollow eyes. He knelt before a massive, two-handed sword of gleaming white, head bowed against it in prayer.

The angel blinked once, letting the blue light fade, and stood. "Josiah Quinn. I didn't think I'd have the honor so soon."

"Michael," I grunted. "I'd stand, but your smiting seems to have taken all the wind out of me."

"Not all or you'd finally shut up." He strode across the roof, armor clinking loudly, and looked down his perfect nose at me, his face smug. "Nice trick, calling Vinè here with a sacrifice and promising him your soul."

"I knew you lot'd step in."

"Of course." Something dark flashed behind Michael's eyes. "The last Nephilim. Do you know how long I've waited for this? To finally purge the world of your stain?"

I lifted my hand from my side and watched blood spurt onto the rooftop. It squished loudly under my hand when I tried to put pressure back on. I had just a few more minutes, if that. "I've still got a ciggy in my pocket. If you wouldn't mind, I'd like to leave this Earth doing what I love."

"A fair request." Michael knelt and retrieved the pack of cigarettes from my pocket, pulling one out for me and offering a light.

"Thanks, mate."

Michael sat. "You know, when that troll and that pet spider of yours summoned an angel, I almost sent Sandalphon in my place. Only once I heard it was you did I decide to come down here personally. You know you're the one piece of unfinished business I have in this world. My one incomplete task."

"Must be embarrassing. Being shown up by a prick like me."

He shrugged. "Doesn't matter now, does it? Remiel hid for a long time, but I got him too. You're the last of his spawn. The youngest. Not even the most clever. You know, some of your half-siblings evaded me for ninety years or more. Yet none of them managed to infuriate and frustrate quite like you. You're like a stubborn gray hair, you Nephilim. Pluck one, two more spring up. But no more. After you, it's over. I can finally move on to focus on what's important."

"Good on ya, mate." I pulled the cigarette out of my mouth and gestured to him with it. "Or it would be if you were actually going to get to kill me."

He narrowed his eyes at me. "Don't think you can wheel and deal your way out of this, Josiah."

I nodded to August's body. "Decimus was one of your commanders, right? Spoke with all the authority of Heaven? Well, he and I had a deal. I save this stinking shithole of a city and kill Danny Monahan, and me and the succubus walk out of the city alive. No interference from Heaven. We had witnesses and everything. Very legit."

Michael said nothing.

"You don't get me this time, Mikey. That is, unless you want to make Decimus—and by extension, you—out to be a liar, in which case you'll have to round up those witnesses. Otherwise, you'll be admitting one of you was fallible. Michael, a sinner. Who'd have thought?"

I could practically see the steam rising from him. His face jerked as if he were about to have a seizure.

"Seein' as how I'm bleeding out though, you'll probably have to heal me if you don't want me to die on your watch. Can't make it out of the city alive if I'm dead."

Michael's hand shot forward and tightened around my windpipe, closing off the air. "I could crush you with one finger."

"Murder's a sin," I gasped out. "So is wrath."

The angel released me and stood, storming back and forth in front of me, shaking his head. He was searching for a way out, but I hadn't given him one. Thanks to Decimus, the deal was ironclad.

Michael stopped and drew his sword. Blue fire raced down the blade. "You want to leave the city? That's fine. Leave. Live. You've dealt a major blow to Hell's forces today and done Heaven a favor." He said the last bit through clenched teeth before turning toward me. "But the minute you pass beyond the city limits, you'll do so with a target on your back. I'll have every legion scouring the Earth for you. You won't last an hour."

I smiled and closed my eyes, suddenly too tired. "You might be surprised. I'm a stubborn bastard, after all."

"Your soul will be mine, Josiah, and when it is, I'll personally spend the next two millennia redefining the word pain for you." Michael jabbed his sword in my side, filling me with painful heat.

30

KHALEDA

They escorted me to an empty exam room and left me there for hours without explanation. I didn't know if Josiah was alive or dead, but he must've succeeded because the rest of New York looked just fine. At least, what I'd seen of it while they escorted me out of the building in handcuffs did.

While I waited, I searched the room, looking for anything I could use as a weapon. They could've killed me at any time, but maybe they'd been waiting to do so in a sterile environment. Freaks like God's Hand would want to dissect me, figure out how I worked. Like hell would I ever let them lay a hand on me.

While I was trying to pull a cord from the wall, the door buzzed open and the woman from before stepped in. She was still wearing that ugly white pantsuit. Two armed guards followed her in, taking up positions next to the door, the threat clear. If I tried to leave, they'd shoot me before I could. Between the three of them, they might even succeed in killing me. Even if they didn't, I didn't know my way out, and the place was probably crawling with armed men. I'd never make it out alive.

"Evening," said the woman.

I stepped away from the cord in the wall. "If you're going to kill me, just get it over with. Otherwise, this is unlawful imprisonment."

One side of her face twitched, but she didn't move otherwise. "My name is Petra. I don't want to waste any more of my time with you than I have to, so let's not mince words, Ms. Morningstar. We know who you are, what you can do, and where you're from. We also know why you were assisting Mr. Quinn."

"Is Josiah alive?" I took two hasty steps forward and stopped when the armed guards shifted their rifles.

Petra made a slight turn and they lowered their guns. "For now," she said, turning back to me. "As long as you behave yourself, he and the troll will keep breathing. Cause trouble, and all three of you will be terminated, and your bodies dumped in the river with cinderblocks attached."

I folded my arms. If it was just the troll, maybe I would've tried to fight my way out. I didn't care about him. He was Josiah's friend, not mine. Hell, for that matter I shouldn't have hesitated over Josiah. He was a selfish asshole who would've left me to die, given the chance.

Except he hadn't. He'd helped me even when it

would've been easier to turn his back on me. Even when I was a total bitch and drunk, he put up with me. The man had carried me out of Hell. The least I could do was try to keep him alive.

"All right," I said. "I'm listening."

Petra pulled a metal chair away from the wall and sat. "You wanted the missing piece of your soul back. We're prepared to give it to you if certain conditions are met."

"What conditions?"

Her thin lips stretched into a smile that looked unnatural on her face. "First, you will provide us with an accurate account of everything that happened since you arrived in New York. You will detail everywhere you stayed, everyone you spoke to, and everything you witnessed Josiah Quinn do, including any magic or spells he used. You will also detail when and how you took control of Agent Victis. Afterward, you will submit to providing us with a sample of your blood for testing. Failure to comply with any one of these demands is grounds for termination. Do you understand?"

I didn't like the idea of giving them my blood, but they weren't giving me a choice. If they killed me, they'd just take it anyway. "Is that all?"

"No." Petra stood and crossed the room to stand toe to toe with me.

She was an inch or two shorter, but that didn't stop her from pretending she was a foot taller and twice as strong as me. Josiah had inferred that she was possessed by an angel. I didn't know if I could take an angel in a fight, especially unarmed. Part of me wanted to try, just to see if I could.

"I don't like you," she said after a moment. "If it were up to me, I would've let my operatives shoot you when we found you. But Michael says we all have a role to play in God's plan. Even you, Khaleda." She reached out to brush some hair away from my face. "There are legions in Hell that would still follow you, you know."

I grabbed her by the wrist and squeezed as the guards fumbled to raise their guns. They wouldn't get a clear shot, not with the way she was positioned.

"I don't want to rule Hell," I told her. "I don't want anything to do with my father's empire. Let it burn for all I care."

"Good. We want the same thing then." Petra jerked her arm away. "When we call on you, you will renounce your claim to the crown. Publicly. And when we demand it, you will fully endorse whatever candidate we put forward for the job."

I stared at her, bile creeping up my throat. Heaven wanted to pick the next Devil? "What do you care who runs Hell? Unless you've got someone sympathetic to your cause already lined up?"

The corner of her mouth quirked up. "I can't divulge that information at this time."

"Bullshit. Michael hasn't told you, has he? You're just an underling. Not important enough to warrant him passing on his master plan."

Petra scowled and ground her teeth. She leaned in so close I could smell lunch on her breath. "You know nothing about him. Say anything out of line again, and this meeting will be over. When I walk out that door, so does your chance at getting your soul back. Think carefully about whatever it is you want to say next."

"My mistake." I sat down on the edge of the exam table. "Say I agree. What leverage do you have once I leave this room? Once I've got my soul back, I've got no reason to talk to you, let alone keep my end of the deal."

"I'm glad you asked." Petra snapped her fingers.

One of the guards stepped forward, opened a pouch on his vest, and drew out a clear plastic container that he placed in her hand. A nauseatingly powerful wave of magic washed through the room. The lights dimmed.

A solid, human-like form flickered into being in front of me. Features sharpened. Short, dark hair, pointed chin, dark eyes, high cheekbones...

My heart skipped a beat as I recognized my dead brother. "Osric?"

His eyes widened. "Khaleda!" His voice was distant and echo-y, as if he were somewhere far away instead of in the room with me.

Osric darted forward, arms outstretched. I tried to embrace him, but Petra did something, and the magic faded. Osric disappeared, reduced to nothing more than a glowing pale green orb inside her plastic container.

Petra smirked. "We have your brother's soul. Step out of line, even an inch, and I give it to your enemies to do with as they please. Keep your end of the bargain, and he'll be free to rest once this is all over."

"You bitch! Let him go!" I drew back a fist, but the guards were on me, holding me back before I could throw the punch.

"Now, now," said Petra, standing. "Language. Is that any way for a servant of God to speak?"

I tore free of the guards and stepped back, still fuming. It was one thing to threaten me, but Osric was dead. He deserved the chance to rest after everything he'd been through. For them to hold him over me, especially since I hadn't seen him in twenty years… It felt like they'd torn open an old wound to let it bleed fresh.

"Fine," I spat, "I'll say whatever it is you want me to say, do what it is you want me to do. But you let him go."

Petra tucked the container into her jacket pocket. "I'm glad we could come to an agreement." She went to the door and rapped on it twice. "You'll be debriefed and released in due time, provided Josiah agrees to our terms."

"That wasn't part of the deal!" I shouted, but she didn't even turn back.

Petra went through the door, and the guards followed. I tried to go after them, but the door slammed shut in my face, and an electronic lock held it firm.

31

JOSIAH

Muffled, underwater voices floated around me in a meaningless fog. Despite the whole-body ache, a strange calm settled over me. For a long time, I drifted in that hazy sleep, my dreams filled with rooftop views of Central Park, deflating balloons, and distant sirens.

The harsh, astringent smell of cleaning chemicals burning my nose woke me. I thought I should sneeze, but knew that if I did, something would break. A grim-faced doctor leaned over me, stethoscope dangling. Ice gripped my forehead and tapped on my chest.

She looked across the room. "Get Petra. He's coming around." Her voice still sounded like it was moving through miles of water. "Don't try to talk, and for God's sake, don't move."

Fine with me. I was still so tired, and I hurt everywhere. The vague need to piss and smoke stabbed my spine, but even that felt like too much. I drifted back into the fog, where it was safe and quiet.

The next thing I knew, I was sitting upright in a pristine white room. Sitting on a white chair next to me was a woman in a white pantsuit. Her short, dark hair was combed and parted to one side, making her look more like a petite man than a woman. If not for the chest, I'd have thought she was a man. She sat with her arms crossed, one knee resting over the other.

I closed my eyes, took a breath, and winced, reaching for my side.

"The knife perforated your lung, Mr. Quinn," said the woman. "You're very lucky to be alive."

"And who do I have to thank for that?" I cracked one eye open.

Her face was still as hard as the side of a mountain. "If it were up to me, I'd have left you on that rooftop for the feds to find. You would've spent your last moments in the custody of Homeland Security, being interrogated, before you succumbed."

"You must be Petra." I tried to push myself up more, but a painful pressure in the inside bend of my arm made me stop. "I take it I'm not in hospital?"

"You're in a secure bunker on Staten Island," Petra said. "One of the many owned by *Manus Dei*. Before you think about trying to kill me and make your escape, you should know that your safety is guaranteed only as long as you cooperate."

"My deal with Decimus—"

Petra tilted her head. "It stipulates only that you may leave the city alive, Mr. Quinn. It doesn't say my agents can't walk you across the border, cut off your head, and bring it back to me so I can mount it on my wall."

Christ, she wasn't messing around. I had to play this carefully or I was done for. "Considering you haven't done that yet, would it be safe to assume you want something from me aside from my head on your wall?"

She gritted her teeth. I could practically hear them grinding against each other, wearing down to dust. "I have been instructed to extend to you a one-time offer of employment as a sub-contractor for our organization. You will be provided with a phone where you receive instructions, a small stipend and travel allowance, and necessary equipment to carry out your work. In return, you'll be allowed to live. Between assignments, you may work and travel as you see fit, so long as you do not interfere with *Manus Dei* operations. Is that clear?"

"Didn't sound like there was a question in there."

Her gaze was practically glacial. "There wasn't."

I looked around the room. No sign of Khaleda, and Petra hadn't mentioned her either. She'd also failed to mention how I got off the roof and to this underground bunker. "Last I heard, I was a wanted criminal. Terrorist, according to Danny. Might be difficult for me to get around with that hanging over my head."

"*Manus Dei* has cleared you of all charges."

Petra uncrossed her arms and stood, pulling a remote control from her pocket. She pointed it at a television in the corner and pressed the power button.

A news station appeared on the screen, the anchorman calmly recounting a story labeled: Thanksgiving Terror Threat. "...the body of millionaire CEO Daniel Monahan was recovered. CNN Investigates has since uncovered dozens of travel documents, detailing Monahan's many investments in overseas radical organizations, including ISIS. Monahan and a group of twenty-five other radicalized terrorists took control of the 432 Park Avenue high-rise Thursday morning. A joint anti-terrorism task force breached the building shortly after the stand-off began, but they were unable to apprehend Monahan and his men before several of the terrorists activated small explosive devices, causing localized damage to the structure and killing themselves. While specific details concerning Monahan's death have not yet been released, a source wishing to remain anonymous stated that Monahan's wounds appeared to be self-inflicted."

"That's a lie," I said as she muted the screen. "And not even a good one. Anyone who looks too close will know it."

Petra dropped the remote onto the bed next to me. "No one looks closely at dead terrorists. People just want them to go away so they can enjoy the illusion of safety again. Tell the people there's a terror threat and they'll believe and do anything we say. Fear is a powerful motivator not to pay attention, Mr. Quinn."

I stared at her smug face, wishing it would melt right off. Danny deserved better than to have his name dragged through the mud after his death. Not that I was expecting a celebration for him or anything. He had planned to kill millions. But he was still a person. To see his existence reduced so easily to less than nothing... It wasn't right.

There's fuck all I can do about it, I thought, *at least now*. I knew the truth about Danny, about what really happened on that rooftop. It didn't feel like enough, but it would have to be. The weight of that realization settled into my bones and made them ache. "What about Khaleda?"

She smiled and paced to the end of the bed, blocking my view of the television. "Your friends are safe, both the succubus and the troll. They'll continue breathing as long as I know you're going to behave yourself. So, do we have a deal, Mr. Quinn?"

I didn't like it. I also hadn't forgotten that Michael promised to put a target on my back the minute I left New York City limits. Making me an agent of *Manus Dei* would be the easiest way to do that. They'd bully me into accepting impossible jobs, jobs that would probably get me killed. If I didn't, they'd send the full force of Heaven after me, Khaleda, and Reggie. I was good, but I wasn't good enough to take on an Archangel like Michael.

I narrowed my eyes at her. "On two conditions. I want access to *Manus Dei* resources whenever requested, and I don't just mean weapons. I mean databases. Computers. Safehouses. All of it. If I'm going to work for you, let's not piss about."

Petra crossed her arms and gave me an appraising look. "I think we can arrange that."

"Second," I said, holding up two fingers, "You'll release Danny's body to me for a proper burial, service and everything. A quiet one. He doesn't deserve the lie, not even after everything he did. I owe him a service and a headstone at the very least."

She gave a one-shouldered shrug. "If it's on your dime, and doesn't hit the press, that's a concession I'm willing to make."

I extended my hand stiffly. "Then you have yourself a deal."

***

It took another two days before I was able to get on my feet. They brought me a set of clothes, near-identical to the ones I'd been wearing on the rooftop. After I dressed, an armed guard escorted me down a long, empty hallway with mechanically locked doors that made the place look more like a prison than a safe house.

At the end of the hallway, they put me in a meeting room to wait and left a single guard behind. I sat in one of the chairs on wheels and tapped my fingers on the tabletop, restless. They'd only been letting me smoke twice a day, and it was getting to me. All I wanted to do was pace, move around. I was on edge and couldn't wait to get the hell out of there. First thing I was going to do was pick up a pack of smokes and work my way through the whole thing out of spite.

The doors opened, and more armed guards

ushered Khaleda and Reggie into the room. Reggie looked no worse for wear aside from seeming jumpy, but Khaleda looked like hell. Small cuts littered her face, and she walked with a hesitant gait that said she was working hard to hide a leg injury.

Khaleda squeezed me hard enough it made everything hurt. "Get me the hell out of here," she snarled into my ear.

I smiled. "Thought you'd never ask."

God's Hand made us sign a mountain of releases and non-disclosure agreements, covering their asses. They didn't technically do it at gunpoint, but having an armed guard by the door sure made it feel that way. Poor Reggie was so nervous, his hand shook the entire time. Mine did too, but all I needed was a little nicotine to calm my nerves. He'd be a wreck for weeks to come.

All the paperwork behind us, they took us to a lift, up two stories, and down another long corridor to a small lobby. There, we found our personal belongings tagged, inventoried, and laid out on long tables.

I went straight for my leather bag and opened it, smiling when I found everything exactly as I'd left it. I pulled out Milly's container and popped open the lid. "Hello, beautiful. Did ya miss me?"

If spiders could glower, I got the distinct feeling Milly would've. *Well, at least you're not dead. And you smell better than the troll.*

"Everything good?" Reggie zipped up his hoodie. "Wasn't easy getting that, you know. Police had the whole downed building blocked off. I had to climb up a building in freezing rain, a building that looked like it might topple at any second."

"Thanks, Reg." I put the lid back on Milly's container. She'd be hungry. After all her hard work, I owed her a couple of nice, fat crickets.

A buzzer sounded, and an unassuming glass door popped open. The three of us gathered our belongings and stepped out into the sunlight as free people.

Reggie pulled the hood on his hoodie tighter around his face before shaking my hand. "Well, Josiah, I'd say it was good working with you again but it kind of sucked. As usual."

I pried my hand from his death grip. "Will ya be going back to the 76 Station then? Not worried God's Hand will give you trouble?"

He grunted and tugged the sleeves down to hide his hands. "Maybe they will, but I know better than to stick with you. I'd rather keep the trouble I have than add more. Besides, I'm just a boring old troll. They'll forget about me in a few days if I lay low. Where are you guys headed?"

I looked at Khaleda and shrugged.

"Don't look at me," she snapped. "I finally got my passport and ID, though I'm sure God's Hand has them flagged so that they're notified every time I use them. Won't be able to go anywhere without them watching. Thanks for that, Josiah."

"No worries."

We walked to the metal gate at the end of the parking lot. It rolled aside at our approach, and we moved onto the sidewalk. It felt like walking out of prison. The world was suddenly bigger somehow, and I didn't know which way to go.

Reggie waved and turned to go up the street. He'd catch the ferry back to Manhattan and ride the subway until the end of the line. An hour, maybe two, and he'd be home in his own bed.

I stuck my hands in my pockets. They felt heavier now, despite having only added a cell phone to the lighter and cigarettes. A cell phone that trapped me working for the God Squad. Maybe I could ditch it, though I had a feeling they'd find a way to contact me even without the damn thing. Persistent assholes, angels.

Khaleda and I turned the other way and started walking.

"So," I said, pulling out the cigarettes and lighter, "what's your plan? You're a free woman now."

She stopped abruptly, and I looked up. A black car waited at the end of the street with the rear window rolled down. Staring out at us from the back seat was the familiar face of the Winter Knight. Her pretty face was scarred almost beyond recognition, but I'd know that icy glare anywhere.

I frowned. "I thought you said she fell fifty stories down an elevator shaft?"

The succubus' eyes blazed. "I did."

Noelle waited until she was sure we'd seen her, then smiled and rolled up the window. Tires squealed as the car pulled out into the intersection and sped away.

"Demons, angels, the FBI, Homeland Security, and now the Winter fae," Khaleda muttered and shook her head. "Is there anyone you didn't piss off trying to save New York, Josiah?"

"At least I'm still on good terms with a succubus." I gave her a wink and a smile before putting the cigarette in my mouth.

"Those things are going to be the death of you, Josiah."

"They're welcome to try."

Khaleda huffed and started walking. "Come on. Let's get some decent food before we leave town. I'm starving. And next time you want to save the world, we're doing it somewhere warm." She walked to the end of the sidewalk and stopped before turning around, arms crossed. "Well? Are you coming or what?"

"Wouldn't miss it for the world." I lit a cigarette and followed.

ALSO IN THIS SERIES

ABOUT THE AUTHOR

E.A. Copen is a wizard and herder of cats. For her day job, she writes books about magic, mayhem, and murder. She is the author of several urban fantasy series, including Hellbent Halo, The Lazarus Codex, and The Judah Black Novels, as well as the historical urban fantasy novel Beasts of Babylon. Her space opera, Broken Empire, was published with Bolide Publishing in the UK.

E.A. lives in a tiny apartment in Bowling Green, Kentucky with her family and a whole zoo of pets. Shen she's not chained to the keyboard working on her next release, she's likely watching movies, playing video games or reading comic books.

Connect with her at www.grimcatpress.com/eacopen or on Facebook at www.facebook.com/eacopen.

www.ingramcontent.com/pod-product-compliance
Lightning Source LLC
Chambersburg PA
CBHW031121210626
46816CB00016B/1750